THE
REAL
MICHAEL SWANN

ALSO BY BRYAN REARDON

Finding Jake

THE

REAL
MICHAEL SWANN

A Novel

Bryan Reardon

DUTTON

DUTTON

An imprint of Penguin Random House LLC
375 Hudson Street
New York, New York 10014

LIBRARY OF CONGRESS CATALOGING-IN-PUBLICATION DATA

Names: Reardon, Bryan, author.
Title: The real Michael Swann / Bryan Reardon.
Description: First edition. | New York, New York : Dutton, [2018]
Identifiers: LCCN 2017023211| ISBN 9781524742324 (hardcover) | ISBN 9781524742331 (ebook)
Classification: LCC PS3618.E22535 T47 2018 | DDC 813/.6—dc23
LC record available at https://lccn.loc.gov/2017023211

Printed in the United States of America
1   3   5   7   9   10   8   6   4   2

Set in Adobe Garamond Pro
Designed by Cassandra Garruzzo

*To my wife, Michelle, who after twenty years
deserves far more than this dedication.*

THE
REAL
MICHAEL SWANN

INTRODUCTIONS

Today's the day. Therapy, which means it is a Tuesday, or a Thursday. I close my eyes, trying to figure out which one. The emptiness frustrates me. Out of an old habit now, I touch my left temple. There is no physical reminder of what happened. Only memories; some mine, some not.

The therapist walks in right on time. Dressed, as she always is, in a long colorful dress and warm-looking jacket, she leaves no doubt as to her profession, not in here at least. Her name is Marci Simmons. And like I said, today is the day.

She sits across the table from me. A video screen is poised between us, ready to begin. She looks me in the eyes, which is something that only happens on Tuesdays and Thursdays.

"Are you sure you're ready for this?"

I nod, so she hits play.

The video is grainy, painted in the shades of a surveillance camera—gray-green. The first shot shows the back of someone's head as he pushes through a mass of people until he reaches the down escalator. He carries a common-looking briefcase in his left hand. Someone in a dark uniform puts a hand up, but the other man pushes past and bolts down and out of the shot.

Next, what appears to be the same man, still carrying the case, sprints along the platform of a subway station. After that, a series of short clips show him running through the darkness of a tunnel. At one point, Marci Simmons pauses the video.

"This is it," she says.

I nod again, so she continues. The next shot is hard to understand. The man runs. The camera shakes. Something comes crashing down from the ceiling of the tunnel, striking the man, knocking him off his feet. Suddenly, a wall of smoke or dust, strangely alien in the greenish tint of the surveillance camera, swallows everything.

"That's me?" I ask.

This time, she nods. "Do you remember?"

I can only laugh at that.

———

This isn't really my story. It's hers, though I have no idea where she is. As the long days turn to longer nights, when I close my eyes I still see her face, the look in her eye, even. It's all I have. That, and this story of hers.

I imagine that if anyone is to read this, they would wonder how I can know everything that happened. Well, the truth is that this story doesn't come from the words of others. Words are undependable, memories even worse. Instead, her tale comes from my soul, from our souls. That is why I can assure you that it is nothing but real.

On a Friday in August, a bomb was detonated under New York City. Hundreds were killed and thousands injured. It happened at a time when our country already teetered on the edge. It touched all of our lives, changing everything, changing the world. It confounded our realities, challenging every basic principle of an aging society. It caused us all to suspect those around us. Who are our friends; who are our enemies? It caused us to question our neighbors, even our families. Even ourselves. You may ask, who am I to tell this story? To that, this is my answer.

PART
ONE

1

I can see her every day. I close my eyes and she appears out of the darkness, a brightness that I simply don't deserve. I can still picture her on that day. She wore a white tank top and capri pants, although it took me months to remember that is what they are called. She stood in the light, its beams touching the soft skin of her cheeks and the heart-stopping strength in her eyes. Her dark hair was pulled back, highlighting the lines of her face and classically long neck. She looked like a runner and a leader, a mother and a timeless beauty, at least to me. And I saw the ring on her finger, silver and simple. Her name was Julia. Julia Swann.

On the day it happened, she sat on her back porch with two neighbors, Evelyn and Tara. Their kids played out in the yard with large and expensive water guns. Their excited screams echoed throughout the tight-knit, established neighborhood nestled in the countryside outside Philadelphia.

"Can you believe the riots last night?" Julia asked.

"Crazy, right? I don't get it."

"Me, either," Evelyn said. "These protests are sort of like the wrestling my brother used to watch when he was a kid."

Julia laughed. "Yeah, but that was fake. This is real."

"I think they should just arrest them all," Tara said, her tone sharper than the others'. "They're full of it. Screaming about promises and that damn wall! No one even seems to care that so many people are losing their jobs."

Evelyn and Julia didn't say anything for a moment. They knew full well how charged this topic could be, especially with Tara. Yet Julia also knew how worried her friend was. And she wanted to give her a chance to let it out. Maybe it would help.

"Over a thousand layoffs?" she asked, her brow rising and her glass of chardonnay tipping in her right hand. Tara nodded. Her eyes reddened as she looked away. Most of the neighborhood knew that she and her family probably would have to move if her husband couldn't find a new job.

"It's just so messed up," Tara said. "I mean, I thought he'd work there for his entire career. That's what my dad did."

"Everything's so different now," the third mother, Evelyn Chase, added. She had short dark hair and wore coordinating Athleta running clothes.

Julia leaned back and watched the children. Her boys, Evan, 12, and Thomas, 8, were close friends with Evelyn's oldest, Brady. At that moment, they stood with their heads close together, like they were planning the perfect coordinated attack on the other children.

"Is it definite?" Julia asked.

"I think so, but they haven't announced who's getting cut. I guess there was a big meeting today, but I haven't heard anything yet."

"Can he find something local?"

Tara shook her head and laughed. "I doubt it. He's a plant geneticist. The jobs, if there are any, are going to be in the Midwest." She laughed again, but this time a tear ran down her cheek. "Can you just picture it? Me in Iowa?"

"It's really nice out there," Evelyn said. "That's what I hear. Frannie Goode moved there a few years ago and loves it."

"Really?" Tara asked.

"Yeah," Evelyn said. "You'll be okay. It'll be hard at first, but any change is. And you'll see, the kids will be great. I mean, look at them. They get along with everyone. And with their sports, it'll be great."

"What if they don't make a team?"

Julia shook her head. "Yeah, right."

The three of them stopped talking for a second. They sipped their wine with a practiced synchrony. The kids continued to laugh and call out as a neighbor drove by, honking her horn in greeting. The three smiled and waved.

"She just started working at the library," Julia mentioned, absently.

"Karen?"

"Yup."

"At the school?"

"No, in the borough."

"Really?"

Julia nodded.

"That's great," Evelyn said.

Julia's phone vibrated. It sat on the arm of the Adirondack chair she and Michael bought when they went to the beach in June. She glanced at the screen and saw the call came from her husband.

"I have to take this."

"No problem," Evelyn said.

Julia shot a quick glance at Tara, finding her watching the kids. It looked like her friend might cry at any moment. As she rose from the chair, phone in one hand and wine on the armrest, she touched Tara's shoulder. Their eyes met and Julia smiled. The movement of her mouth was subtle and kind. Tara's eyes lowered, and she placed a hand softly atop Julia's, for just a second. As Julia walked back toward the house, the pit of her stomach lightly rolled.

"Hi," she answered the call.

"Hey," her husband, Michael, said.

She heard thick noise in the background. "Where are you? It sounds like a party."

"At Penn Station. Just walking down the steps."

She took a breath. "How'd it go?"

"It went great," he said. She heard the tone he used. It had recently become more recognizable in the way it sounded, as if his words were meant more to convince himself than anything else. "I think it did. The questions were pretty standard. I think I did really well answering them. The HR rep took me to lunch. You would love her. She's got two kids just a little younger than ours."

Julia touched her belly and looked out the window. "Did you like the offices?"

"Definitely."

"The people?"

"Yeah, pretty much."

"Pretty much?" she asked.

"I mean, it was—"

"Huh."

The world outside took on focus when one of the boys screamed. She saw her younger son, Thomas, holding his forehead. His shaggy blond bangs nearly swallowed his thin fingers. But she saw his eyes wide—with pain or anger, she couldn't tell.

"Gotta go," she said.

"Everything okay?"

"Yeah, Tara and Evelyn are here. I think Thomas hit his head or something."

"Bad?"

She laughed. "Probably not."

"How's Tara doing?" he asked.

She sighed. "Doesn't look good. She's pretty sure they'll have to move."

"That sucks," Michael said.

No one said anything for a moment.

"Yeah."

Thomas pushed open the door into the kitchen. His cry echoed through the phone connection.

"Whoa," Michael said. "Take care of him. I should be home in about three hours, assuming the train's on time."

"Love you," she said.

"Love you, too."

Julia hung up just as Evan came through the back door and reached Thomas. He bent and spoke softly to his little brother, a hand on the smaller boy's shoulder. In moments like that, Julia noticed so much of his father in Evan, with his red-blond hair and blue eyes. He was a baseball player, like his dad. In the moment, her son's maturity caught her off guard.

"They're growing up so fast," she whispered.

With a smile, Evan returned to the kids outside and Thomas came to Julia. He was no longer crying, but she took him in her arms and kissed the top of his head. The coarse hair there smelled of the sun, and a surprising heat touched her lips.

"What happened?" she whispered, holding him tightly.

His words stuttered like a chronic cough. "Brady hit me in the head."

"On purpose?" she asked.

"Probably."

Julia turned her head, resting her cheek on the warmth of her son's head and fighting back the urge to laugh. A wide smile crossed her face and she rubbed his back.

"Guess what I bought yesterday?"

His sobbing stopped on a dime. "What?"

"Those popsicles you like with the cream inside."

He pulled back and looked up at her. "Can I have one?"

"Only if you bring some out for everyone."

His bare feet danced on their porcelain-tiled floor. "Okay."

"Is your head okay?"

"Yeah!"

The feeling Julia had in that moment was hard to describe. She had it often, but mostly at the oddest of times. Silently listening from the other room as her boys discussed something trivial with the absolute earnestness of the young. The way Evan's brow furrowed when he worked on his math homework. Or when Thomas stomped around the house in his father's size-thirteen shoes. In a way, that feeling, a flutter high in her midriff, might be called a physical manifestation of pure love. Yet it seemed at once more and less than that. It felt primal to her, utterly undeniable but far too fleeting. The rest of the day she never truly thought about it, yet its absence lurked, waiting for life to slow down just enough for it to flare up once again.

Regardless, it felt simple and good. She tousled his hair and opened the freezer. She was about to hand the box to him, but she stopped. Feeling light for no particular reason, she dug through the popsicles until she found a red one, her favorite. She took that for herself before handing the box to Thomas.

"Remember, share," she said.

"I will."

"And start with the adults."

Julia followed Thomas out. He scurried over to Evelyn and Tara and offered cream-filled popsicles with the utmost politeness. The two women thought to protest. With big smiles, they saw Julia, her lips already a deeper red and a childish sparkle in her eyes, standing behind her son. Giggling, Evelyn took a purple one, Tara a green. The three women shared popsicles and chardonnay as they watched their children play under the hot summer sun.

2

The truck rolled down a narrow access road at approximately 4:10 P.M. The man driving knew he was early. He'd driven the road three times in preparation. He followed the same path, about half a mile from where the road ended, replaced by a vast meadow of dry hay grass. When he coasted to a stop, he had already decided the spot was perfect for two reasons. One, it was absolutely remote. For the weeks he'd watched the entrance, not a single vehicle had traveled in or out on that road. Two, that particular bend came within fifty yards of the Amtrak rails. He got out and looked east toward the tracks and the dry grass between that spot and where he stood.

He did not smile. His face remained set in a hard yet emotionless expression as he walked around the side of the truck. He released the tailgate and leaned forward, his hands reaching for two red canisters of gasoline. Straightening, he stepped to the edge of the grass and placed one on the ground. The second he carried as he moved off the road toward the tracks. The hay swayed around him, brushing his thighs and waist. His one hand reached out slightly, and he let it trail atop the blades. Dry. Perfect.

He spoke softly to himself as he uncapped the canister and slowly poured out the gasoline as he walked a serpentine trail along the tracks.

"When the time comes," he said, his tone strangely flat despite the slight accent, "I'll be remembered as the patriot that made things right again, not that liar. I'm the *real* American. They won't get it at first.

They might see me as the bad guy. That's okay. History will see it differently. I am the one . . . versus the one hundred. That much I know."

When the last drops fell from the first canister, he proceeded to seed the field with the second. When that was done as well, he walked back to the truck. Leaning against the side panel, his hand slipped into the front pocket of his blue jeans. His fingers wrapped around the matches. When he pulled them out, the summer sun reflected off the stars and stripes on the top of the box.

Before pulling out a single match, the man licked a finger and held it into the air, testing the wind. Dry and hot, it blew east, toward the distant Atlantic Ocean. He nodded and removed the match.

"God bless America," the man said, striking the red tip.

A tear of flame licked from the frail wood. Left alone, it could only burn for an instant before running out of fuel. Instead, though, the man flicked the match, the careless gesture of someone who worked with his hands. Maybe he had lit hundreds of charcoal grills in his backyard, grilled up thousands of burgers for his family. The match turned a lazy arc through the air, landing five feet into the brush. In the blink of an eye, a larger flame whipped into the air. It widened, running the path the man had walked a moment before. Thick gray smoke billowed into the air. The man watched it for a second before returning to his truck.

Before driving away, he leaned to the side and entered a combination into a leather briefcase on the passenger seat. It popped open and he looked at the contents, nodding. Then he drove away, back onto the turnpike and toward the Lincoln Tunnel.

———

At 4:25, the engineer on an Acela Express out of Washington with stops in Baltimore, Wilmington, Philadelphia, and points north could not believe his eyes. He stared out the window of the engine as it raced forward at 135 miles per hour along the straightaway outside Newark, New Jersey, just before the slowdown approaching the station. He blinked, but the heavy smoke drifting across the tracks did not disappear.

He grabbed the handheld radio at his belt. After identifying himself and giving his location, he said, "There's considerable smoke drifting across the tracks."

The engineer of a transit train joined in, reporting the same thing. Chatter grew as the Acela engineer slowed his train to thirty miles per hour. He entered the smoke. To his left, he could see flames rising among the brush and grass near the track.

"There's a fire about ten feet from the rails. Wind is blowing the smoke and flames across both the north- and southbound lines."

Both the Acela and the first transit train to respond made it cautiously past. Within two minutes of the engineer's first report, all other traffic was stopped on the track or held at the stations north and south of the fire until further notice.

3

Julia stood on her deck, watching the two women walk up the hill, their children pulling ahead. She could not hear their conversation, but she caught their hands moving with expression. They looked back once and waved. Thomas opened the slider behind her.

"When's dinner?"

"Half an hour," she said without turning.

She heard the door slide shut, and she sat back down in her chair. She wondered what they might be talking about. For a second, she wondered if serving popsicles was a weird thing to do. She could still feel the artificial cherry coating her tongue. Evelyn only ate organic at her house. Julia wondered if it might have offended her that Julia allowed the kids to have them without checking first.

Sometimes, Julia thought she had two brains. Or, more accurately, two distinct halves to her brain. One from her career days and one since she started staying home with the kids. At times, she had to slow it down, be less premeditated, more primal. Kids plus summer equals popsicles. It could be as simple as that.

Just as she was about to get up and start fixing dinner, a chicken dish that had sat in the slow cooker for about four hours, her phone vibrated again. It was Michael. At first, she didn't recognize the number. A few weeks before, he had purchased a new phone. Before that, for years, he had only used his work-issued cell. He still carried both. Every time she saw them, though, it bothered her, like a constant reminder of the type of change that hadn't been one hundred percent their idea.

"Hey," she said, laughing. "I'm still not used to this new number of yours."

"Sorry," he said.

When they paused, she noticed the background noise. It seemed even louder than before.

"Wow," she said. "What's going on?"

When he spoke, she had to concentrate to hear him over the din. "They closed the rails north of Philly. Both ways. You should see it in here. The station is getting pretty crowded."

"Was it an accident?"

"I don't think so. A guy I was talking to has Amtrak alerts on his Twitter. It said that there's a brush fire in New Jersey."

"That's not good," she said.

"Yeah, that's what I was thinking. I might head out and just rent a car. It'll cost more, but this could go on all night."

"Yeah," she said, distractedly.

Evelyn and Tara passed out of her line of sight. She stood, resting her free hand on the railing of the deck.

"Whatever you need to do," she said. "Love you."

"I love you back," he said. "I'll text you if I hear anything or if I decide to change plans. Tell those monkeys of ours that I love them, too."

"I will."

"See you soon, babe."

"Can't wait. Stay safe."

"I will."

She hung up. Looking up the hill toward the more wooded section of the neighborhood, she closed her eyes for a second.

"Huh . . . ," she whispered.

She used to take the train to Washington all the time for her work.

That was before the kids, but she'd never heard of anything like the tracks being closed because of a brush fire.

"Mom," Evan called out behind her.

Her eyes shot open and the span of her backyard came into focus, with its wooden play set and lacrosse pitch back. The grass needed to be cut, but they had the weekend for that.

"Yup," she said, turning.

"Thomas just called me a bully."

She shook her head. "I'm coming in."

———————

Julia flipped through her phone as the kids ate at the counter.

"Are you having any?" Thomas asked.

"I will . . . in a minute."

She'd found both the Amtrak Twitter account and another website reporting the status of the track closures. The latest tweet said that the tracks were closed indefinitely. She closed her eyes and ran a hand across her mouth.

"You okay, Mom?" Evan asked.

"Oh, yeah, sure. It's just Daddy's going to be really late," she said.

"What about the game?" Evan asked.

Michael had hopes that he would be home to watch the end of the Phillies-Mets game on TV with them. She glanced at the clock. There was no way he'd make it in time.

"I'll watch it with you guys," she said.

Thomas's eyes widened. "You will?"

She laughed. "Of course I will."

"But you hate the Phillies," Evan said.

"I do not."

"Yes, you do," they said together.

"Well," she said with a grin, "tonight I don't."

Julia really didn't want to watch the game. She would rather read out on the back porch, listening to the sounds of their perfect neighborhood as it slowly quieted down after a long summer day. But that wasn't in the cards. She'd be okay with that.

On a whim, she dialed Evelyn's number.

"Miss me already?" her friend joked.

"Definitely. Hey, I was just thinking. We should put together a girls' night for Tara. She could use it, with everything that's going on."

"Totally," Evelyn said. "You want me to start the group text or you?"

"I can," Julia said. It would give her something to do during the game. "Should we invite Karen?"

"She's kind of a drag," Evelyn said.

"I like her."

"Then invite her if you want. She makes Tara uncomfortable, though." Evelyn laughed. "It's like she sees right into your soul."

"Ev!"

"Sorry."

Julia shook her head. "She probably won't want to come anyway. Right?"

"Probably not."

"Okay. I'll send something out after dinner."

"Great."

When she hung up, Julia called Michael. He answered after three rings.

"Hey," he said.

"Wow, it's even louder," she said.

"Yeah. It's getting crazy. There has to be about a thousand people down here. The place is packed."

"Where are you?"

"I'm in the Acela lounge, so it's not as bad. Still standing room only. I'm about to head out and take a look at the board, though. See if I can get an idea about when this might clear up. It looks like a mosh pit filled with business suits out there."

She laughed. Michael always kept things light. It was one of the things that had drawn her to him almost twenty years before.

"It looks bad," she said. "Have you thought more about getting a car?"

"I called around."

"What?" she asked. "I couldn't hear you."

"I called around," he said, louder. "Sounds like people beat me to it. I might just get a room. Would that be okay?"

"Where?"

He paused. "The Paramount might not be too bad."

"Probably three hundred a night," she said.

"You're right."

Julia immediately regretted what she said. A few months before, she would not have mentioned it at all. Yet uncertainty had crept into her thoughts, and suddenly $300 sounded like a lot of money for a hotel room.

"But . . . whatever you want to do is fine. I mean, if everything works out, we'll be fine."

She heard what sounded like a bark. She blinked.

"Was that a dog?"

"I don't—"

In the midst of Michael's sentence, the line went dead.

4

Within ten minutes of the track closure, the crowd in Penn Station started to bulge. It did not happen all at once. The usual trickle of passengers arriving for future departures continued. After twenty minutes, two trains that had boarded but not pulled away from the station let their passengers out of the cars. They pressed back up the stairs and into the station. After an hour, hundreds of people milled around the giant message board in front of the ticketing area. It listed dozens of trains either coming or going. By that time, every status read *delayed*.

Dispatchers, men and woman inside the Penn Station Control Center, stared at a massive screen across the wall. Over seventy feet wide, it showed the location of every train within a 150-mile radius of the city. Normally, the dispatchers tracked movement. On that day, their mouths hung open at the utter standstill each and every one of them witnessed.

On a typical day, over a thousand trains ran in and out of the station that sat like a labyrinth beneath Madison Square Garden. Hundreds of thousands of commuters filtered in and out aboard trains, boarding subway cars or climbing stairs or escalators to the bustling city above. The dispatchers in the control center were tasked with somehow putting the pieces of this massive and moving puzzle into the right places, all the while knowing that the crowds outside seethed at even a fifteen-minute delay. Every minute that ticked off the giant digital clock above the screen simply stoked their anxiety. They had seen bad days. But few had seen a day worse than that Friday in August.

These dispatchers, more so than most, understood what was about to happen. In a manner of speaking, the fire had dammed up the flow of commuters through Penn Station. Just as water would pool on one side of the blockage, people continued to press into the station. More and more arrived, and fewer and fewer left. First the cavernous center of the station filled to capacity. Then the area around the bookstores, pizza shops, and other vendors. People leaned against walls, milled in thick groups wherever space opened, or dipped their heads, hands cupped over ears, trying to update loved ones on the delay.

Word of the brush fire spread throughout the station, adding to people's reluctance to leave. Something like that, they thought, might be cleared at any moment. Without simple alternatives, most waited it out as hundreds more arrived. Within an hour, over two thousand people milled around Penn Station, making the best of a bad situation.

By 5:43 P.M., the number of New York City Transit Police there doubled. Men in dark uniforms moved among the crowds, eyes scanning, lips thin. Handlers led trained dogs along the edges, looking for signs of the unthinkable. The temperature rose, and the smell of sweat and damp wool hung in the humid air, clinging to people like cobwebs.

At 5:58, a sharp bark pierced the underlying noise. Voices rose in response. A deep male voice shouted out in alarm, then with a series of orders. People froze from one side of the crowded station to the other. Two minutes later, at 6:00 P.M. sharp, a bomb detonated. The explosion ripped through people and walls alike. Shards of blue plastic from the chairs in the Acela lounge pierced cement-block walls beyond ticketing. Smoke, fire, and chaos swallowed New York's Penn Station, killing or injuring hundreds instantaneously. The subsequent rupture and explosion of natural gas lines killed even more, and left thousands injured, bleeding, blind, deafened, and changed forever.

5

"Michael?" Julia said after the line went silent.

She paced out of the kitchen. Whatever conversation the boys had been sharing trailed off. They listened in nervous silence as she walked to the far end of her living room and stared out the window. Outside, life was peaceful. Birds sang as the summer sun still hung above the easy hills to the west. A car rolled slowly by, someone's father just getting home from work. She heard the faintest sound of children laughing from somewhere down the street.

"Michael?"

She pulled the phone away from her ear. The call had ended. She dialed his number, but it went straight to voicemail. She tried his other cell phone, the work-issued one; same thing. Figuring he was dialing her as she dialed him, she ended that call without leaving a message. To be honest, she hadn't expected him to pick up the call to his old cell number. He hadn't been using it much recently. It was probably in his briefcase. Plus, calls got dropped all the time, she thought.

It was nothing, she kept saying to herself. Unfortunately, the more she repeated it, the more worried she felt.

6

My eyes opened to nothing. At first, I thought I couldn't see. Everything was white, everywhere. It surrounded me, cutting me off from whatever was around me. I existed within a color, alone and inhuman.

What am I?

That was the first thought. In that moment, I had no idea. I could not see my hands or my arms or my legs. I could not feel my face or my body. Instead, I seemed to float outside reality, more a thought than a real physical being.

Who am I?

That came when sound returned to my world. The silence around me simply ceased. In its place, horrid noise pressed in on me like the crushing hands of some awful giant. They pressed and squeezed, screams of pain and moans of the dying. The crash and crumble of concrete and the shriek of rending metal. Alarms, sharp and so loud, sounded all around me.

Next came the smell. It filled my mouth like thick liquid, like some bitter poison. Tinny and sweet with a hint of putridity, it came from everywhere all at once. Instinctively, for that was the only level of brain function I managed in those first few moments, I took air in through my mouth. The dust coated my throat and filled my lungs. I hacked and coughed, and with each shudder a splitting pain radiated out of my head like an iron spike had been driven through my temple.

Somehow, my hand moved. Although I cannot say I controlled the movement yet, it still rose out of the debris more from reflex than thought. The motion brought with it a fragment of reality. *I move*, I thought. *Therefore, I must live.*

My hand rose slowly. It hovered just outside the halo of my pain. Cringing, I pushed through that invisible barrier and felt a brittle crust. Dust and fragments of ceiling tiles and specks of pulverized cinder block coated my hair like fallen snow. I brushed at it, and the pain flared exponentially, forcing me to close my eyes. My hand remained still as I fought to keep myself conscious. It hurt so bad I felt waves of nausea. But I knew that if I lurched, the pain would be too much to take.

As that first tidal wave of agony lessened, I slipped my hand back down. One eye opened, and I looked at chalky-white fingers, the tips coated in the brightest red I have ever seen. It burned into my eyes and everything wavered. I blinked, and only then realized it was blood.

Those alarms would not stop. They surrounded me. In a way, the noise reminded me of insects in the late summer, with that same cadence but mind-splittingly loud. At the same time, they sounded like shrill fire alarms. Opening my other eye, I tried to focus my vision. At first, everything remained white. Slowly, though, I saw a shape. It looked like a protective mask, the glass cracked, and a large metal tank. A rubber line spread across the jagged floor, disappearing under a large mass of what I took to be asphalt or crumbled concrete.

My hand moved again, but this time it seemed like a conscious decision. I reached out, gently touching the smooth surface of the mask. When my hand came back, I noticed a streak of red on the glass. I remember staring at that, for how long I have no idea. And I remember wondering if the blood had been there before or if it came from my finger.

The alarm continued. I had to move. The sound tore at the nerve endings inside my head like a fire burning beneath my skull. I put my hand down, the first step in attempting to stand. The ground shifted under me. That's when I realized there was no floor, only sprawling debris.

I struggled and the pain intensified. The more I tried to move, the darker my world seemed to get. As the fog-like dust settled, I realized that the only light came from a ways off. I couldn't tell if it was sunlight or artificial. The air felt so heavy and smelled so bad that I assumed it was the latter, but it was all I had.

Eventually, I rose to my knees. I felt so dizzy. But I fought through that. I had to. For some reason, that part of the brain that has remained unchanged since humans first walked with two legs took over. It called the shots. It told me to move, to get out. Something awful had happened. Something big. There was alarm and devastation. I couldn't even find a floor. Above that metallic smell, something new filled my nose. I didn't place it right away, but I knew it meant danger. I believe, looking back, that it might have been the sulfur smell of natural gas. At the time, I just somehow knew nothing good could come of it.

When I got to my feet, the dizziness worsened. So did the nausea. I heaved, but nothing came out except a groan from the pain. I dropped to a knee, my hands cradling my head. I wanted to scream, but I knew that would be even worse. I needed to move.

Pushing through it all, I rose again. I took a step, stumbling in the rubble and falling. But this time I got up right away. I took another step, passing the mask and the tank. I stopped for a second, distracted by the fact that at least one of the alarm sounds came from that equipment.

I cannot and will not ever claim to understand the human brain. Nor will I ever really get what happened that day. Yet I have this one memory. It is so vivid and it happened as I looked down at the mask and tank just after passing them. A single word filled the void that had existed in my head a second before.

Firefighter.

I knew what that meant. Nothing else made any sense, but I understood. Someone had been wearing that mask. Someone had been trying to help people. Now, they were gone. I followed the rubber hose, even bending down to touch it. I traced it to the crack beside my feet. When I looked closer, I realized it was poured cement, a jagged hunk that had to be at least twenty feet long and twice that wide.

For some reason, I bent at the waist and slipped my bloodstained fingers under the crease where the hose disappeared. I grunted. To be honest I have no idea how hard I tried to lift that slab. Maybe not at all. Maybe with everything I had. It didn't move, though. Nothing did. Except me.

7

Her husband never called back. Julia's gut told her something awful had happened. Calls got disconnected all the time. Phones lost their charge. They were dropped. Even more common, thick fingers accidently hung up. So did cheeks and chins and God knew what else. But that didn't make it any better.

"Mom, are you coming?"

That's when she realized she was pacing. Evan had swim team in the morning. After that, they had planned to canoe down the Brandywine. It was expensive, considering all you really did was rent an old green or red canoe for a couple of hours, but the kids loved it.

Michael didn't, she thought. He felt the place got too crowded. Julia was pretty sure that he had decided canoeing in general was boring. Nonetheless, he would go for her and for the kids. He would put on a good face about it. *That's just how Michael was,* she thought.

Is, she should have thought, not *was. Is.*

"Mom."

"I'm coming," she said a little more sharply than she had intended.

Julia shook her head. This wasn't the first time she'd feared that something had happened to Michael. She liked to think that every mom had these moments, times when a husband didn't answer the phone when she thought he would. Maybe a message not being responded to for half a day, even when his calendar had been clear. There had even been dropped calls. She remembered one during a snow-storm two years before. She had been sure something awful had happened. Julia had envisioned tires locking up, maybe a semi plowing into her husband from behind. His car careening off the road, maybe into a frozen pond.

"Shit," she whispered.

Julia was sure other people had thoughts like that. They had to. Without thinking about it, she dialed his number again. The call went to voicemail, so she decided to text him. Although he had asked her to keep everything on his new phone, she started a chain with both numbers.

Hey, call me. I'm worried

Julia stared, watching for the three dots that would tell her a response was coming. The screen remained unchanged. Closing her eyes, she remembered that night two years ago during the storm. She had tried to call him back right away then, too. And probably texted as well. After five minutes, her phone rang. He was laughing, actually, telling her how he had dropped the phone and hung up when he tried to pick it up off the floor of the car. She even chastised him, lightly, telling him that he should drive more carefully. He thought that was cute.

No matter how much she didn't want to, Julia had to go watch the Phillies game. The boys expected it. She remained standing there, her phone in her hand, not necessarily due to the feeling deep in the pit of her being. That was part of it, but although she would admit it to no one, she had spent the last twelve years doing things that she really didn't want to do because it made her children happy, or well fed, or alive and safe, even. Those selfless decisions added up, no matter how much she told herself they didn't. The game was just the next one to throw atop that pile. A pile that was getting harder and harder to climb.

I can't do this alone.

The thought invaded like a fly that swoops into the house as you are shutting the door. No matter how fast she might have been, how careful, it was getting inside. And once it was there, it could not be ignored.

The thought buzzed by again, but like an echo, softer and further away. She felt a wave of self-centeredness, both for the thought and the delay in watching the game with her boys. She was better than that, she thought. Stronger. So, putting the phone in her pocket, she joined Evan and Thomas in the family room. She even laughed a little to herself, thinking she was crazy for all that worry.

8

That's when I saw the other finger. It, too, was stained with blood, someone else's blood. It was someone else's finger. It's unnerving to think about. Not that the finger of a corpse rested inches away from me. Nor that it lay in the rubble utterly alone, with no sign of who it might have belonged to. All those things might have overwhelmed someone under normal circumstances. For me, right then, and thinking back to that moment even more so, it was something else.

I see that finger every day of my life, now. It hovers just beyond every thought and every memory I have. I don't know if I can describe that moment, really. Before seeing it, my mind felt, in a lot of ways, new. Not blank, necessarily. Not empty of thoughts or even empty of memories, though it was. Instead, it felt like a clear white sheet of sparkling paper, perfectly devoid of any mark whatsoever. On that pristine surface, the very core of what would be rebuilt as me over time, that finger painted itself in vivid horror. It became my genesis, my new beginning.

I stared at it. Once again, time diffused around me. I stood in a bubble where seconds flew yet hours never existed. My head tilted and a drop of blood slipped into the corner of my eye, quickly coagulating among my dust-covered eyelashes. I did not even try to brush it away. I felt frozen, somehow attached to this disjointed body part.

I never thought to crouch down and pick it up. I never even considered touching it. I did look at the mask and the tank and the tubing that disappeared under the rubble. I heard the blaring alarms, and I wondered if it belonged to some rescue worker.

Why would a rescue worker be here?

I'm sure that thought seems idiotic or, worse, fabricated. Yet that's where my mind went. At the moment, I still hadn't figured out that I had just survived what would eventually be called a terrorist attack on US soil.

Instead, I took a step. And then another. I moved toward the light and away from the shrill, jarring alarms that called out around me like the lost souls of the dead. With every step I took, I thought I rose to the land of the living. It would take me time to know how wrong I was. For instead of up, I traveled further and further down.

9

Julia stared at the television. As each moment passed, her thoughts floated further and further away. Her mind scrambled for answers, ones that might explain questions that scared her to death. She repeated over and over again: *He'll call. Any second, now, he'll call.*

At one point, she stood. Maybe, at first, she thought to go to the bathroom, or clean up some of the dishes from dinner. The boys, engrossed with a pregame interview, sounded like two grown men laying out the pros and cons of the designated hitter.

On a normal evening, that might tickle her. She might think about how raptly they paid attention. She might wish that they would pay that much attention at school, regardless of their exceptional grades. Inside, she might even feel an unspoken pride that her boys liked sports so much. How lucky that was.

None of that came to mind. She looped to the kitchen and moved to the front window. Her fingers pinched the seam of the drape. She moved the fabric slowly, like a young child might turn the crank of a creepy jack-in-the-box. She stood there, listening. When she heard the first car engine, she thought it was him, that he was home. But that hope was quickly snuffed out. Michael was in New York City. He wouldn't be home for hours . . .

If at all.

God. She pressed in on her temples, trying to clear away those thoughts. She laughed, even, finding herself being childish. She had been a stay-at-home mom for over ten years with a husband that traveled more days than he spent at home. Michael being early should have shocked her more. Nonetheless, her gut just wouldn't stop churning, itching at her nerves, telling them a tale that her brain just couldn't handle.

Slowly, she paced one more circle and then rejoined the boys. By then, the first pitch was still almost an hour away. Without looking at her, Evan and Thomas made space between them on the couch. She settled in, and they inched closer to her, pressing into her, gently. Thomas's head rested on her arm. Carefully, she wrapped him up and held him even closer.

The news broke two minutes later. For two minutes, Julia led her normal life. She had her children. And she had plausible deniability. Looking back, maybe she should have cherished that time more. Each second should have been placed on a pedestal to be worshipped. Instead, it passed too quickly and a new, shattering reality screamed out at her from, of all places, the television.

The red banner flashed across the top of the screen.

BREAKING NEWS: EXPLOSION AT NYC PENN STATION.

Julia saw it. She read it. But it didn't register. Not as if she didn't understand the words. They made perfect sense. Instead, for a moment, they felt like part of the show. Like lines in a movie in which a family unknowingly watched a ball game while tragedy struck from far away. She blinked.

In a time when presidential campaigns became reality television and news programs resembled the satirical shows that mocked them late on Saturday nights, Julia watched like this drama was happening to someone else, some fictional mother of two who lived in a Lifetime movie.

What will she do?

It was Julia's thought. Her question. But she asked it about some-one else, some heroine who must somehow overcome this . . . A high, tentative, heartbreakingly young voice made it all real.

"Mom?"

The switch turned. That young voice cut through the veil between technology and real life.

No.

Julia slowly turned. Evan, eyes wide, stared back at her. His mouth opened and his lips quivered just slightly. Like he'd used the only word that he could form.

The feeling rose up through Julia. Like a flood of molten lava start-ing at her waist and burning through her stomach, behind her ribs, and up her throat. It built there, solidifying, choking her.

Evan started to shake. Thomas, oblivious to the banner, noticed this. He leaned forward. One look at his brother, he burst into tears. He sobbed, sputtering out sounds meant to be words. But Evan just shook. His face turned red while Julia watched, frozen in a few sec-onds that spread out longer than a lifetime.

Julia grabbed her sons. She squeezed them to her, burying their heads, maybe as much for her survival as theirs. Her brain misfired, shooting rapid thoughts out as if she hoped to hit a different target than the one being announced on the television.

Maybe he wasn't at Penn Station . . . Maybe he was already on the train . . . Maybe I read the banner wrong . . .

But she hadn't. And his phone had gone dead.

Julia didn't cry, not at first. Nor did she breathe. She held her boys and listened.

"At 6:00 P.M. this evening, reports confirm, at least one explosion tore through Penn Station in the heart of New York City. Emergency crews arrived on the scene immediately. As they worked to find survi-vors, a portion of the building directly above the station collapsed. At this time, authorities are unsure if a second explosion occurred or if damage from the first weakened the foundation of the arena. It's being reported that first responders were killed in the collapse. And that at least one subway train crashed. Natural gas leaks are hampering rescue efforts. We go to Farin Glass on the scene."

Julia shook, too, although she didn't know it at the time. Evan pushed away from her, a primal noise escaping as he stood.

"It's okay, baby," Julia said.

She thought, at twelve, he couldn't know that Michael was there. Maybe she didn't even know. Maybe this was all a dream. But then she looked at him. And his eyes looked so much like his father's. It was all too much.

"Call Daddy," he said.

"I . . ."

"Call Daddy."

Julia did not know what to say. She didn't know what to do. No thoughts formed. No decisions. She needed to feel this, to comprehend and process what she had heard on the television. At the same time, she had to be there for the boys. She couldn't be herself. She had to be someone else, someone above this. Someone who could remain calm. Could handle this. She had to do that for Evan, and for Thomas.

"Okay," Julia said.

She dialed Michael's number. It went directly to voicemail. She looked into Evan's eyes. She didn't see the pain and fear. Instead, she felt it deep inside her own heart. Her own soul. And she did something then that could never be undone.

"Hi," she said to the sound of her husband's recorded voice. "You're okay, right?"

It happened without premeditation. She never dreamed that was what she would do. She'd always tried to be honest with them. When the small bumps of childhood occurred, she tried to let them navigate them. They needed that because life could be hard. It could be cruel.

It was cruel. For as she spoke, his mouth opened. This time, the corners rose. It was the most genuine and heartfelt smile she had ever seen cross her son's face. And it pushed her down the rabbit hole.

"So you won't be home until tomorrow," she said.

Thomas squirmed. He looked up and saw his brother's reaction. He started to laugh. Julia felt like she was going to be sick. She thought, *What have I done?* At the same time, it was too far now to turn back.

"Okay," she said. "I love you."

Julia pretended to hang up the phone. Evan wrapped himself around her.

"I knew it. I knew it. I knew he was okay."

10

I didn't know if it was smoke or more dust, though my thoughts remained so vague, like headlines instead of full stories. If it was smoke, I knew I wouldn't make it. I'd suffocate there in the dark, stumbling along on a ground that seemed to move every time I took a step. If it was dust, I would still die, just twenty years from now, of cancer.

I knew these things. They appeared on the blank page right below the dismembered finger. The beginnings of what felt like a new existence, not someone else's life but not my own. More like an empty vessel slowly filling with a trickle of experiences.

Through the haze, I could see the light. It looked odd, not right somehow. I stopped, staring at it. I willed it to be something else. I tried to see it as warm and yellow. Instead, it was harsh and white.

"It's not the sun," I said.

Those were the first words I'd spoken since opening my eyes. They came out as if dipped in shards of broken glass, scraping up my throat and cracking my tongue. I stared at the light, down at the light, and nothing made sense.

My chest shook and my hands tightened into fists. My head throbbed, and I hate saying this, but I cried. It came out like the words, sharp and cutting. My body convulsed as tears fought through the dust and grime on my face.

But I still moved. I took a step, and then another, as I descended into darkness, chasing the light.

———————

A train. I stood just on the outskirts of the light. It cut through the thick air, illuminating a beam of particles that seemed almost alive in their movement. The light shined out from the front of a subway engine, although I didn't know what it was at first. A web of jagged cracks radiated out from a large hole in the glass. The smell of gas choked me and I coughed.

As if in answer, I heard voices. They echoed back up the way I had come.

"This way. Hurry."

"Hello," I called out, but my voice sounded frail and shallow compared to whoever had spoken. No answer came back. Yet I heard movement, shuffling, scraping sounds that harkened more to a wounded animal than anything else.

Nothing made sense. I looked around, really looked around, and realized that the train sat below me still. The ground on which I walked seemed to slope down like a ramp. For some reason, I felt frightened. Something inside me screamed, telling me to return to the darkness, to hide from this abominable sight. But the voices sounded again. A little farther away. So I moved.

My foot caught on something. I stumbled, putting a hand on the wall. Something cut the skin of my palm. When I looked, it was, I think, an exposed iron beam of some kind. It jutted out of the wall. That's when I saw the opening below me. The floor was gone. Well, not gone, really. A part of it, at least, dropped like an enormous ramp. A white tile slid down and struck something metallic. It shattered into pieces.

Then, stupidly, I turned my head, looking down to see what had caught my foot. It was a body, I think the engineer from the train. Maybe he had been thrown through the hole in the windshield. How could I be expected to know?

The picture around me suddenly made sense. I may be wrong, as everything still had a dreamlike feeling to it, but it looked like the ceiling above a subway tunnel had collapsed and a train slammed into the debris.

I stared at the body for a moment. To be honest, I felt nothing. It was like I was so detached from everything, I had no idea *how* to feel. Nor did this dawning understanding of what I was seeing have any association for me. I had no memories to draw on, nothing to compare this to. They had been severed, like everything around me. Like that finger.

Eventually, I moved toward the voices again. When I saw the first person moving, that overwhelming feeling of something, maybe sadness, maybe caution, stopped me again. The tears started up. So did the shaking. I stumbled, almost fell. But this time, someone caught me.

"We've got another one here," a voice said.

Hands reached for me, supported me. And the world spun and spun until I closed my eyes again.

11

"You can sleep in Evan's room."

The words were robotic. Julia moved like someone else: the old Julia, the Julia who existed before she heard what she heard, before she shut off the television, like the Julia who called the shots. She told the boys they needed to get into bed. She watched them, still as stone, as they brushed their teeth. She turned off their light and silently closed the door. And neither of them said a word, even though it was hours before their bedtime. Both Evan and Thomas avoided looking directly at their mother and did what they were asked without hesitation.

They sensed something, surely. Yet they would never ask. Life hadn't yet turned on that part of the brain that might need to face the fear they felt. Instead, they would sit in the darkness of their room and feign sleep.

The second Julia reached the stairs, the tears started. She did not sob, or really even cry. Not really. Instead, she walked with a firm, otherworldly purpose. She called Evelyn.

"He's not there, right?" she said.

Julia didn't answer right away. She couldn't. "Is Tom home?"

"Yeah. Do you need me . . . ?"

"Can you come over and sit for the kids? They're in bed."

"I'm on my way," she answered, too quickly.

Julia put her shoes on. She got her keys. She opened the garage door and backed the car out, pulling out onto the street. Evelyn's car came around the bend, tires squealing. It slowed and then stopped beside hers. They rolled their windows down.

"Oh, God, Julia."

"I'm going to find him," she simply said. And drove away.

———————

He's alive. I feel it.

Julia wouldn't put on the radio. She couldn't listen to that. It meant nothing. Instead, she drove on pure instinct, never once questioning her route. Her car sped across Route 202 and merged onto the Pennsylvania Turnpike as if it drove itself.

What am I going to do?

Once again, the thought invaded. She pushed it back. A strange smile lifted the corners of her mouth.

"He's okay," she said aloud. "I'd know if he wasn't."

Can I do this alone?

That had never been a part of the plan. They were partners. They were supposed to be partners forever. Years should have spread out in front of them like the highway on which she drove, no ending in sight. It had been a promise, made even before their wedding day. One that simply could not be broken.

"Stop," she whispered.

Her thoughts no longer listened to reason. They bounced and crashed with the numbness of circumstance. One minute, the thoughts of the future nearly suffocated her. The next, memories of the past threatened to break her forever.

AN INTRODUCTION

Julia was twenty-one when she met him. Of all places, in a bar. At the time, she was due to graduate in less than a year. She was majoring in political science and had just started as a volunteer coordinator for a candidate in Delaware running against an incumbent for statewide office. It was an uphill battle, one destined to be lost. Yet, as that summer started, she felt as alive as she ever had before, with one foot in the future and one dancing to the live music at the most crowded club in Dewey Beach.

"You need anything?" her friend Mary Beth asked, shouting to be heard over the music.

Julia shook her head. She stood by the back of the bar, just above the deck that stretched out to the Delaware Bay. It was hot for Memorial Day, in the eighties, and summer had infected everyone in the place. As the band played a fusion of calypso and hip-hop, people stood shoulder to shoulder, all smiles and sunburns.

"You sure? There's a guy buying."

"Who?"

With a Cheshire smile, Mary Beth shrugged. "Some frat boy from Delaware."

Julia laughed. "I'll take a Tanqueray and tonic, then."

Just as Mary Beth walked away, Julia caught sight of three friends from the campaign. They came over, exchanging loud hugs. They merged effortlessly with Julia, Mary Beth, and all of their friends. Julia sipped at her gin and tonic, dancing and laughing and sweating the hours away.

"You want another?" Mary Beth eventually asked.

"Is your buddy still here?"

She pointed. Julia lifted to her toes, trying to get a look. The place had just gotten more crowded. Something distracted her friend and the pointing finger swayed, but not before Julia caught sight of a group of guys near the far corner of the bar. One stood a head above the others. Leaner than his friends, he certainly had the look of a Delaware frat boy in his white T-shirt, slicked-back hair, and Ray-Bans. His glasses hung low on his nose when their eyes met. Honestly, in the moment, she couldn't know that. They were too far away. Yet she did think he saw her just as she saw him.

He was the exact type she tried to ignore. She should have laughed him off and asked Mary Beth for another free drink. That's not what happened, though. Something passed between them. Some inevitable force cut through the humid, smoky air. Later in life, some of her friends would mention similar experiences the first time they saw their future husbands. None of them, however, could truly explain it. No factor stood out. There was physical attraction, certainly, yet the place had a good number of hot guys. From a mundane point of view, though, it could be nothing else. They never spoke. They knew nothing about each other. Yet she felt drawn to him, like if she gave in just a little, she'd find herself wandering across the bar and introducing herself, a truly uncharacteristic move.

Just as it got dangerous, the moment passed. The music blared and the party around her raged. Her heels touched the ground and she danced, convincing herself she would forget the guy in minutes.

Months later, Julia sat at her computer in the corner of the campaign headquarters. Volunteers milled around her, stuffing letters into envelopes and using small pink sponges to seal them. Out of the blue, she thought about the guy at the bar. His face appeared at random occasions, never called for and always just a little bit distracting. She tucked a lock of hair behind her ear and looked at the blank white wall. A smile came and went and she shook her head, feeling childish. She had a mountain of work to do, and she certainly didn't have time for anything so frivolous as daydreaming about a guy.

"Julia, come here for a minute."

She blinked, turning away from the wall and looking across the room. The campaign manager, a twenty-nine-year-old former staffer for one of the state legislators, now hitching his career aspirations to a long shot, waved her to the back office.

"Hey," he began. "Would you be interested in working the event tomorrow?"

Her heart beat faster. The election was two days away. The president of the United States was scheduled to visit Wilmington the next afternoon to stump for one of the other statewide candidates, a long-shot challenger to the sitting US senator and a possible swing seat.

"Um, of course," she said.

Julia left the meeting feeling light-headed and severely unfocused. She spent the rest of the day alternating between uncontrollable excitement and a simmering fear as she prepared, and overprepared, for the next day. At one point, one of her volunteers, a seventy-six-year-old retired nurse, lightly touched her arm. She looked up into the woman's eyes. They looked milky and damp, but the woman stood as straight as an old oak tree. She'd come to the campaign at its start, sitting a seat away from anyone else and constantly humming under her breath. But when Julia's gaze met hers, she truly noticed the woman for the first time.

"Are you feeling okay?" the woman asked.

Julia smiled ear to ear. "I'm going to meet the president tomorrow."

The woman patted her. "Doesn't surprise me at all."

Julia's head tilted. "Why's that?"

"You're heading for big things," the woman said. "I can see it all over you."

———————

Julia sat under a life-sized bronze statue, chatting with a friend who worked for the county executive. In her excitement, she arrived an hour early for the event at Rodney Square, a block of green grass in the center of a gray city.

"Who's the guy on the horse?" her friend asked, thumbing up at the sculpture.

"It's Caesar Rodney," she said.

"Who?"

"One of Delaware's delegates to the Continental Congress . . ."

"Oh," she said, though Julia could tell she didn't care.

Shading the morning sun from her eyes, she looked across the square and watched as more volunteers arrived. The day was cool and smelled of drying leaves and coffee. A steady but not overwhelming line of traffic passed on the street behind her. She could hear a police officer directing cars around the five trucks unloading equipment for the afternoon's event.

About five minutes before they were scheduled to start canvassing the city with flyers, a straggler appeared at the far side of the square.

He dressed like he belonged in a much bigger city, with fitted black jeans, cool urban boots, and a zip-up gray fleece under a slightly darker sports jacket. What caught her eye, though, were the Ray-Bans.

Julia watched him walk toward the group. He seemed to watch her as well. The moment was like a near-death experience in reverse. Instead of her past life flashing before her eyes, Julia saw her future. It passed at the speed of light, pictures painted more in emotion than in color. If asked to describe what she saw, or, more accurately, what she felt, words fell short. Instead, she would feel the flutter of destiny rise up to her chest, and her answer would be nothing but a knowing smile.

For the first few minutes, the two orbited each other. At one point, Julia lost sight of him for a second, but when she turned around, there he stood. His glasses were off and he looked down at her with large blue eyes.

"You look familiar," he said.

She took a step back. "Um, hi."

"Oh, sorry. I just saw you and it's driving me crazy. I know I've met you, but I can't place it."

She looked at him. His hair was styled perfectly. He had wide cheekbones but a sharp chin, and his mouth looked locked into a perpetual smile. She recognized him immediately. Not that she would let him know that, though.

"Can't tell you," she said.

He shook his head in earnest. "We need to figure this out."

They crossed paths over and over again that day. Each time, he spent a minute trying to connect the dots and she spent the rest getting to know him. He learned that Julia was an only child and that both her parents worked for DuLac Chemicals, the state's top employer. She learned that he was the older of two and worked in the governor's office, though she couldn't quite figure out exactly what he did there.

They ended up in the same group for lunch. Five or six of them walked a few blocks to a small out-of-the-way pizza place. They found a table in the back, so shadowed that it was hard to read the menu. They sat next to each other, and as each minute passed, her perception narrowed more and more. Even before their lunch arrived, it might as well have been just the two of them in the restaurant.

"What do you love?" she asked, feeling empowered by the energy of the day.

"Me?" he asked.

"Yeah, you."

"Baseball, I guess. I played through college . . . and I miss it sometimes."

"Wow," she said.

"What about you?" he asked.

"I don't know yet," she said. "I love what I do." She smiled. "I love today."

"That's cool."

"Where do you think you'll be in five years?" she asked, her elbow on the table and her cheek resting in her palm.

"I'll run for office. Maybe you can be my campaign manager."

She laughed. "Or your opponent's."

"Ouch. From what I can tell, you could probably run against both of us and win."

"Sure." She shook her head. "But I have no interest in being the candidate. I just want to do something that, I don't know . . . means something."

"I hear that," he said.

"What about baseball?" she asked.

He laughed. "Hitting a ball with a stick can only get you so far in life. So I thought, 'Why not politics?' Anyone's good enough for that, right?"

Shockingly, she can barely remember any of the event, even the moment when she shook the president's hand. Later, when she developed the film from her camera, she would find two pictures of POTUS and twenty-two of her mysterious new friend. In the moment, though, it all felt so natural.

When everything was over, he walked Julia to her car. "Are you going to O'Friel's?"

Everyone who worked the event was meeting up there later that night. She nodded, though before that moment she had been on the fence.

"Can I pick you up?"

Whoa, she thought. But she nodded again.

"Great. Can I have your number?"

She gave it to him. It was the first time she had given her number to a boy, ever. She'd been too busy and, frankly, unimpressed before that day. True to his word, he picked her up, complimenting her outfit and asking her thoughtful questions for the entire ride to the bar. They spent the night mingling with the group and coming back together. He touched her hand and, out of the blue, she touched his hair. When everyone sat down at a long table, she sat at one end, talking to a few of her friends. He glanced at her, lifted his beer, and sat at the other. She paused then, realizing something was very different. He wasn't blowing her off. He was giving her space. She had never met a guy with the confidence to do something like that.

As the hour got late, they met back up, sitting together at a quiet two-top in the corner. He looked her in the eyes.

"Memorial Day," he said.

"What?" she asked.

"That's when I saw you. I can't believe it. You were across the bar."

"Oh, yeah," she said, patting his shoulder. "You were buying drinks for us."

He looked confused. "Me?"

"I thought it was you."

"Huh, I don't remember that."

As he dropped her off that night, they shared their first kiss. It would be over a year until she admitted that she knew exactly who he was when he first appeared that day. It would be a year and a half before he admitted that he had, indeed, bought her and her friend drinks at the bar on Memorial Day.

12

No matter how hard she tried, her memories of the past could never be enough to will away the present. The fears crashed back like a storming ocean, and Julia drove with abandon. As the sun set and news of the bombing held the world in its unyielding grip, her journey took on an even more surreal nature. No drivers made even fleeting eye contact as they moved along the New Jersey Turnpike. Everyone had windows closed and looked to be listening raptly to reports of the attack. At the same time, people made way for the faster-moving traffic, as if they somehow understood that, for this night alone, others might have more pressing needs than their own.

When Julia saw the sign for 16E, Lincoln Tunnel, she swerved to the right. She entered the ramp going about sixty miles per hour. She failed to notice the glowing red brake lights ahead. By the time she did, she had to slam her foot down on the brake. Adrenaline widened her eyes and somehow tightened her grip on the wheel. The tires locked up and she swerved into the shoulder, coming within an inch of the white SUV in front of her.

As the endorphin boost left her system, she sagged into the seat. Trying to catch her breath, Julia stared out the windshield. The line of red lights stretched out for what looked like miles as it bent away from the turnpike and onto the access road leading to the tunnel.

She couldn't move. She was so close to the city. She could see the first twinkle of light across the river. This couldn't stop her, though. Slowly, she inched the car all the way into the shoulder and crawled closer and closer to the tunnel.

Within about a hundred yards, she had to stop again. A line of cars blocked the shoulder ahead. Without making a sound, the tears now dried on her skin, Julia locked the brakes again. This time, she swung the driver-side door open and stepped out of the car. Someone behind her honked a horn as she walked between the cars in the shoulder and the cars in the rightmost lane.

Eyes followed her. Some of the drivers looked angry, frustrated, and even afraid. Others stared like they saw a ghost among them as she strode, head up, among the motionless traffic, her white shirt reflecting light as she moved from one set of headlight beams to another.

Julia saw none of this. She barely saw the cars. She simply saw a path ahead, the way she must take. In that moment, everything had left her mind. All memories of the past. All hopes for the future. It all melted into a single, primal need. She had to get into the city. And nothing could get in her way.

Strobing red lights mingled with the more constant illumination of the endless traffic. Julia heard voices. Instead of moving toward them, however, she slipped between two cars and proceeded along the concrete barrier wall. The voices stopped. Then she heard the foot-steps approaching behind her. Her pace quickened and she stared straight ahead.

"Ma'am," a man's voice said.

Julia stiffened, and she moved even faster. The steps behind her sped up as the man, a New Jersey State police officer, jogged toward her.

"Ma'am, I need you to stop."

Julia shook her head. The officer caught up to her. He passed her and looked into her face.

"Please. I need you to stop. The tunnel is closed. There's no getting

into the city right now. You can get hurt out here. Let's get you back
to your vehicle."

She never once looked at him. Julia simply put one foot in front of
the other, every step getting her closer to Michael.

That's when the officer reached out. He grabbed her biceps, lightly.
Yet his touch might as well have set Julia afire. Her arm snapped out
of his grip and she spun on him. Her words came out sharp and loud.

"No! No!"

His hand reached for her again.

"NO!" she screamed. "Don't touch me."

Another officer approached from in front of her, yet Julia never
saw him. She swung her attention back to the path ahead. She walked.

"Please, ma'am. I can't let you do this. I need to get you back to
your car."

"No," she whispered.

Then the other officer reached her. He blocked her path forward.
The first officer stepped back, boxing Julia in. She stopped, looked
from one to the other. Her body tensed. Her scream turned to a cry
of visceral pain.

"No! Let me go. I need to find him."

They moved closer. Their arms reached out, calming, pleading
with Julia. The second officer spoke then. His voice was soothing and,
in a way, wise.

"I understand. I do. Your husband's over there, isn't he?"

The question seemed to slip into Julia like a needle. His words
coursed through her blood, quieting the raging emotion, easing the
overwhelming shock. Julia blinked, and for the first time truly saw
her surroundings. Cars and trucks idled all around her. Exhaust filled
her lungs. The heat of all those engines mixed with the humidity of a
summer night on the East Coast. It clung to every part of her and she
realized she couldn't breathe. She had to, but she couldn't.

Julia's chest heaved. Her eyes widened. The second officer came to her. And in a moment of humanity, he hugged her. Julia fell into this man, this stranger. Her body shook as she fought to take in air.

"It's okay," the officer said softly.

"It's my fault," she whispered.

"It's okay," he repeated.

She felt like she might pass out as memories of the past month threatened to crush her to dust. Her words came out thinner than the air. "It is."

"I can help. I promise. Just come with me."

Julia, utterly spent, hyperventilating and succumbing to the shock, nodded. She let the man lead her to a squad car and help her into the backseat. Air-conditioning surrounded her like a cool mist, and her chest loosened. Her body seemed to deflate as the officer got into the front seat. He placed a sturdy laptop on his legs and turned his head.

"What's your husband's name?"

The question brought a picture to Julia's mind. She saw Michael's blue eyes, his sharp chin, his easy smile. But the lines seemed to soften. The edges faded away. She blinked again. And the tears returned, silently running down her cheeks. "Michael," she said. "His name *is* Michael Swann."

13

'm okay. I can walk."

I said it without thinking, really. I felt awful, very dizzy and disjointed from reality. Yet something inside me, a very primal urge, told me to flee. I felt the need to cover my head and run as far away from this place as I could. I kept looking up, like the ceiling might collapse right on top of me. And I flinched at every loud noise that echoed down the tunnel behind us.

My nerves buzzed as I moved slowly in a long line as we headed up the stairs of the subway platform. The man behind me, dressed in a tattered and stained NYC Transit uniform, had helped me for almost half an hour as we all shuffled through the darkness. Once we stepped up to the station—I have no idea which one, but maybe it was 34th or probably 28th—the urge to get out became overwhelming.

"You lost consciousness back there," the man said in an accent.

I tried to sound okay, but my "I'm fine" came out more of a mutter.

"You're bleeding."

My hand, the one already stained with my blood, lifted. My hair still felt damp.

"It's okay."

The man reached for my other hand. "Can I help you with your bag?"

That's when I stopped walking. The man behind the transit worker bumped him. I barely noticed. Instead, I stared down at my other hand. In it, I held a brown leather briefcase. I guess I'd had it since I first stood up. I never noticed. I never knew.

"No," I snapped, jerking forward again.

I needed to get the hell out of there. I needed air. I needed to be free. The walls seemed to press into my chest, crushing the air out of my lungs. The need to escape quickly matched the need to breathe. I pushed past the guy in front of me as he stumbled into the wall. Someone shouted, but I kept going.

"I need to get out," I said.

People moved to the side. I staggered up the stairs, never looking at the case again. But I kept thinking about it. In a way, it made me panic. I just kept going over and over it in my head. Where did the briefcase come from? Had I been carrying it that whole time?

Near the top of the stairs, a firefighter appeared. He wore no helmet, but he did have an oxygen tank on his back. Seeing it, I slowed. I remembered the tank and the mask . . . and the finger. The dizziness got worse. I reached out for the tiled wall, but my hand slipped. I fell back into the people behind me. Their weight, their mass, kept me on my feet, but just barely. Then the firefighter got to me. He touched me, gently, and I didn't stop him. He didn't try to take the case. Instead, he put my other arm over his neck and he led me up into the night.

14

The patrol car's siren burped out a series of staccato wails. Traffic gave way, grudgingly, as the officer piloted them with astounding expertise to a space beside Julia's car. The other officer jumped out, and Julia watched him slip behind her wheel and start the engine. Her car followed as they muscled through impossibly narrow spaces until they reached the left shoulder. There, the cruiser and Julia's car U-turned onto an exit ramp and left the turnpike behind.

She felt so empty. Like nothing she had ever experienced before. She couldn't think of anything at first. She never saw the police officer check his mirror. He saw her face.

Without another word to Julia, he got on the radio. He called in the car's license plate number and Julia's name. Within minutes, they arrived at a station somewhere outside Weehawken, New Jersey. The officer helped her out and led her inside to a waiting area, all without saying another word. She sat, and he leaned forward and spoke softly to the dispatcher.

A minute later, he led Julia back to a small room. A comfortable chair had been placed next to a small desk with a dated computer on the top. They both sat, and he leaned toward her, his large hands on his knees.

"I checked with NYPD. There's still no word," he said, calmly.

"Your car is in our lot, but I think it might be best if you take a little time before you drive home. Should we call someone for you?"

Julia nodded. She looked at the man. He had a dark complexion and a strong, wide mouth that looked unused to smiling. He was huge, well over six feet and built as solidly as a lineman. But it was his eyes she remembered after that day. A deep compassion shined in the soft brown of his irises. They looked at her and seemed to understand that what was happening was progressing faster than she could comprehend. They didn't judge her at all. Yet they made his desire to help her so clear.

"Thank you," she whispered.

She felt tired. Her eyes actually closed.

"Who do you need me to call?" he asked.

She gave him Evelyn's cell. "Tell her I'm sorry. I just . . . I didn't even think about it. I never thought the tunnel would be closed. I shouldn't have just left the kids . . ."

"She'll understand, Ms. Swann. I guarantee you that." He paused. "In just a few minutes, a therapist is going to come in. She specializes in dealing with events like this. We just want you to talk to her, not long. Just so we know you'll be okay getting home. Is that something you're willing to do?"

She nodded.

———————

Not five minutes later, a woman walked in wearing a long paisley skirt and reading glasses that hung from a gold chain around her neck. Her long hair, more gray than brown, was pulled away from her face. She had the type of eyes, inviting yet sharp, that immediately reminded Julia of an old friend, one she'd purposely drifted away from years ago. Every time she and her friend had spoken, words would pour out of Julia like her filter had suddenly disappeared. Then, the second she walked away, Julia would be left second-guessing everything she had said.

"Julia?" Marci asked.

"Yes."

The therapist handed her a bottled water. The condensation off the cold plastic wet her fingers.

"My name is Marci Simmons. I wondered if we could talk for a minute."

Julia nodded. Her gut roiled. Although her thoughts remained disjointed, foggy, she wondered what they would talk about. None of the possibilities seemed even close to bearable, yet those eyes were already tugging at her, almost pleading with her to speak.

"I need to get home to the kids," she said.

"Officer Franklin was able to get ahold of your friend Evelyn. She's got everything under control. We also have someone out front checking for any news on your husband's whereabouts. For now, I'm going to ask you something that is going to be very hard for you to do. I'm going to ask you to take care of you. I know all you can think about is your husband. And that's totally understandable. But I want to make sure you are okay first."

"I don't know," Julia whispered. "I . . ."

Julia's throat tightened. Marci Simmons leaned forward. "It's okay."

"I . . ." She started to cry again. Her strength, what was left of it, simply gave way to the surge of fear and uncertainty. She thought of Evan and Thomas, and her heart broke over and over again. "I didn't know what to do when . . ."

"You can talk to me, Mrs. Swann. That's why I'm here."

"I lied to my son. He was there when I found out about the . . . what happened. He looked at me and I just . . . I don't know. I pretended to talk to Michael on the phone."

The therapist nodded, waiting to see if Julia would continue. When she didn't, Marci Simmons handed her a box of tissues. Julia grabbed one. It felt rough against the skin of her face.

"Life isn't always easy. And it's never perfect. When things get tough, we go into crisis mode. Sometimes, we might snap at someone we love. Or maybe we'll do something worse without even thinking about it. Unfortunately, the rest of us, the people around the person dealing with some stress or tragedy, family and friends, they don't always understand that. Sometimes they get it and sometimes they don't. Often, they are so caught up in their own lives, they don't even notice that their loved one is struggling at all.

"In my practice, I've heard story after story about it. When someone hurting calls out for help and people that they love respond with cold detachment. They might judge someone's pain as overreaction, saying something like, 'People survive worse every day.' As the person navigating those moments of pain or stress, we need to ignore that judgment. We need to forgive ourselves.

"I guarantee that your son will forgive you. I have absolutely no doubt. Just make sure that you forgive yourself. Do you understand?"

Julia nodded, but her eyes looked distant. "I should have just told him to get a hotel room," she whispered.

"Excuse me?"

"I was worried about the money. He already had the train ticket. If I had just . . ."

Julia broke down again. She sobbed uncontrollably. The therapist watched for a second. Then, putting professionalism aside, she leaned forward and hugged her.

"It's not your fault," Marci said. "Just know that. It's not your fault."

But all Julia could think about was that she would never see Michael again.

THE FIRST TIME

Three weeks after they *officially* met, he came by her apartment after work. Julia had finished classes early that day and had spent the afternoon on the phone with a woman she met during the campaign who was the assistant director of the Delaware State Housing Authority. The woman had recruited Julia, hard, promising her a job in which she could make a true difference developing policies to help lower-income families find safe and affordable housing. Julia went into the conversation with trepidation. To be honest, she was aiming way bigger than that. She had dreams of moving out west and working for next to nothing for an organization that assisted on a Native American reservation. Conversely, she also dreamed of moving to Washington, DC, and conquering the world.

"Hey," she said to Michael after opening the door.

He stood with his hands in the pockets of his jeans. He must have stopped home first, because his hair was also in weekend mode, no longer slicked back but swept back and unruly. His smile, as usual, hinted at supreme confidence and the sense to laugh it off. On a whim, she rushed into his arms, rose to her tiptoes, and kissed him.

"Wow," he said.

She stepped back and looked at him again, took him in for the thousandth time. And he simply smiled back at her, like this evening promised to be even more fun than the last.

"I thought you had to work late?" she asked.

"I did. But I couldn't stay away."

They laughed. Since their meeting, not a day had passed without them seeing each other. They'd gone to over a dozen restaurants. They spent nights hanging out with her friends, as well as nights with his. On two occasions, the two groups met. It had been beyond fun, and Julia kept finding herself smiling like a fool after every good-night kiss.

She acted out her best version of a swoon. "Oh, me, too."

He grabbed her hand. "Let's go for a walk."

She glanced out her apartment window. It was already dark. "Now?"

"Sure," he said, pulling her gently out of the doorway.

Julia locked the door and they headed down the stairs. Once outside, he led the way through the adjoining neighborhood as they talked about their day. She lived in a college town. Family homes sat beside two-story frat houses. Sheets painted with Greek letters hung across Ionic columns. A party raged at one. Michael slowed, motioning with his head. She smiled and shook hers. So they kept walking, holding hands and listening to the songs of the night.

Without notice, he veered directly into someone's side yard. Julia laughed nervously.

"What are you doing?"

"Come on," he said.

Julia was, and always would be, a rule follower. She felt on edge as she hurried through the damp grass. When they reached a tree line in the backyard and he pushed his way through the thinning underbrush, she let out a deep breath.

"You're crazy," she said through a huge smile that belied her words.

"Nope," he answered, simply, as they wove between the stark, straight trunks of a copse of oak trees.

The nearly full moon shined down through the bare branches overhead. Julia watched the faint speckles they cast on the forest floor. The sight of shadows at night, ones she had never noticed before, felt at once magical and disconcerting, almost dangerous. When she reached out and grabbed his hand, she snorted out a laugh. Julia considered herself a strong, independent woman, yet she let a shadow frighten her into holding a man's hand. How gauche! Mind you, she didn't let go.

He continued to lead and she continued to follow. Her anticipation countered any desire to change that. She looked around, listening to the utter silence. Although it wasn't too cool that night, maybe low fifties, the first freeze had hit less than a week before, and crickets had quieted since.

"Where are we going?" she whispered.

"Almost there," he said.

He was right. Not ten paces more and they stepped from the trees into a clearing. She glanced back through the trees and could still see the back of the homes behind them. When she looked forward again, she saw two dark lines running off into the distance.

"Are those train tracks?"

"Yup."

He led her just a little farther. To her surprise, they came across six perfectly cross-sectioned stumps, probably cut from some fallen oak. By the way the wood cracked and the bark had all peeled away, she assumed they had been there for some time. He offered her one as a seat.

"It's the best one," he said.

"How do you know?"

He smiled. "I used to come here all the time when I was in school."

She hit him in the arm. "With all your *girls*?"

"No," he said, smiling. "Usually with beer."

The laughter burst from her. Then she motioned to the stump he offered her.

"You take it," she said. "You led us here."

He protested but was cut short when she put a hand on her hip. Shaking his head, he sat and she chose the stump next to his. They looked at each other for a moment in the moonlight. Their features appeared timeless in the pale light, and Julia had a fleeting wish that this exact moment might last forever.

"How'd your call go?" he asked.

It took her a second to come out of the moment and answer him.

"Great," Julia said. "I think it would be great working for Karen. She's amazing, and so smart. They're doing some great stuff down there with tax credit financing."

"Yeah, Karen's got a great reputation. You know she sits on the governor's cabinet?"

"She told me. She said if I took the position, I would staff her for the meeting."

"Nice."

"I know."

He leaned forward. For the first time, his smile faded just a little. His eyes took on an earnestness that she'd never seen before.

"So, do you think you'll take it?"

"I don't know," Julia said, glancing up at the stars. "It sounds great. I just . . . I thought I'd travel, you know." She laughed softly. "Can I be honest?"

"Of course," he said.

"I . . . Since I was little, I always felt like I was supposed to *do* something. It probably sounds crazy. I just feel like it all has a reason, you know. That we have a place, but it's not guaranteed that we'll find it." She paused. "But I need to. I mean, I think about it all the time. I feel like there's something guiding me."

She looked at him, fearing he might see her in a new light. He might have, but it wasn't the one that she expected.

"I know," he said, softly.

"What do you mean, you know?"

He laughed but didn't answer.

"Do you think about money?" she asked after a brief silence.

"Sure," he said. "All the time. But I also, sometimes, think it gets in the way. It's like this insidious little distraction that keeps us from doing something meaningful with the time we have."

"Holy crap," she said, smacking him again. "That's exactly how I feel all the time. That's crazy."

"No, it's not," he said. He looked her in the eyes. She could see the blue even through the dim light. "I sort of knew it. When I saw you that first day, it's like I could see it. It might sound weird, but there were so many people working that day. They were everywhere, and they all kind of meshed into a single thing, like a ball pit filled with just one colored ball. But you, you stood out. Not in how you looked or how you were dressed. It was more like I could see the way you looked at things. There was something important. Not broody or anything. Just . . . I don't know . . . it was like I could tell you had this great purpose. And I wanted in on it."

She stared at him, thinking, *How could he know that? How could he see something like that?* It made no sense. Yet she had sensed it that day, too. She felt whatever it was he described. Like him, her words would be nothing compared to what actually happened. But they had shared it, like their meeting had been preordained, some spark in the great movements of the universe.

Just then, she heard a soft rumble in the distance.

"It's coming," he said.

"What? The train?" she asked.

Out of the night, a single beam of light appeared. It panned along the line of trees until it shined directly at them. At the same time, a steady tremor shook the ground. The sound moved closer and closer, seeming to speed up. Julia flinched, feeling the need to flee, yet his hand on her leg gave her the courage to remain still. The air pushed against her face and she held her breath.

"Oh, God," she said.

The train passed. Her world shook. As the cars roared by, she felt the force pulling her, sucking her toward the mass of crushing metal. It pulled her to the edge of the stump. She screamed.

That's when she heard him laugh. His hands shot up like he was riding on some breathtaking roller coaster. His eyes widened, full of wonder, feeding on the thrill and the danger. When she saw this, when she saw his face, the moment took on a new clarity. Her mouth opened, and a surge of excitement tingled from head to toe.

As the last few cars passed, he rose. She sat and watched him as the vibration ran through her body, stimulating every nerve, making her feel beyond alive. It pulsed inside her, the rhythm syncing with her racing heartbeat. Her toes curled.

She saw the force moving him closer and closer to the track, inch by inch. Then, as fast as it had appeared, the train passed. He went with the momentum, sprinting toward the track and jumping clear across. He hooted with excitement. And she ran to meet him.

He fell to the ground. She fell atop him.

"You're crazy," she said, out of breath.

His smile encompassed everything. "I know."

Her mouth met his. They had kissed, but not like that, not yet. As they pressed into each other, their hands moved in the darkness, peeling away the layers of clothing that separated them. Neither felt the dampness or the chill. Not until after. In the moment, they felt afire, burning up from within.

Astride him, she guided them together. They moved faster than the train had, and her scream, so different this time, echoed down the tracks. A dog barked in the yards beyond the trees. She crumbled atop him, laughing, burning, and utterly breathless.

"Wow," she said.

He closed his eyes. "Wow."

Through the years, Julia would think often about that night, and how she felt. Although they wouldn't say it for some time, it was the moment they fell in love. But there was something else, too. Something that bound him to her even more deeply. As they came together as one, both before and after, she remembered this feeling. It was like the world around her shrunk. The night pushed away. She felt so safe, but it was something more. Years later, after their two kids were born, she put a word to it. She never quite knew if it was exactly right or not. But the word was *trust*.

15

I sat on a curb. It's odd how, sometimes, the loneliest feelings occur when you are surrounded by people. So many, some wounded physically, all damaged emotionally, we all existed in some other world. Dust still hung on the air, filling my throat and diffusing the beams of light from the portable lamps above. It cast haunting shadows across the street. People moved in and out of the light, creating a cadence of the dead shuffling from their graves. The moans of pain, punctuated by cries of agony, only worsened the shroud of horror that surrounded me, surrounded us all.

Half a block away, the lights from two ambulances flashed blue and red. I glanced up and saw a man in a window maybe three floors above. Although he was distorted by the haze and the lights, I think he wore a business suit and held a cell phone to his ear. He stared down at us, never blinking, as his lips moved quickly.

"We need triage down here," someone called out.

I touched my head again. It hurt like hell. Then I looked down at the case. My knuckles around the handle glowed white, then red, then blue. For the first time, I thought to open it. I needed to, suddenly. I still didn't fully understand why, but I needed to open it.

"Sir?"

I looked up. A young woman, maybe in her midtwenties, bent at the waist. She carried a leather medical bag that looked disturbingly out of place, like we had just survived a shootout in some dying western town.

"Yes," I said.

"I'd like to take a look at your head, if that would be okay?"

I paused, but nodded. She came closer, kneeling on the pavement. A blanket seemed to materialize in her hands, and she wrapped it around my shoulders and then probed the wound on my head. Her touch was gentle and surprisingly confident for her age and for the surroundings.

"My name's Fiona," she said. "I'm a resident at Presbyterian. What's your name?"

I said nothing. She shined a light in my eyes, first the left and then the right. It felt oddly familiar yet totally foreign to me, so I simply remained still. At the same time, I tried desperately to break through the fog that surrounded me and seemed to fill my skull. Yet all I seemed to return to was the severed finger. And the headlight of the subway car.

"The cell service in the city is down. They say it's because too many people are trying to call. They don't expect it to be working anytime soon, but landlines are working sometimes. Do you have anyone that you want contacted?" she asked as she continued to do her work.

I still said nothing. I had no answer for either question. Nothing seemed to make sense. I knew I should be able to answer them. That it should be instantaneous. Yet there was just nothing but a gray emptiness when I tried.

The resident's eyes widened slightly. She looked not concerned, maybe attentive. She stood.

"I'll be right back with an orderly. I'm going to have them take you straight to the hospital. Okay?"

I nodded. The pain was excruciating, but I tried not to show it. I watched her walk away; then I looked down at the case again.

Calmly, I stood. On the sidewalk, people hovered about, survivors in haphazard jerks and emergency workers with practiced intention. I merged with them, trying to act natural. A few people looked at me. One man who appeared to be a paramedic saw the blood on my face and hair. He was working on another patient. By the time he gained the attention of someone else, I had reached the corner. I turned onto one of the avenues—I have no idea which—and I kept walking. When the case brushed up against my thigh, my steps lengthened.

I can't say I had a reason to walk away, at least not one I knew at the time. Yet one thing had suddenly become clear. And maybe that's what caused me to get out of there. When the woman asked my name and I couldn't answer, it started something. A little bit of the fog in my brain lifted. Just enough for me to truly understand. Confusion surrounded me, yet one fact became clear: I had no idea who I was. Or, for that matter, where I was. And unlike everyone else, I still didn't know what had happened under the city that night. Yet something deep inside told me to get out, to find safety. So I left behind those who might care for me and fled.

16

The therapist walked her out to her car. She paused before handing over the keys, looking into Julia's eyes.

"Are you sure you're okay?"

She nodded.

"We can have someone drive you."

"No, I promise. I'm okay. I just want to get back to our kids."

The therapist's eyes narrowed, but then she nodded. She handed Julia the keys.

"Thanks for your help. You'll call me right away if you hear anything, right?"

"We will. I promise. And you promise you're heading home, right?"

"Yes," Julia whispered.

When she started the engine, the radio came on. The officer who had driven her car from the turnpike must have turned it on and found a news station on the satellite radio band. Julia backed out, thinking she'd turn it off, but got distracted as she followed the signs to the southbound exit. By the time she merged into one of the two middle lanes of the turnpike, she'd forgotten the radio altogether.

"It's a terrorist attack, plain and simple," a woman with a strong but shrill voice said over the speakers. "What happened with banning Muslims from this country? See what the liberals got us. Innocent Americans dead. Children dead. Mothers and fathers dead."

A man's voice rose in response. "Weren't you the same person that suggested that African Americans were to blame for all these police

shootings? Didn't you suggest building a wall along the border to
Mexico? Didn't you support bank deregulation right before the collapse? Here's what I think. It's the people like you, warmongering,
unethical fascists who support would-be dictators and line their pockets with money earned at the cost of those less fortunate. You've raped
this country for over a century."

A calmer, more professional voice broke in at that point. "Frank,
as the leader of a political party associated with socialistic leanings,
what do you suggest we do?"

"I suggest that we lock up every politician in Washington, career
or otherwise. That's what I suggest."

The woman broke in with a laugh. "So you can run things with
your merry band of jobless millennials. Oh, that would be great. The
economy would go right down the toilet."

"At least we wouldn't be in the middle of a race war!"

"Oh, did I offend you? Is that your *trigger*?"

Julia heard none of this, the chatter becoming white noise. Every
mile she drove back toward Pennsylvania seemed to take her farther
from home. She couldn't stop thinking about Michael. She tried to
remember what he had said right before their last call went dead. Was
it important? Had they argued? She had no idea.

Her head spun around, seeing an access road between the two
directions of the highway. She thought about slamming on the brakes,
veering off the road and going back. The urge to find him felt impossible to ignore. She remembered what the officer had said. No one was
getting into the city. She had to get home.

Yet every mile she drove seemed to push her memories of Michael
further and further away. Her hands tightened on the wheel as her
vision grew blurry. In the past, every time she worried about some
ethereal misfortune following a late call, she somehow never considered it a real possibility. Speeding along the turnpike toward exit 6, it
hit her for the first time. Her husband could be dead.

"No," she said aloud. "No."

Can we afford the house?

Stop!

Will the kids ever be okay?

Her palm slammed the wheel. Julia turned her head, left and right, looking for signs. She needed to turn around and go back. She had to find him. There was no other way.

Her phone rang. She stared at the display on her dashboard. It was Evelyn. Her finger hovered over the button on the wheel that would accept the call. The air left her lungs.

"Hello."

"Are you still at the police station?" Evelyn asked.

Julia heard the tension in her friend's voice. Her head cleared, just a little, and she thought about the kids. She couldn't even get to the city. She had to get home to them. She had to make sure they were okay. After that, she could figure things out. There was nothing she could do in the unending traffic outside the tunnel. The thought suddenly seemed utterly absurd.

"Are the kids okay?" she asked.

"Evan is up," Evelyn answered, guardedly.

Julia's stomach flipped. "Is he . . . ?"

"How long until you're home?"

Julia glanced at the GPS display. "I'll be home by eleven."

She heard Evelyn repeat that to her son. He said something back, but it was too far away for her to understand.

"Is he okay? Put him on."

"You'll be home soon," Evelyn said. "We'll be okay until then."

Julia noticed that Evelyn would not put her son on the phone. That meant Evan wasn't okay. No one was. No one ever would be.

"I need to be strong," she said to the emptiness.

Oh, Michael, is what she thought.

FREEDOM

It is funny how, when times are good, memories paint the past in shades of perfection. We think back to Christmas mornings and see ourselves all smiles, surrounded by bounty and adoration. We remember a single soccer game, one of dozens played in our youth, and we replay the perfect shot, the exhilaration of the small band of parents cheering us on. At the same time, we file away the disappointment of unmet expectations and embarrassing failures. Those memories only rise back up in the low moments, those times when we find ourselves questioning everything.

Driving home, Julia's mind seemed to finger through the tabs, finding one of those moments. One day, not long after her campaign work ended, while sitting in her new office at the housing authority, she had gotten the call. It started out normally. Someone she'd worked with at the US senator's office wanting to touch base. In no time, though, Julia knew this conversation was different. When the woman—her name was Geri, and she was the director of the state office—asked where Julia saw herself in five years, her life shifted. Not drastically, at first. More like an earthquake in agonizingly slow motion.

"Me?" she asked.

"Um, yes," Geri said.

Julia paused. Her mind moved like an old-fashioned typewriter. It jerked forward, rumbling to a point, but something kept sending it slamming back to the present.

"I don't know," she said, more buying time than anything else.

Geri jumped on that. She was a powerful woman in her late thirties. Unmarried, she loved her job like family and was known for being on the clock 24/7. She also scared the crap out of most of the people who worked in government, at least those in Delaware.

"Really," she said. "I'd expect an up-and-comer like you to have a pretty intense plan."

She laughed. "I have several."

"Like what?"

Julia froze up. She had no idea why, though. Most likely, it had just been the moment, the surprise of the call. She surely had plans. Within a week after the campaign ended, she had been hired by the housing authority. She'd held the job for a couple of months, and everything still felt so new. She'd plunged into learning everything she could. And maybe that had distracted her ambition for a moment. Nothing more, though.

"I . . ." The words still wouldn't come. She cleared her throat. "I want to help people. I mean, I love politics. I loved the campaign, the speed of it. The energy." She laughed, nervously. "Does that make sense?"

"Totally," Geri said. "Totally."

I'm striking out, she thought. She didn't know why, or for what, but she felt it nonetheless. And once the thought crossed her mind, another followed. She'd never used a baseball analogy before when thinking about work. *What could that mean?*

The conversation continued for a couple of minutes, but Julia never felt like she found her balance. She sensed Geri's impatience. At the same time, she wanted the woman to at least hint at why she had called in the first place. Unfortunately, that never happened.

"Okay, then," Geri said. "We should get coffee sometime."

"I'd love that," Julia said.

"Good. I'll be in touch."

When the call ended, Julia doubted that would ever happen.

That afternoon, she sat outside the state building on a retaining wall, waiting for Michael and watching three women, all between forty and sixty, smoking cigarettes. One did all the talking. Though Julia couldn't hear, the woman's lips moved with the beat of familiar anger as her hands waved in the air as if conducting the music of discord. Her head tilted slightly as she watched, and the thick feeling that pressed against her breastbone made Julia wish she could jump out of her skin.

Striking out? That thought kept rolling in her head. The phone call, and her performance during it, had put Julia on edge. She felt like she'd just bombed an interview for the best job on the planet. At the same time, it was as if she had barely survived some awful ambush, or lost a game she didn't even know she was playing. Every statement she made during the conversation replayed in her head like a false start or a wrong turn. She regretted everything.

These feelings were new to her. Julia had glided ever forward when it came to school and work. She'd been tested multiple times. Certainly during the campaign. Yet she'd risen to those challenges without premeditation or scheming. Instead, she did what she'd always done, worked twice as hard as everyone else. For some reason, though, this one call had somehow erased her store of confidence like a flash flood. And she was left wondering what had changed.

Distracted, she didn't notice Michael's arrival. She looked up and he stood before her, all smiles.

"Hi, beautiful," he said.

"You're late," she answered.

Her attitude hadn't been intentional. Nor did Michael react to it. Instead, he put a hand out to help her up.

"Sorry. How about I buy you lunch to make up for it."

She smiled, accepting his apology. Yet as they walked to the restaurant, the same pizza place they'd gone to on the day they met, that thought returned again and again. *Striking out.* By the time they found a table and ordered, her mood had darkened even further. When Michael started talking about their weekend plans, her teeth clicked together.

"I think we should tell Jen we can't make that fund-raiser on Saturday. We could just rent a movie and chill."

He said it with a smile. In fact, on any other day, she might not have been able to imagine a more innocuous sentence. Instead, though, Julia snapped.

"Have you even thought that maybe I need to go? That the fund-raiser is important?"

Michael blinked, still smiling. "It's just Charlie. Even he knows no one under the age of sixty is going to show up. Plus, I already told him and he doesn't care at all, as long as I still give him the check."

She glared at him. "You told him? Without talking to me first?"

"Well, yes."

"So you're speaking for me now."

"Um, no. I told him that *I* wasn't going."

"God, Michael. Not everything is funny, you know. I have to go." She got up. His eyes widened. "We already ordered."

She shrugged. "Maybe I just need a little space."

Julia walked out of the restaurant without looking back once.

———

An hour later, she called Michael.

"I am so sorry," she said before he could speak.

"You okay?" he asked.

"Just a rough day. And I took it out on you. I don't—"

"So you're not mad at me?" he interrupted.

"No, I—"

"Thank *God*!"

Her eyes narrowed. "What?"

"I have to go," he said.

"Um, okay."

Michael hung up. Julia spent the next five minutes feeling totally confused. Then, out of nowhere, he appeared at the door to her office. His hand reached out for her, and the smile on his face outshined everything that had happened that day.

"Come on," he said.

"What?"

"Let's go."

She stared at his outstretched hand but didn't move. "Are you feeling okay?"

"Now I am," he said.

He reached out a hand. Slowly, somewhat confused, she took it. Michael nodded to Julia's secretary, who was all smiles.

"Um, okay," Julia said, sensing she alone had no idea what was going on.

Michael's smile just grew larger somehow. "I'm whisking you away for the weekend."

He tapped the down button when they reached the elevator. She squinted up at him.

"Oh, are you?"

"Yup."

It wasn't until she sat in the front seat of his car as he headed south on I-95 toward the Maryland line that Julia had time to think again.

"I don't have any clothes."

"Yes, you do," he said, thumbing toward the backseat.

She turned and noticed her overnight bag sitting next to his. "You packed for me?"

He nodded.

"So, this was all before our fight?" she asked.

"Our *first* fight," he said. "Yup."

She laughed. "Thank God. That would have been creepy."

———————

Julia sat on the bench near the back of the boat, her head on Michael's shoulder and the sun setting behind the Chesapeake Bay. Michael had planned the entire weekend in St. Michaels, Maryland, down to the sunset tour aboard a single-mast skipjack. They had sat with the small group aboard for the tour as the captain talked about the bay and fishing for oysters. After his presentation, though, they had slipped away, as far as they could on such a small boat, to just enjoy the beauty of the evening.

A cool, salty breeze rippled the sparkling water, and Julia snuggled in closer. Michael wrapped her in his arms. But they said nothing for a while. Instead, the moment seemed to gently brush away the stresses of the working world, so by the time they docked, Julia felt loose and strangely free as they stepped out onto the pier. Michael nodded to the crab shack sitting right on the water.

"Should we get a drink?"

"Sounds great," she said.

Michael found a small table right on the water. The breeze rustled the awning above them, and he gave her his fleece to wear. She slipped it over her head, pausing for just a second to take in his smell.

"I am so sorry," she said.

"I know, you said that already," he said.

She shook her head. "It had nothing to do with you."

He nodded. And she told him about the call. He listened without a word until she got everything out, except the baseball analogy.

"Geri's a piece of work," Michael said.

"I know, right."

He took her hand. "I want you to know something."

"What?"

"I'll never hold you back," he said.

"I know that."

"No, really. If you want to head to Washington, go for it. Maybe I'll go with you. Sounds like an adventure."

A twinge followed his words. She looked up at the fading colors of the sunset.

"Who knows?" she said. "It's crazy. Maybe it was the way I was raised, but I've always just done what I wanted to do. I mean, I thought about my parents and everything, sure. But that's different. It was always *my* life. You know?"

"It still is," Michael said.

Maybe a little part of her wanted that to be true. Maybe she had felt *held back* by her relationship. Maybe that was why she'd stumbled during the call. Maybe responsibility had already crept in and wrapped its long fingers around her freedom.

"Maybe," she said instead.

And they both turned to look out at the water and the sky.

On the drive home, Michael tapped the wheel while softly singing along to a Pearl Jam song. At one point, Julia watched him. Her mind slipped back to the call. It was as if she could hear Geri's voice again.

But this time, it sounded shrill and suffocating. Maybe she didn't want to work with her anyway. She couldn't even fathom why she had gotten upset with Michael in the first place. Instead, she felt a surge of love as she looked at his profile and was amazed anew by how deeply he already understood her.

A week later, Geri's secretary called and set a time for coffee. Julia showed up in her best outfit feeling as nervous as she ever had before in her life. Geri swept into the shop like a golden-age movie star. She got right to the point.

"I was wondering, we are looking to hire a new press secretary. Do you know anyone that would be great?"

Julia gave Geri a couple of names, though she knew neither of them would even get an interview. Geri's question had, instead, been a condemnation. It said that Julia was officially off her radar. As she left the meeting, she felt sick to her stomach. At the same time, she felt a competing sense of utter relief.

17

Dread followed Julia into the garage. Getting out of the car was an effort. Without realizing it, Julia held her breath as she opened the door into the family room. She saw Evelyn first, sitting in a chair against the opposite wall. Her friend's eyes flashed to the couch on the far wall, where her son sat. His shaggy red-blond hair was a mess, wisps shooting out in all directions. And the red around his big eyes turned them an even deeper shade of blue. He stood as the door opened.

For just an instant, Julia felt a flood of relief. She had expected to find her son hysterical. At first glance, he appeared calm. Fine, really. He didn't take a step; he stood across the room looking at her, waiting.

Then she noticed. He looked peaked. His skin was too pale. His eyes glassy. He swayed gently, like the last dangling leaf of fall before the icy wind harboring the oncoming winter tears it free. His mouth opened, and she never had felt such dread before. Not for how he looked, but for what he would say.

"He's dead," Evan said, flatly.

A lump rose inside Julia, like a plug holding in raging emotion. A tingle vibrated behind her forehead and her eyes burned. She couldn't breathe. The true weight of being a parent, that utter responsibility that makes you forget everything, most of all yourself, took over. Her movements took on a thick calm. And the strength behind Julia's voice surprised her.

"We don't know that," she said.

Evan quivered like a current had run up his spine. "He is."

She went to her son. There were no words she could say. Nothing else she could do. Holding him to her, letting him shake her, all her worry shed away. Her questions vanished. Her fears dried up. They would return, tenfold, but in that instant, Julia remembered the most basic of truths. She was a mother. And her son needed her now more than ever.

"It's going to be okay," she said, stroking his thick hair.

She meant it, too, at least in the moment. It would be okay. They would be okay. She'd get them through this. Holding Evan, she understood that now. There were no other options. She had no choice in the matter, really. Her decision to run off, to try, for some incomprehensible reason, to find Michael, haunted her. It seemed so selfish now. So thoughtless. But in truth, it wasn't. She wouldn't understand that then. Maybe she never would. But in that moment of crisis, as the crushing potential for tragedy suffocated her, she acted. It was real, primal. And she should have felt no guilt. Yet she did nonetheless.

"It's going to be okay," she repeated.

A keening came from Evan then. It filled the room. Evelyn stood but didn't come any closer. It rose in pitch. His balled-up hands struck his mother's back. Not hard and not out of violence. His chest heaved as he fought to breathe. The shrill sound of agony faded.

"No," he gasped, his entire body heaving. "No."

The tears threatened to rip their way out of her face. Fighting them back, she pulled her son even closer.

She needed to say something. There had to be a word she could find that would help him. Some emotional bandage she could wrap him up with. But what? She could . . . That's when Julia remembered. And that's when Evan reminded her.

"You talked to him, right?"

Julia froze.

His eyes somehow grew even wider. "You did, right?"

No matter how she tried, Julia could not summon up the lie a second time. That look on her son's face made such a thought utterly impossible. The first time, it had burst from her without a thought. This time, it lodged in her throat, like a cap atop her breaking heart.

"You lied," he screamed. "You told me he was coming home. You lied!"

And the weight of it all threatened to crush Julia to oblivion.

18

As I walked slowly along the darkened street, the sounds of chaos filtered down every alley and around every corner. I heard sirens and loud voices. Traffic on most of the streets had been blocked off, yet police and emergency vehicles moved up and down blocks, alternating between a slow crawl to sudden, engine-screaming acceleration.

Bodies pushed against me, penned me in, as waving arms seemed to appear out of the darkness, directing the crowd forward as if we had all merged into one slow-moving animal. Some officers held flashlights, and the beams cut through the dust like searchlights. My eye caught a different color, a greenish-yellow glow that tugged at something inside, some innocent yet lost memory of long ago. I turned to see one emergency worker waving a glow stick, the type a child might carry on Halloween. I whipped my head back around, unable to look at it for even a second. And the press swallowed me anew, pushing and prodding us down the street like cattle.

Every few steps I looked at the bag. It was my only clue. I saw it as a key, one that might open up whatever door had closed off my brain. Although I could not have formulated the thought at that moment, I felt like a balloon slipping out of a child's hand. I floated up and up, knowing that at some point I would get too high, out of the reach of any help. That bag was the single string dangling down, the last hope of stopping me from drifting away to nowhere.

My thoughts still felt disjointed, yet a thread of consistency began to form. It started small, a quick glance to the side. A feeling of unease, like I might suddenly turn inside out. A jarring crash sounded behind me, and I startled, spinning around, ready to break into flight. I saw a man standing over some kind of scaffolding that had fallen to the concrete.

That's when the tightness in my chest hit its limit. I veered, bumping into a woman with a torn shirt and her left arm in a sling. She made a sound, either in protest or in pain, I have no idea. I had to shoulder through the rest of them, get out of the mass of bodies, break free before it was too late. I had no idea why I felt that way. But I could not deny it.

After that, I felt eyes on me. They came from everywhere. I felt the need to run, or hide. I reached the sidewalk, the fringe of the shuffling mob of lost souls. My head hurt. I was still bleeding. I needed medical attention. I knew that. Though as rational as that thought might seem, my instincts railed against it. I slipped into an alley.

My pace quickened. I was suddenly sure someone was chasing me. The feeling only grew as my head swiveled this way and that, looking for some hidden danger. It got worse and worse. I could feel my heart pounding against my ribs, like it might burst.

I turned left and right, always following the path of least resistance. The throng of people thinned, becoming smaller pods. They stood with their heads close together, like long-lost friends. Yet not a name was used in their conversation. They wore anonymity like armor against the unknown.

Suddenly, right in front of me, a door opened. Two young men, speaking in quick bursts to each other, exploded out onto the street. Instinctively, I reached for the door. They held it in surprising solidarity.

"Dude, you okay?" one asked.

"Were you there? Do you need help?"

My hand went to my head. "No, I just ran into something."

"Is it bad out there?"

I didn't know what to say to that. "I just need to sit down."

"Sure. No problem. Can you get up to your place okay?"

I moved into the doorway. "Sure. Yeah."

They trotted off toward the destruction. I let the door close. Looking around, I found myself in a narrow hallway leading to an elevator. A bank of mailboxes covered a portion of the adjacent wall. The slight but pungent smell of natural gas and smoldering plastic merged with the earthier tang of mildew. The combination hurt my head.

Silence wrapped me up. I took a step, and my back touched the other wall. I slid down it, sitting on the cool, hard floor. The studs on the briefcase pinged against the threadbare carpet like each strand was woven of steel. Taking a deep breath, I swung it onto my lap. My head throbbed, but my fingers found some strength. They undid the latch.

The case fell open. Belongings spilled out around me, manila folders, a leather portfolio, a small vial of what looked like some kind of analgesic, even an iPhone with no case—a cornucopia of clues.

I grabbed the phone first. I felt a burst of excited energy. For, when I hit the home button, I saw her name: *Julia*. The screen read:

Julia
Missed Call

Those words meant little to me. But that name. It stirred something. It hinted at something intimate and real. I had *missed Julia*. Like I missed some lifeline that might lead me back to . . . myself.

When I swiped the screen, I just stared at the field to insert the passcode to unlock the phone. I tried to dig through the malaise, force my mind to come up with an answer I surely knew. It was my phone.

I set the passcode. The harder I tried, however, the more blank my mind felt. With it came a very deep and feral anxiousness. It was like I held my breath too long, like the nothingness drowned me.

I dropped the phone, grabbing the folders. My fingers flew through the papers, like I'd done it every day of my life. Yet the words melded together. I saw names, but one after another after another. So much that it became meaningless.

Frustrated, I slammed the case on the ground. Things flew into the air. One caught my eye. A small white sticker folded in two, the sticky side inward. It floated to the carpet. Black letters blazed from the side facing up.

GUE

MICHAE

I stared at those letters. Everything that was me focused downward. My vision blurred and then focused again. Slowly, I reached out. I touched the edge of the paper, softly, like someone might touch a newborn. Then I slipped my bloodstained thumb under the edge and flipped it to the other side.

ST

L SWANN

19

Parents make mistakes. It is, and always will be, inevitable. The irony is, they rarely know the big ones when they happen. Julia remembered one summer night sitting on the back deck of her childhood home. Her mother sat across from her and they sipped white wine. Her mother had placed a single ice cube in each glass, and they clinked every so often, harmonizing with the sound of katydids and crickets.

They talked with a candor that can only be earned once a child has reached adulthood. They laughed about Julia's minor youthful indiscretions. The time she snuck out of the house to hang with her friends, and how her mother locked her window, forcing Julia to walk, head hung low, through the front door and into the waiting gaze of both of her parents. They recalled her junior prom and how sad her date looked when she politely let him know they were just friends.

At one point, the stories turned to something that still harbored emotion on Julia's end. It boiled up innocently, as part of a different story involving the car. Her mother sensed it when they mentioned an old Nissan that her parents traded in when Julia was a senior.

"You know, you promised me that car," Julia said.

Her mother looked surprised. "I did?"

Julia nodded. "It was after I got that award from Key Club. You were so happy. I remember you telling me how nothing made you as proud as hearing that your daughter had good character. And you said, since I was so responsible, that maybe you'd let me have the Nissan."

"Oh," her mom said. "I . . . Maybe I did. I'm sorry."

Julia wanted to let it stand there, but she kept going. "I just felt like you didn't trust me. After that sneaking-out thing. And that's why you didn't give me the car. That you changed your mind."

"Nope." Her mother laughed. "I just totally forgot."

There was a minute or so of silence. Her mother tilted her head, looking at Julia.

"That really bothered you," she said.

Her daughter nodded.

"And it still does?"

Julia shook her head slowly. "Not anymore."

"Truthfully."

"Okay, maybe a little."

"I'm so sorry," her mom said. "I never knew."

They laughed about it after that. At one point, as their glasses sat on the end table, empty, her mother looked thoughtful.

"Do you remember when I told you that you couldn't go to acting camp?"

"Acting camp?"

Her mother smiled. "You really wanted to go. And when I said no, you were so disappointed. I remember stewing about that one for years. Honestly, I said no because I was just being a little lazy. The camp was about forty minutes away."

"I don't even remember," Julia said.

"It's funny," her mom said. "In the end, it seems like the moments we thought we messed up were nothing. And we can't even remember the stuff we really screwed up."

She laughed. So did Julia.

"You were great, Mom."

She nodded, looking out at the night. "I tried to do my best."

————————

Evan's head rested on Julia's shoulder. The house was silent except for his breathing. It finally calmed but not until he had clearly been asleep for about ten minutes. As for Julia, her adrenaline had all faded away, leaving her a spent shell.

She never really got Evan to calm down. His fear mixed with anger. He lashed out at her and cried for almost an hour. She had nothing to say, really. She had lied. And he had been sharp enough to figure it out. She somehow knew that this was different. Unlike what her mother said, she knew she had screwed up pretty badly. She also knew that Evan would probably never forget this one.

Yet all those thoughts hung out on the fringe of her mind, mixing in and out with the myriad of worries, fears, and dreads that swirled nonstop. She looked down at Evan, at the top of his unruly light hair, and knew that no matter what grand statement she might whisper to herself, she would probably make more mistakes. They were pioneers, blazing a trail unlike any she had experienced. She had no answers, but the gnawing cloud of loss kept inching closer and closer, tugging at her head and her heart, threatening to tear them free and devour her and her family in a single lifeless gulp.

Stop.

She'd had that thought so many times now. Her inner monologue had become manic. It spun and slashed like a raging tornado. When she focused, she could slow it down. But once it grew quiet, her thoughts came back, more rampant than before.

Her eyebrows furrowed. Julia reached out and grabbed the remote without disturbing Evan. The thought of turning on the news turned her stomach. But she needed to know. She needed to gather information, make informed decisions. She had to be responsible. Not for her sake, but for the boys.

As her finger hovered over the power button, she thought of Thomas. She felt envy. He slept soundly upstairs, unaware. In the morning, that would surely change. This nightmare would be his, too. And way too soon. That broke her heart, but he had a few wonderful hours of ignorance. A life raft of minutes holding him above the floodwaters.

Julia turned on the television. She thought she would have to find the news, but it appeared on the screen immediately. Every channel had had nonstop coverage since minutes after the attack. She adjusted the volume so that she could just hear it. Evan didn't stir, so she watched, swallowing down her pain with every image that flashed on the screen.

The first channel, like most, showed a moderator and three panelists, all on split screen.

"So far, no group has claimed responsibility."

"So, are you saying this wasn't a terrorist attack?"

"I'm saying we don't know enough to say anything."

"Oh, I know enough. We all do. We know exactly who did this and why. What I need to know is what we're going to do about it!"

"I blame the left's liberal agenda in Congress. They've constantly tried to block any real change. Let's say it like it is. They just don't care about Americans."

"That's awfully inflammatory."

"Well, I'll put it another way. They just care about everyone else on the planet and their *feelings* more. Everyone's so afraid to offend someone. You know what that makes us? A soft target, that's what."

Julia changed the channel. She needed to know what was happening.

"Have you thought that maybe this was a targeted attack? New York City is the most forward-thinking metropolis in the world. People of all races and religions live together in relative harmony every day. Maybe that's what was being targeted here. Maybe it was an assault on freedom."

"I totally agree. There are people out there that see other people as less than human. They hate anyone who's not like themselves. How else can you explain the candidates that have won recent elections? The right has tried over and over again to elect a dictator. That's what's next. Mark my words."

Julia's hand shook as she changed the channel again.

"Stop lying to the American people. The truth is out there, and we need to uncover it. The government manipulates every part of our lives. Before you protest, really think about it. We can't even vote for the president. Sure, there's this charade of the general election, but—"

Click.

"Close our doors! It's as simple as that. We need to make America shine again. And the only way to do that is to take care of Americans first."

Click.

The next station might have been the most painful. Julia stared at a live shot of the streets around Penn Station. Portable lights had already been put up, and an eerie white glow shined down on dozens of people sitting on the curb and moving slowly, aimlessly about. Some people darted with obvious purpose, clearly there to help. Some of those wore uniforms—firefighters, paramedics, police officers—yet others were in plainclothes, as if they had been home eating their dinner when tragedy struck and they raced out to do what they could. The camera panned through the crowd, shifting in and out of focus. Julia leaned forward, forgetting Evan slept on her chest. Her eyes burned as she searched the faces on the screen.

The picture went grainy as it panned farther away. When it paused, the focus cut back in on a single police officer in riot gear standing at the entrance to a subway station. He carried a military-grade weapon.

Then another video played, this one obviously from someone's cell phone. It started out so strangely—at least Julia found it so. It showed a group of girls, maybe late teens, posing with someone dressed as Elmo. The girls pursed their lips and cocked their legs just so. Flashes went off. The person taking the video could be heard laughing. Then the scene erupted. The shot jumped, and then a deep, awful thump could be heard, like some fictional giant falling dead. The camera shook violently and then fell to the pavement. It obviously landed faceup, for it kept shooting, showing flashes of light and dark that eventually looked like legs. A hand grabbed the screen just as a plume of smoke, or maybe dust, whited out the entire image. It was as if all the people had been swallowed down to oblivion. A final scream could be heard and then the video ended.

Julia closed her eyes. Her finger held the down arrow and the channels flipped by for a couple of seconds. When she opened them, she let up, slowing the progression. Something caught her attention and she stopped. She had to go back two channels to get to the one that she had noticed, but when she did, she saw a single anchorman facing the camera. Something about the composition of the shot felt familiar, comfortable. She immediately trusted the man. It took a second for Julia to realize it reminded her of the news when she was a child, like a regal Dan Rather might reappear to cut through the chaos and set the world at ease.

"As of this time, over a thousand people are unaccounted for. Continued gas leaks have hampered emergency workers as they try to break through the rubble covering the lower levels of the station. We have now confirmed the earlier report that Eileen Kass, the CEO of DuLac Chemicals, is among the missing, along with seven of the company's board of directors. According to a statement issued by the company, the group was scheduled to board the 6:05 Acela to Wilmington, Delaware."

A fresh wave of pain pressed in on Julia's chest. That had been Michael's train. As the tears came again, a graphic appeared on the screen. It was a running scroll of names, ten on the screen at any one time. It moved quickly—ten, twenty, thirty, forty names—as the anchor spoke.

"Hampering the effort to account for survivors, cell service in the city has been overwhelmed by incoming and outgoing calls, nearly all of which are failing to connect. Service providers are working on the issue but do not expect normal communications in the areas surrounding New York City anytime soon. In addition, hundreds of thousands of people are without power.

"This just in. The Department of Homeland Security has issued a list of those people currently known to be missing but thought to be at the station during the time of the attack."

She slipped out from under her son and fell to the carpet. On her knees, she scurried closer to the screen. Her eyes burned as she tried to keep up. The names passed so quickly. There were so many. She reached toward the screen, as if she might be able to slow them down.

At that instant, her cell phone rang. She froze. At first, she didn't even want to look at it. But she grabbed it off the ottoman and saw a New Jersey extension.

Another wave of emotion crashed. She answered it, feeling a surge of hope laced with crushing dread.

"Yes."

"Ms. Swann?"

"Yes."

"This is Marci Simmons. We spoke earlier tonight. I'm calling to let you know that, although we have no new news on your husband's whereabouts, his name is on the list that was just released."

"Okay."

"Ms. Swann, are you okay?"

"Mrs.," she said, softly.

"I'm sorry?"

"I'm a Mrs."

They remained silent for a second. Then Julia said, "Thank you."

She hung up. Slowly, she made her way on the floor to the couch. Her back leaned against the plush leather and her hand reached back, eventually finding the remote. She turned off the television and closed her eyes, thinking only about her missing husband. As she did, Julia cried without making the slightest sound.

20

The second call came minutes later. This time it was from a number in New York City. Julia fumbled the phone once and then answered.

"Hello?"

"Mrs. Swann?"

"Yes."

In the pause before he continued, she heard a bank of voices in the background, along with the sound of multiple phones ringing. It reminded her, strangely, of the old telethons she'd seen on public television as a child.

"My name is David Gregor. I'm with the New York City emergency response team. I'm calling about your husband, Michael Swann."

Her legs felt suddenly useless. But Julia turned and looked at her sleeping son. Her back straightened.

"Yes?"

"I understand that to the best of your knowledge he was inside Penn Station at approximately 6:00 P.M. yesterday?"

Instinctively, she glanced at the clock over the mantel. It had, indeed, passed midnight. She closed her eyes as she spoke.

"Yes. I was on the phone with him. He said that all the trains were delayed. He was going to look for a rental. Or maybe . . ." Her voice cracked. "Get a hotel room."

"Have you heard anything from him since that phone call?"

"No."

"Thank you, Mrs. Swann. As of now, your husband is included on the list of missing people following the incident at Penn Station. I'm going to give you a number to call if you hear from him in the next few hours."

Her eyes shot open. "Is that possible? Were there survivors?"

"Right now, ma'am, there are hundreds of survivors either receiving emergency treatment or en route to the hospital. And not all survivors that have already been taken to a hospital have been conscious, so some identifications may take some time. The hospitals are having trouble getting calls out from the city, too. People, some likely survivors, are taking boats out of the city. Ferry service between Manhattan and Port Imperial is planning to run throughout the night.

"I can't say what happened to your husband. But I will say that we are working as hard as possible to help everyone we can, and to notify the loved ones of those affected by what happened this evening."

"Thank you," she whispered.

As the man gave Julia the number, she heard a soft knock on the door to the garage. She turned as it opened, slowly. Her mother, Kate Fine, stepped carefully through the threshold. Her eyes seemed to find her grandson first. Julia watched her face. She saw the sorrow there. But her mother hid it quickly when she caught sight of her daughter.

"I'm sorry," Julia said, looking at her mother. "Can you repeat that?"

She felt so drained. For some reason, seeing her mother made that worse. Or possibly, it simply didn't make it better. That fact felt heavy, almost unbearable. Julia jotted the number on an envelope beside the television as her mother stood with her arms at her side, watching and waiting.

"Okay," Julia said. "Thank you again."

She ended the call. Her mother took a step toward her and stopped. Julia saw the helplessness then. Her mother, like Julia herself, had no idea what to do.

———————

Two hours later, they sat at the kitchen table sipping coffee and listening to Evan shift around on the couch. They remained still until he quieted.

"I can't just sit here," Julia said. "I know I should. The kids need me. But I can't get what that man said out of my head. They might have already found Michael. Maybe he's in the hospital . . . or something. I mean, I tried to call, but they're saying phone service is a mess . . . Did you see the videos?"

"Some," her mother said.

At just under sixty, Kate looked a perfect cross between a favorite schoolteacher and an actress playing a favorite schoolteacher in some edgy drama. Her white hair was cut short and tight, and she favored crisp black outfits and sensible shoes. When she spoke, people tended to listen. When she smiled, it felt like you had earned it. She had been Julia's rock for most of her life. Since the kids, though, their relationship had changed. Julia had begun to feel a nagging yet insensible dichotomy. She wanted more help from her mother, yet at the same time wasn't a huge fan when she showed up unannounced. For this night, however, all that was forgotten. They were two women feeling the first clawing fingers of loss, and neither was able to sit still and let that hand pull them down without a fight.

"They said ferry service is running again. The roads might be open now, too. Do you think they'd be okay if . . . ?"

"I know they will be," her mother said. "I'm here until you kick me out." She laughed softly. "Maybe longer."

Julia leaned forward and hugged her mother over the table. "Go," her mom said. "Find him."

Just past 2:00 A.M., Julia crouched in the bedroom they used as an office. She moved quickly but silently, stopping at times to be sure that Thomas didn't stir. Then she continued to shuffle through a stack of photos, looking for one she could use.

Her frustration grew. She dropped one handful back in the box and grabbed another. So many pictures, yet so few with Michael in them. From pictures of the kids as babies, to candid shots of them riding on a miniature roller coaster or playing in the ocean during one of their many day-trips to the beach. A pattern arose. Neither Julia nor Michael showed up in a single one.

She watched her life unfold like one of those old-fashioned penny arcade Mutoscopes. The stop-motion story played out as if Evan and Thomas were orphans, making their way from one adventure to another without a parent in sight. For Julia was behind the camera for almost every shot. And Michael was at work.

She had to dig deeper and deeper into the box of photos. Finally, she came across the first with both her and her husband. They stood under a streetlamp outside a minor-league baseball stadium, the light surrounding them like a halo that pushed back the darkness. She cried, looking at that picture. She remembered the moment like it was yesterday. But so much had changed since. Life had piled up like a game of Jenga. She and Michael had done their best to ease through each step—parenting, work, money. Regardless, the years had taken a toll. Their tower had started to sway and had threatened to topple, making the sweetness and perfection of the beginning that much harder to remember.

ENGAGED

Photographs. We pause the moments of our lives. We see them through artificial lenses. As the cameras click away, we feel so sure of the utter rightness that we never question. Instead, we pride ourselves on encapsulating our happiness, storing it away for some moment far in the future when we can pop the cork and drink of its beauty once again, as if joy moves in a perpetual loop.

That's not how it works. When our fingers pinch the corner of some captured memory, we hold it before our eyes as a tingle starts in the chest. It rises, pushing moisture into the corner of our eyes. We see what once was. It dangles before us like unreachable perfection, made all the worse because we are convinced we held that moment, that most perfect experience, in our hand once, too. But it's gone, reduced to a two-dimensional image that does nothing but fade more and more each day.

See, photographs are not what they appear. They are not little gifts from the past, bringing with them the glow of Christmas morning. Instead, they are paper-thin slices of loss that we insist on reliving in the guise of romantic nostalgia.

Just over one year after starting at the Delaware State Housing Authority not long after her call with Geri, Julia was promoted to assistant director. At only twenty-four, she already supervised career employees over twice her age. Now she was responsible for most of the daily operation of the agency while her boss wielded gilded shovels and oversized shears at groundbreakings and ribbon cuttings. By her third year in the job, the rumbles had grown deafening. The governor's policy adviser for social issues had announced that he would be stepping down. The job had, in all intents and purposes, been placed in Julia's lap. She felt overwhelmed but excited about the entire thing, but it wasn't the best news that the young couple would receive. One Thursday, Julia's secretary leaned back and called into her office.

"It's Michael," she said.

"I'll pick it up. Thanks."

She lifted the cradle and hit the blinking light. "Hey."

"Guess what," he said.

She could hear the pure joy in his voice. "You got the job? Are you serious?"

"Yup."

Not long after they met, Michael became disillusioned with politics. It started slow, but his passion waned and the weight he felt could be seen when his everlasting smile faded. When the state made a play to attract a minor-league baseball team, he was asked to lead the task force. His job satisfaction waxed, but a new seed was planted.

They succeeded and the team came to town. Michael, having rubbed elbows with management throughout the process, was courted within weeks. They called him in for an interview, and he'd been like his old self since.

"That is awesome!"

He started to laugh. "They want me to start on Monday."

"What about giving notice?"

"No problem. I already told Kent all about it. He knows. In fact, he's going crazy outside my door right now. Let's celebrate tonight."

"Definitely. I'll meet you at home."

For the rest of the day, Julia alternated between a giant smile and checking the clock. He was waiting for her when she finally got home. They jumped into his Mazda, and he drove to a new seafood restaurant on the riverfront. The food was amazing, but just listening to how happy he sounded made it even better.

With faux thoughtfulness, she said, "So, did they ask you about playing in college?"

He laughed. "Somehow, they already knew."

"It's not like every applicant can say they played Division I baseball."

He smirked in fun. "I think I was the *only* applicant."

"I am so happy for you."

They sat together at a small two-top. The music played softly in the background, and they spoke louder than they meant to, lost in the excitement. She found herself staring at his smile. His face always seemed to look happy, even when she watched him sleep some mornings as she got ready for work. That night, it was different, though. Julia would swear that his mood radiated out, embracing the entire restaurant. The place buzzed from the minute they got there until the minute they walked out, hand in hand.

"Come on," he said.

She had an idea where they were heading. But when they reached the minor-league stadium a couple miles west of the restaurant, he surprised her. The fence on the first base side along the outfield was low. With a quick look around, he vaulted it. Beaming, he turned to help her across. Caught in the moment, she shook off his assistance and slipped gracefully over the fence. She felt alive, emboldened by their transgression, and she kissed him deeply under the darkened lights of the ballfield.

He took her hand again and led her out toward the field.

"What if someone's here?"

"So what."

Her cheeks reddened. "But they just hired you. If they catch you breaking in, they'll—"

"They'll know how excited I am."

She shook her head but let the moment take her. Julia's whole life had been planned out. She attended the best private schools in the state. She sat on student government and played field hockey and basketball, all perfect additions to her college application. She graduated with a 3.9 average and landed a job within days. He was her one spark, her one chance-taker. She loved when he pushed her, albeit gently, out of her comfort zone. Over the years, she'd learned to go with it. Knowing she could trust him.

He strode right up to the pitcher's mound. There he stopped and looked around.

"You miss it?" she asked.

He nodded. "Yeah. Honestly, when I graduated, I felt this hole inside me. I had played baseball all my life, since I was six. Sometimes it felt like that was all I ever did. I practiced all the time. And we played hard, man. Intense. All the time. And, I guess, I liked the attention, too. My parents bragged all the time. All the students knew me. The way the graduate assistants took care of everything. I guess I got a little caught up in it.

"When school ended and I stopped playing, all that just disappeared. That first year was tough. I kept trying to find something to fill it up. I felt like I couldn't sit still. I got angry all the time. In a way, I felt like an addict going cold turkey." He turned and looked her in the eyes. "If it wasn't for you, I might have stayed that way. Once I met you, though, things changed. I felt like I had a purpose. Sure, getting hired to work here, even if it's just marketing and ticket sales, it feels like I'm home. But you know it's less money."

"Who cares," Julia said.

Michael smiled. He leaned down and took her face in his hands. They were strong and dry, and his thumb cupped her chin softly. They kissed.

"I love you," she whispered.

He tilted her head and their eyes locked. She saw something come over him. He looked suddenly even more alive, even more impulsive. He let go and dropped to a knee.

"Will you marry me, Julia Fine?"

She took his hands. A tear rolled out of her eye and met the corner of her smile.

"Are you serious?" she whispered.

"One hundred percent."

"Then yes."

He popped up to his feet and lifted her into the air. Squealing, she put her head back and closed her eyes. When he brought her down, and they kissed, he pulled back.

"I don't have the ring yet. I . . . I didn't plan this or anything."

"I know," she said. "That's why I love you, Michael Swann."

Giddy, and lost in the moment still, neither noticed the night guard as they climbed back over the fence. When he stopped them, they both burst out laughing.

"We just got engaged," Julia said.

The man smiled, and Michael shook his hand and asked him to take their picture. The guy was a total sport. He took his time, an intense look on his face. When he finally snapped the photo, he nodded to himself.

"Now you'll have it always," he said.

No single statement could have been more, and less, true.

21

I have no idea how long I stared at the sticker. Like the ticking of some old clock, I just kept flipping it from one side to the other.

GUE

MICHAE

Flip.

ST

L SWANN

Flip.

GUE

MICHAE

Flip.

ST

L SWANN

Guest—Michael Swann. Michael Swann. Michael Swann.

It was like I tried to force those words back into my head. Like I could actually manipulate the neural pathways, tie off the synapses, make them connect this name to something inside me. I needed some kind of miraculous conception, for those letters to merge together, then find some purchase among my failing thoughts where they could divide and grow and thrive. Instead, to be honest, they meant nothing at all.

My hand began to shake. My entire body shook. I couldn't sit still. My foot pounded against the wall under the mailboxes, the sound echoing through the empty hallway. I kept hitting it over and over again. Then my hands pulled at my hair, causing fresh blood to inch down my temple, into my ear. I wiped it off and left a new stain on the old carpet.

"Michael Swann," I said out loud. And repeated it over and over again.

I heard the footsteps, but I didn't care. I heard the elevator door open. I saw the people. And it all meant nothing to me. My foot kept pounding and pounding.

"Hey, stop," a man said. Then he paused, his head tilted. "You okay, man? Holy shit, were you in the explosion?"

Explosion, explosion, explosion. I kicked the wall every time that word flashed in my head. I didn't look at the guy. I couldn't, for some reason. Instead, my heart just beat faster and faster, harder and harder. I wanted to scream.

"You don't look good," the man said.

He took a step toward me. He reached out. I am sure he meant to help me. But something snapped inside me. Out of nowhere, I was sure this man was going to try to take my case.

I don't even know what happened next. I know I suddenly felt very unsafe. I felt like I was in danger. Like I was being attacked. Like the world was pressing in on me. The sound of this man's voice became like the shriek of some awful demon. I swear I smelled him, the smell of blood and death and sulfur.

In a way, it was like I blacked out. Yet I saw it all as if it were happening on the television or something. I sprang to my feet and lurched at the man. My hands struck his chest and I sent him stumbling backwards. He hit the closing elevator door and fell to the ground. I stood over him. I even saw the blood on his chest. I thought nothing about that, really. I wasn't really worried that I had hurt him. Nor did I realize that it was my blood, not his, placed there when I struck this stranger. I thought nothing. In a way, I felt like an animal.

"Stop," the man cried out. "No!"

I stood over him. Maybe it was his tone, halfway between a whine and a call for help. Maybe I just came to my senses. Because all I wanted to do at that point was get the hell out of there. I turned and bolted, grabbing the case just before slamming into the door. It swung open and people passing by stared as I staggered out. They shied away from me as I took two awkward steps and then ran off into the shell-shocked city.

22

As Julia stood before her mother, the photo from the night of their engagement hung from her long fingers.

"Thanks for knowing," Julia whispered.

As if in answer, someone softly knocked on the front door. Startled, Julia swung around and answered it. Evelyn, Tara, and two other women from the neighborhood stood on her front porch. Evelyn smiled, yet she had clearly been crying. Tara did not make eye contact. The others were the first to step into the Swanns' home. They wrapped themselves around Julia like a protective blanket. It was well after 2:00 A.M.

"How'd you know?" Julia asked, fresh tears following well-worn tracks down her cheeks.

Evelyn stepped into the house next. The others parted, and it was her turn to hug Julia. They held each other for a time, while everyone else in the foyer stood awkwardly watching. Evelyn let out a choked laugh.

"I told them," she said. "I had to. What can we do to help?"

Julia felt her heart about to burst. She couldn't believe that her friends would be there, at that time, to help. It was so overwhelming.

"My mom's going to stay," she said.

Evelyn hugged Kate next. She'd known Julia's mom for some time, as had Tara. Yet the latter seemed frozen on the doorstep, unsure what to do.

"Well, I'm guessing we aren't going to sleep, so we'll want some coffee." Evelyn's hand lingered on Kate's shoulder as she moved into the kitchen. Julia followed her while the other women spoke softly to her mother.

"What about your kids?" Julia asked.

"Stop. Everything's covered. We're here whether you like it or not."

"But my mom . . . I'm going back."

Evelyn nodded. "I know. Just get going. When your kids are up, I'm taking them and everyone else's to my house. Your mom can get some sleep then. What about you?"

"I'm fine. I don't think I'll ever sleep again."

"You will," Evelyn said, as if she knew firsthand. "Now get going. We got this."

Julia grabbed her keys and snuck quietly out of the house, pausing for just a second to watch Evan asleep on the couch.

"We'll be okay," she whispered.

Julia slipped out and drove away.

———————

Julia arrived at the twenty-four-hour express shipping store in Wilmington just before 3:00 A.M. The glowing window was the only one lit for blocks. She parked on the empty street outside and hurried in. A single young man in thickly framed glasses and a handlebar mustache looked up from a small television.

"Can I help you?"

Julia didn't know what to say. She stood staring at the guy, holding nothing but the photo. Her plan was to print flyers that she could put up around the city. Yet she hadn't made them up. She hadn't done anything. Instead, Julia walked into the store with a photo in her hand and a look of desperation on her face.

"Are you okay?" he asked.

"I . . . I wanted to make up a flyer." She laughed, a nervous sound that caused the guy to reach down and turn off the television. "I should have thought about it. Made it up on my computer." She held out the photo like that might make sense. "I have this."

A phenomenon occurs during tragedy. People become more human. They are connected by something common and larger. Like adherents of a temporary religion, they come together in peace and love and understanding. This young man was no different. He stepped out from behind the counter and gently took the photo from her hand. Then he walked over to the single computer terminal in the shop. Julia followed slowly.

"I didn't know where else to go," she said softly as the guy took a seat. "I don't even know if you have a copier or anything."

"We'll get it done," he said.

She stood behind him as he booted up the computer and opened the presentation-making program. He leaned over and placed the photo on a scanner. Within five minutes, he had the template for exactly what Julia had envisioned. And he'd done all that, gotten to that point, before asking her a single question.

"Is he missing?" he finally asked, looking up at her.

She nodded. "He was in Penn Station."

He nodded. She saw the thought he had. It showed like a projection behind his eyes. He thought that Michael was dead. He felt pity for her, but maybe more. Possibly relief, that he and those close to him had been spared. Or maybe something else . . . morbid curiosity? Yet he said nothing. He added words to the flyer, somehow reading her mind again. He only asked for her name, her husband's name, and her cell phone number, which he added at the end. When he was done, he tilted the monitor up and waited. She looked at the flyer and her heart fluttered, because of what it said and what this stranger had done. Out of the worst night of her life, she had somehow found the purest example of caring she had ever witnessed. The moment burned into her soul, the kind of thing that she knew she would never forget. Though her memories, like a photograph, would be two-dimensional. This man became an angel. And that could never change.

Julia held the flyer in her hand. The heading simply read *MISS-ING*. Below that was the picture of Michael and her. She remembered thinking how young they looked, how people might not even recognize that face compared to his present, more aged appearance. But there was nothing to do about that.

She continued to read. The flyer stated that he was last seen in Penn Station and asked anyone who might have seen him or had any information of his whereabouts to call Julia on her cell. Crying, she nodded.

"Thank you so much," she said.

"I wish I could do more," he replied.

He printed her three hundred copies and placed them in a sturdy accordion file. When she tried to pay, he refused.

"No way," he said. "Just come back and tell me when you find him."

23

Julia listened to the radio for the entire ride up to New York. It took her more than half a dozen tries to find a station that reported news as opposed to opinion. Most of what she heard covered the ongoing rescue efforts.

"Although not confirmed, investigators believe the explosive used in the attack to be a newly developed application of octanitrocubane. It is thought that researchers at the DuLac Chemical Company in Wilmington, Delaware, stabilized the high-density crystal structure earlier last year. It is not known if this product is being used by the US military at this time.

"As people all over the country look for ways to help, the Department of Homeland Security has issued a list of supplies that emergency workers are running low on. Items include dust masks and respirators, work boots in all sizes, and protective socks for the specially trained dogs. A full list is available on our webpage.

"At this time, rescue workers have cleared debris from the main stairway leading down to the majority of the station. They expect it will be some time before the area is secure enough for people to enter, due to the structural damage caused by the partial collapse of Madison Square Garden.

"Near the site of the attack, survivors from the subway crash following the collapse are still being attended to by emergency workers.

Witnesses claim that the ceiling above the tracks collapsed and the train hit the debris at full speed.

"Cell service in and around Manhattan is still down, although sporadic calls seem to be getting through as providers work on the problem."

Julia grabbed her phone. She tried Michael's new number first. It went directly to voicemail. She tried his old work number and almost swerved off the road when it rang. Once, twice . . . Her heart raced and her fingers ground into the steering wheel.

The ringing stopped. Her eyes widened.

"Michael. Are you there? Michael!"

The line crackled and then went utterly silent.

"Michael," she said, softly.

When she looked at the screen, she knew the call had been ended, or dropped. Maybe it never went through. She stared back out the windshield at the darkness and at the glowing white street lines under her headlights. Her head throbbed and she let out a long breath, while the radio continued to report on the explosion.

City officials were interviewed, as were staff from Homeland Security and the NYPD. Julia went back to listening to those reports. Yet when a survivor from the station was introduced, her hand shot to the dial and almost turned the radio off. Something stopped her. Hope, maybe.

"I was just walking down the stairway at the corner of 33rd and 7th Avenue when the bomb went off," the man said. His voice sounded hoarse, like he had been a heavy smoker for decades. "At first I didn't even know what happened. I didn't hear it, not really. Instead, it was like something huge hit me. Not in one place, though. That was what was so weird. It hit me everywhere, every part of me in the front." He paused and his voice cracked often as he continued to speak. "There was a flash of light. Not yellow or red or anything like fire. It seemed bright white. But I hit my head, so that might have been what it was. I know I woke up back up on the street, right on the sidewalk. I don't know how I got there . . ."

The man coughed uncontrollably. The sound cut right through Julia.

"It's okay," the interviewer said. "You can stop if you want."

"Someone was on top of me. She was—"

Julia's hand slammed into the dial and the radio cut off. She looked back at the road and saw traffic at a dead stop. She slammed on the brakes. The tires locked up and she skidded. Turning the wheel at the last second, Julia barely avoided the bumper of a Ford.

"Jesus," she whispered.

The traffic snaked for as far as her eyes could see. A frozen line of soft red lights. She cursed under her breath just as her eyes caught sight of the flashing sign up ahead.

LINCOLN TUNNEL CLOSED.

———

Sitting dead still in the traffic, Julia screamed. Her frustration vibrated off the glass, buffeting back against her frayed nerves. She slapped the steering wheel twice.

"Damn it," she said.

She wanted to pull her own hair out. She hadn't thought to take a different route. Or even check to see if the tunnel had reopened. When she heard ferry service was running, she just assumed. Worse, maybe she just hoped it was open, like her wish could make it so, her will could make everything go back to normal, like none of this had ever happened. She rushed forward blindly, for care and thought meant seeing and accepting the situation.

Her eyes closed. There was nothing she could do. She couldn't turn back. That option never occurred to Julia. For a moment, she thought of accelerating, slamming into the cars in front of her, tossing them out of the way like in a Michael Bay movie. She might have tried, even, until something caught her eyes. She saw an opening in the divider between the oncoming traffic. She blinked, and then looked around. She was on the ramp off the turnpike at exit 16. She glanced at the break in the median again. Julia couldn't be sure, but it looked identical to the one that the police cruiser took her through hours before. Without another thought, she banked left and nosed between two cars. It wasn't until she successfully made the U-turn that Julia realized exactly what she intended.

One hand fumbling with her phone and the other steering, she tried to remember the route the police officer had taken earlier. Somehow she dialed the station at Weehawken.

"Can I speak with Marci Simmons?" she asked.

"Please hold."

Julia gripped the wheel. She saw an exit that looked somewhat familiar, so she took it. Within a minute, while hold music played through her Bluetooth, she realized how lost she was.

"Shit," she hissed.

"Excuse me?"

"Oh, sorry, is this Marci?"

"Yes."

"This is Julia Swann. I . . . I'm sorry. I—"

"Are you driving?"

Julia laughed. "I'm in Weehawken, actually."

There was a pause. "Mrs. Swann, you need to go home. There's no way into the city right now. There's nothing you can do. We talked about this. You promised to take care of yourself."

"I know, I just . . . I heard the ferry was running. I thought the tunnel would be opened now."

"Please, Mrs. Swann. You need to go home."

Julia's body shook. Her car drifted out of the lane and a driver behind her lay on the horn. The sound startled her, mixing adrenaline with the staggering weight that seemed to be pressing the life out of her.

Tears filled her eyes. The taillights of the car ahead of her looked like tiny starbursts as her vision clouded. The horn blared again. With a jerk, Julia swerved to the right, pulling over on the shoulder. Her head turned, and she saw the quick flash of a middle finger as the car sped past her.

"Are you okay?" Marci Simmons asked.

"Yes," Julia said.

"It'll be okay. Get yourself home and stay there. Your family needs that right now."

"Okay," she said.

Julia ended the call. As cars whipped past her, her head fell to the steering wheel and she sobbed.

Her car accelerated, tearing up the ramp back to the turnpike. Julia's eyes burned as she picked up speed. Another car horn sounded as she cut someone off, but it didn't matter. Nothing mattered. Someone was going to let her into the city, one way or another. She considered this to be a simple, irrefutable fact.

She saw one path forward. She would find the ferry and take that over to the city. In the moment, it did not occur to her that she had no idea where the station might be. She never considered there being more than one. She just drove with purpose, yet without aim.

In the instant that she realized she needed to slow down and think, her phone rang. It cut through her temporary madness, and her foot came off the gas pedal. Her heart missed a beat. *Maybe they found him.* When she accepted the call, she felt sick to her stomach.

"Hello?" she whispered.

"Mrs. Swann, this is Marci Simmons. Where are you?"

"On the turnpike near exit 15, southbound," she said.

"Pull over onto the shoulder. An officer will be there within a couple of minutes. He'll drive you through the tunnel."

Julia's entire body seemed to inflate. Her face tingled. "Are you serious?"

"Yes, Mrs. Swann."

"Oh, God. Thank you."

"Just stay there," she said.

———————

Not two minutes after the call ended, Julia saw the flashing lights approach. The cruiser pulled up beside her and rolled down a window. The officer was young, in his twenties, and wore sunglasses against the rising sun. A female officer got out of the passenger side. The moment felt like some deranged version of déjà vu.

"You can get in the back," the male officer said. "Officer Reyes will drive your car back to the station."

"What? I thought I'd—"

"No civilian vehicles are permitted through the tunnel."

"Oh, okay," she said.

Julia grabbed her flyers and a roll of tape that the man from the store had given her. Slowly, she got out of the car, leaving the door open. The other officer got in and started the engine. Watching her, feeling very vulnerable, Julia climbed in the back of the police car.

Without a word, he merged onto the highway. The siren rang out and traffic parted before his car. They pulled off the turnpike. Julia watched her car, driven by a stranger, peel away as they reentered the northbound lanes. Without a word, she stared straight ahead as they neared the tunnel. A yellow temporary barrier had been put up across the lanes before they split near the entrance. Men in dark uniforms milled around, holding assault rifles.

The cruiser slowed to a stop. One of the officers stepped up to the driver's window.

"Johnson?"

The officer nodded but didn't speak. He turned back and motioned to the others. Two lifted one end of the barrier and moved it to the side. The patrol car eased through the space and accelerated into the tunnel. Julia stared out the window as they drove under the Hudson River.

When they rose out of the tunnel and into the daylight, the officer turned onto Ninth Avenue. When they reached West Twenty-Fifth Street, she saw blockades to her left. Up ahead, not a single car was parked on the side of the street. The sight seemed postapocalyptic. In a way, maybe it was.

The cruiser pulled up along the deserted curb.

"You can get out here," he said, tersely.

"Okay. Thank you."

He nodded but said nothing. In fact, he didn't turn to look at her. So she got out and walked down the street, glancing back once or twice. Though she couldn't be sure due to the sunglasses and the glare on his windshield, she felt him staring at her.

At the first corner, she turned. Once out of sight, she stopped, leaning against the wall of a building. She had a hard time catching her breath. That's when she realized how nervous she felt. It all seemed so strange, the way they stared at her, the way Marci Simmons changed her mind, the way the officer wouldn't talk to her. *Maybe they're all on edge*, she thought. *They had probably been up all night.*

Taking a breath, she took a step back and looked back around the corner. The cruiser was gone. Julia shook her head. It was all in her head, she thought. Nothing more. She had to focus. She had to find Michael. So she moved again, the accordion file holding the flyers held tightly in her hands, the roll of tape in her front pocket.

At first, she shuffled among the people of New York. They seemed different from the last time she'd visited. Whereas before everyone had seemed to move with intense purpose, heads down and eyes straight ahead, that morning they milled, wandering around, looking into the eyes of the people they passed. Some unspoken connection formed and Julia fed on that. It gave her the strength to hand out her first flyer. She put it in the hands of a middle-aged man in a business suit. He took it and nodded. She smiled, and he was gone, lost in the crowd behind her.

From there, her work got easier. She passed flyers to everyone she could and stopped at any post or window to tape another up. She headed east on 26th. Within a block, she came across the first flyer that someone else had posted. It showed a middle-aged woman's face and a local number. A few steps east, and more faces stared blankly out of more homemade posters. She placed one of hers in an open spot and continued forward, inching closer to the station.

Another block over and flyers dangled from mailboxes and fluttered in the breeze caused by people passing by. They littered the sidewalk and the street. Flyers were everywhere, hundreds of them. Julia moved slowly, fighting a growing panic. She held a flyer in front of her, trying to find space to hang it. There was nowhere. So many faces. Old, young, black, white, male, female. She saw all the faces.

Her head swiveled. Julia looked up and down the street. No one looked at her. No one noticed. They moved like ghosts, like shadows made by someone or something else she couldn't even see. Everything suddenly felt so alien. She felt so alone. Staring at all the flyers, thinking about all the people who had hung them, she felt surrounded yet alone.

Julia slammed a flyer on a window, affixing it atop two others. She swung around and hurried to the end of the block. There, she stopped, her eyes wide and her face going pale. She smelled it first, though. Her nose turned her head and she looked up 8th Avenue. And she saw the line of smoke rising up from Madison Square Garden. It rose into the shockingly blue sky, like the finger of God pointing in judgment of us all.

Others stopped and stared with her. Julia sat down on the sidewalk. As people stutter-stepped around her, most not even taking note, she just stared at the smoke. She didn't cry or shake. She just sat and stared.

24

I don't know when I stopped running. But I know why. Eventually, I fell onto a bench in a small park, one more paved than natural. As cars passed me on all sides, I struggled to find my breath. My chest heaved and I coughed. My head wouldn't stop bleeding. I needed to clean it up. I could feel people watching me. It felt like a net surrounded me and someone in the shadows was pulling it tighter and tighter.

I lifted the case and placed it on my lap. I held it there for a moment.

Michael Swann.

There was still nothing. I remembered nothing. It wasn't like I didn't believe this was my name. I just felt like maybe it was my name from a prior life. Maybe I died in the explosion, for I'd heard people on the street talking about what happened. Maybe I was reincarnated. I knew that made no sense at all.

As I'd run through the city, things at once became more and less clear. I knew where I was going. I can't explain that, either. None of the sights around me looked particularly familiar. Yet I seemed to know where I was nonetheless. As I sat on the bench, this new realization was at odds with how my *self* remained such an utter blank.

Eventually, when the two people on the bench across from me finally walked away, I opened the case. I dug through the contents. The more I shuffled things around, the more frantic I felt. I couldn't find the sticker. I must have left it behind. It might be hard to understand how this made me feel. That sticker was my lifeline. It connected me to my life. It was the only thing. And it was gone.

Without the sticker, I was no one. That realization felt like a current carrying me further and further away. For the first time, I felt exhausted, spent. I lost all will to move, even to breathe. For just a second, I wanted more than anything to blink out, cease to exist.

And that is when my finger brushed against something small, smooth, and cool. I grabbed it, lifting it out from under a stack of papers, and my eyes widened. I held a money clip in my hand. It was my money clip. My money, my credit card, and . . . my driver's license. I pulled that out and held it in my hand. A surge of energy filled me. I vibrated as I read the words on that tiny piece of plastic.

Name: Michael Swann
Height: 6 feet 1 inch
Weight: 200 pounds
Eyes: Blue
Hair: Blond
Address: 443 Glen Meadow Drive, West Chester, PA 19380

Then I looked at the picture. A stranger's eyes seemed to peer back at me. My head tilted. *Who's that?* I thought. He was an utter stranger. Or I was.

Dropping the license, I tore through the rest of the contents of the case. The words I read registered like familiar roots in a foreign language. Singularly I understood, but taken as full sentences, as ideas, those same words merged into a senseless jumble of nonsense.

Eventually, I stopped on a crisp sheet of paper. My name, *Michael Swann*, blazed across the top in large, blunt print. My eyes ran over words like *Education* and *Employment*. I saw *Office of the Governor* and *Axis Sales*. Although I had no idea it was a résumé I read, *my* résumé, I had the sense that these words, taken together, told my story.

My eyes closed and my head throbbed. I felt like I might pass out. Seeing that picture, those words, it all tore away the last shred of hope I had. My being, my self, had been ripped away. I'd lost everything. Yet somehow, through the crushing weight of that moment, a much smaller sensation rose up. I felt the slight press of the case on my lap. My lap. My case. The license had come from *my* case. It was *mine*.

I find revisiting that particular moment to be the most painful. It wasn't like I suddenly wanted to live again. It was somehow more, and less, than that. In some Cartesian way, it was like I burst out of the darkness, into the searing and brutal light. I was reborn. An instant before, I had been nothing. And then I was Michael Swann.

25

Chaos surrounded her. It happened so suddenly. One block seemed almost normal. The next, like a tragic war zone. Julia walked among it, her eyes wide and her nostrils flared. A noxious smell seemed to violate every breath she took, like a slow and deadly poison. She cleared her throat over and over again, and her eyes perpetually teared up.

Emergency workers appeared at every corner. They searched the crowd for people in need of help. At first, Julia didn't understand. But then she saw the first survivor. The woman leaned against a building, her hands shaking. White dust covered most of her body, except for the lines of her tears as they ran down her face. Her left arm hung limp at her side and her eyes were closed. People had already stopped to help her, but she wouldn't talk. The good Samaritans looked around, as if they could not figure out where she had come from.

Julia stopped and watched, caught up in the surreal reality. One of the people called out. A minute later, a paramedic appeared. He cleared the others away and sat the woman on the pavement. Another emergency worker arrived. She asked everyone to make space, to keep moving. So Julia did, or at least a part of her did. Another part of her would stay at that corner for years to come.

———————

For hours, it seemed, Julia wandered around the periphery of the attack. She handed the last of her flyers to a passing woman dressed for
work. The woman took it but did not make eye contact. Julia watched
her walk away and reluctantly dropped the used accordion file into a
trash can.

Once her hands were free, the exhaustion hit her. She stopped
again, looking around. She stood half a block from 9th Avenue now,
three blocks away from Penn Station. It drew her back, the finger of
smoke. She walked to the corner and stared at it.

She was not alone. The living, breathing pulse of the city had
changed that morning. Briskness was replaced by caution. Suspicion
and concern became twin emotions. People looked for villains to
blame and for victims to save. Although a number of people moved
toward some usual destination, the office, breakfast, even coffee, their
journey suddenly felt off, like they'd taken a wrong turn. Everyone
else hung up the charade of normalcy and openly stared at that smoke,
unsure of what it meant, wishing it was all some mass dream.

Eventually, she turned away. She had nowhere else to go. Yet she
couldn't leave. The guilt crept back and she called home. Her mother
answered.

"Any news?" Kate asked.

"No . . . There's so many," Julia said.

"What do you mean?"

She shook her head, staring at all the flyers that hung over everything like an infinite patchwork quilt. "Nothing. Are the kids awake?"

"Thomas is. Evelyn took him to her house to play. Evan's still asleep."

"Is anyone else there?"

"No. Tara just left. She went home earlier and came back with breakfast."

"Are you kidding?"

"No. Your friends are amazing, Julia. I've never seen anything like it."

"I can't believe it."

They paused. Julia was afraid to ask, yet she did.

"Does Thomas know?"

Her mother sighed. "I don't know, really. He didn't say anything. But when he saw me and Evelyn sitting here, I think . . . I didn't make him talk, though. Is that okay?"

A part of Julia wished her mother had. It was a selfish part that turned her stomach. For a second, she dreamed of others shouldering that burden. Others having to watch her younger son's reaction. As the minutes ticked by since the news, hope had slipped away. Practicality replaced it, a pinprick in the loss she felt. Utter dread followed fleeting images of her sitting the kids down and telling them. Or holding them while they sat in a church pew listening to people tell stories about their father, who none of them would see again.

"What are you going to do?" her mom asked.

Julia said nothing. She stood alone on the crowded streets of New York City as the last shards of hope lifted away like the finger of smoke. She felt empty, exhausted. For the first time, she felt like a widow.

"I don't know," she finally said. "I—"

A sharp buzz from the phone interrupted her midsentence. Then nothing.

"Mom? Mom, are you there?"

Julia lowered the phone and looked at the screen, realizing she had lost the call. She hesitated, deciding if she needed to try her back or not. Just as she started to redial her home number, the phone vibrated in her hand. Without noticing whom the call was from, she answered.

"Sorry, Mom. We got—"

"Is this Julia Swann?" a stranger's voice asked.

Julia lowered the phone, quickly looking at the number. It was a New York City extension. A ball of energy rose up and through her. Her head tingled. All her previous thoughts evaporated.

"Yes," she said, holding her breath.

"Um . . . I think I just saw your husband."

26

Carefully, I checked and rechecked to make sure nothing fell out of the case this time. The sticker still haunted me. I had to fight the urge to go back for it. I couldn't. Somehow I knew that. But it called to me like some siren's song, begging me back to that apartment building.

Up ahead, I saw a police officer. He stood in the street, the rising sun behind him like a glowing halo. I stared for a moment. I even thought about walking up to him, asking for help. But something stopped me. It wasn't a thought. It was something more instinctual, something that rose up from my gut. The longer I looked at the man, the more agitated I grew. Instead of moving toward him, I hurried away.

I moved west, away from the sunrise. Yet with each block I passed, more and more emergency workers appeared. They waved and shouted. Nervous, I moved into the crowd, melding with the masses. We shuffled down the street like zombies. When I saw the school bus, of all things, nothing made sense anymore. I felt like I was inching through some endless and pointless dream, one where people and places and things mix in haphazard pairings.

Someone called out, maybe a paramedic, maybe a firefighter, I don't really know. In the type of voice that wore authority like an indelible right, he moved us, ushering us forward, toward the bus that sat unmoving in the middle of what should have been a busy intersection.

At first, I felt penned in again. I needed to run, to get away. My head swiveled, and I looked for a chance to break from the crowd. That's when I really looked and saw the other people around me. They were bloodied, covered in dust. They looked lost, confused, overwhelmed. They coughed and stared forward through glazed, wide eyes.

And the fight left me. Maybe that sight reminded my body just how injured it was. I felt at once connected to these lost souls and haunted by them. They had me, and I was powerless to resist. So my feet moved. My thoughts quieted. And I let myself be led into that school bus like a cow to slaughter.

27

The malaise that hung over the people filling the sidewalk changed in that instant. In the time it took Julia to register what had just happened, the muddled, disjointed movements became obstacles, nothing more. Her phone still clutched under white knuckles, she lurched forward. Other pedestrians barely noticed as she bumped and brushed her way past. More accurately, Julia never noticed anything behind her. She just ran.

The blocks flew by. She was not an expert at navigating New York City. She had only been into the city three times in the last twelve years, and Michael had always led the way. That day, something guided her. She never once thought about directions or wrong turns. It was as if the caller had cast out a line and was reeling her to the apartment building.

When she turned the final corner, her eyes met the woman's immediately. Somehow, Julia was sure this was the person who called her. She stood on the sidewalk beside the entrance to an apartment building. The woman was tall, maybe over six feet, but could not weigh much more than a hundred pounds. Her clothes, the type of outfit that Julia would notice but never fathom putting together herself, hung loose, and she tugged at a frayed edge of her sleeve.

Julia slowed, suddenly and overwhelmingly nervous. She put up a hand and the woman did the same. One step at a time, Julia approached.

"Did you just call me?" she asked.

"Uh, yeah," the woman said. "Look, I messed up. I didn't really see him."

It felt as if she had been struck. Julia took a step back and pressed a hand to her stomach. She looked into the stranger's eyes and saw something different, not a madness but close. She thought about the fact that she had just plastered her cell phone number all over the city. Anyone could call her, mess with her, like this woman had obviously done. Something in Julia snapped. She lashed out.

"You think that's funny?"

The woman's eyes widened. She held out a hand. A small white square of shiny paper dangled between two fingers.

"No . . . wait. I found this."

Julia stared at that paper. She saw, between those bone-thin fingers, two letters—two *n*'s. Her heart thumped and then missed a beat. Her legs felt numb and weak. She wouldn't reach for that paper. She couldn't. Not for a second. And then it hit her. Her hand snaked out and snatched it from the woman's tentative grip. She knew what it was, immediately. Michael's name tag from his interview.

"Where'd you get this?"

"I found it on the floor," the woman said, pointing back at the door. "In the lobby."

The tears welled in her eyes. "He was here?"

The woman's nod exploded inside Julia. It opened up the first real hope she'd felt since her call with Michael had gone dead.

"When?"

"Half an hour ago."

"Was he . . . okay?"

The woman paused. "I don't know. Gino, this guy that lives down the hall, he says that the guy . . . your husband? He attacked him, for no reason. I came down just after. I saw Gino on the ground, and . . . your husband running. He had blood on his hand. And I think his head. That's what Gino told the police."

"The police?"

"Yeah . . . I called them. Then I found that. And when I went out-side, I saw your flyer. And recognized the name. Was he . . . ?"

Julia nodded. "Which way did he go?"

She pointed north. Julia looked out across the sea of people walk-ing up the sidewalk. But that new hope would not be doused. Mi-chael had been in that apartment building. He'd been there less than an hour before. As she thought about it, the flood of relief followed. All her fears, all her dread, vanished. It would be okay. She'd find him and it would be okay. But why hadn't he called? Why run?

"Blood on his head?" Julia asked.

The woman nodded.

"Are the police still here?"

She shook her head.

"If you see him again, will you call?"

"Definitely."

Without another word, Julia turned north. Her pace quickened into a run as she dodged around people in her way. After a block, she noticed the name tag still in her hand. Stuffing it into a pocket, she picked up her speed.

"Michael!" she called out.

Those around her startled, giving her a wide berth as she passed. Julia, however, didn't care. She called for him over and over again, but no one answered.

"Michael . . . Michael!"

The words, his name, echoed back to her, hinting that her husband was close. The very city seemed to shrink around her as she pictured him just around the corner, alone and injured, waiting for her, need-ing her. So Julia ran, her legs carrying her faster than she could have ever dreamed possible. She raced to find her husband.

28

The school bus rattled along 42nd Street, heading toward the river. I stared out the window, watching the faces as they passed by outside. Somehow, I could feel their fear like it was my own. It radiated off them like a sharp smell. It hung over everything. No matter where I looked.

I had no idea where I was, or where I was going. Worse, I had no idea why I had stepped into the bus in the first place. I felt myself slipping again, inching back toward the nothingness, so I pulled out the license, running a finger along the smooth surface to make sure it was real.

Michael Swann, Michael Swann, Michael Swann.

I read the name over and over again. It helped, a little. Yet the second I slipped the money clip back in my pocket, the confusion returned. And when the bus squealed to a stop, I could barely remember having boarded it in the first place.

The others stood up and filed into the aisle. I remained sitting and looked out the window again. We were parked along the Hudson River beside a low glass-faced building. Outside, a line of people stood on a patch of stark concrete.

"Everyone out," the driver said.

I startled and looked around, realizing I was the last passenger sitting. I stood, moving quickly to catch up with the people heading down the steps. Once we were off, someone outside ushered us to the line. It led to a pier jutting out over the river. A big ferry backed up. When it came to a stop, I noticed it was empty.

That's when I realized we were being ferried out of the city. My hand shaking, I pulled the license out again, reading the address. *Pennsylvania.* Though I cannot say I understood where that was, or even where I was, it felt right. Somehow, I'd drifted right to where I needed to be.

When the line started to move, I felt settled for the first time, like I was finally heading in the right direction. Then I noticed the four people holding iPads. They stood just ahead of the stark white railing leading to the slip. As people passed, they spoke to them and typed on the screens.

That visceral feeling returned. I watched those four like I had watched the police officer. My gut told me to run, to get out of there before it was too late. It made no sense to me. I could not logically figure out why I would want to turn away at that point. Why I wouldn't want to board the boat and get out of the city. Yet my hands started to shake.

"No," I whispered.

My vision tunneled. I took a step out of line, but it felt as if the ground under my feet suddenly listed. I stumbled and fell to a knee.

"Are you okay?" someone said behind me.

I touched my head. The pain flared and I thought I'd be sick. Hands grabbed my arm. Fingers wrapped around my elbow.

"I just need to sit down," I said.

"I'll help you get aboard."

I looked up and saw the man helping me. He wore glasses and had a beard. I saw the words *Water Taxi* on his shirt. I let him lift me to my feet and guide me to the front of the line. A woman with one of the iPads waved him through. We passed and she called after us.

"Get his name."

29

Julia eventually stopped. Standing in the middle of the block, she looked around her. So much movement. So many people. Her excitement seethed, pushing her to action, yet she had no idea how to direct the impulse.

Someone bumped into her from behind. The person, an older man with deep lines around his eyes and the hands of a mechanic, looked her in the eye.

"Excuse me," he said in a brisk but meaningful way.

"Sorry," she said.

The lines of his face countered the brief smile, like it might have been his first in years. Then he was gone. She watched him walk away, seeing him meld in with everyone else. It was enough for her to realize that she needed to stop and think, not rush blindly forward. She eased against traffic until she found a spot outside a market. Once out of the way, she closed her eyes.

How can I find him?

The thought came quickly. When Julia was young, her great-grandfather, suffering chronic pneumonia, once got in his car to drive to a grocery store and disappeared for over twelve hours. He eventually came home safe, though a little delirious from the fever, but she remembered her mother calling his credit card company. They had told her that Julia's great-grandfather's card had been used at the grocery store and then at a gas station a hundred miles away.

Not wasting a second, Julia pulled out her wallet and phone. She dialed the number on the back of her card. She had to put in her account number and sit on hold. Her foot tapped along with her nerves as she waited.

"Come on," she said.

Someone walking by noticed. Julia looked down at the pavement, but her foot wouldn't stop tapping. When she finally got a live voice on the phone, she struggled to make sense.

"I need you to help me find my husband," she said.

The customer service rep began a speech about privacy and such, but Julia cut him off. It looked bad until she mentioned the attack on Penn Station. Suddenly, the man on the other end of the call changed. His tone went from annoyed to compassionate midsentence.

"Oh, wow, I'm . . . How can I help?"

Julia explained everything, giving way more detail than she needed. Her voice rose an octave and she could hear him typing.

"Someone saw him. So I thought, maybe . . ."

She held her breath. The typing stopped. There was a long pause.

"I'm sorry," the man said. "It hasn't been used."

Julia's face went pale. She swayed. Her arm holding the phone fell limp to her side. A deep emptiness weighed her down. She wanted to fall to the pavement, to give up. Instead, her head tilted up. She glared at the deep blue sky . . . and screamed.

"MICHAEL!"

People on the street stopped. They stared. Julia barely noticed. She continued to stare at the sky, looking for some hint, some clue that would tell her what to do next.

"Ma'am, are you okay?"

She spun around. A NYPD officer stood beside her, his thumb hooked under his belt. Julia's face burned.

"Sorry, I . . ."

He shook his head. The look in his eyes seemed to accept the humanity of the moment in stride.

"It's been a crazy day. Can I help you with something?"

She had no idea what to ask. She just stared at him.

"Do you need to get somewhere? I'm going off duty, but I can give you a lift on my way home."

"No, it's okay."

She couldn't stop looking into the man's eyes. He would drive home feeling the weight of the day. But it would be temporary. He'd be returning to his perfect family. Family . . . Home . . . That's when the thought hit Julia so hard that she shuffled back a step. In that officer's eyes, she saw her husband. She slipped into his mind. And it became so clear. If Michael was alive, if he was out there, she knew exactly where he would be going, what he would be doing. He would be trying to get home.

"The ferry?" she asked, suddenly.

"It's running between Manhattan and Port Imperial," he said. "Homeland's been trying to get as many people off the island as they can since the attack."

"I think my husband may have gone there."

———

As the police car pulled up to the curb at West 39th Street, Julia saw the mass of people moving toward the pier. She jumped out of the car and ran, totally forgetting to thank the officer. She bolted right past the line and out onto the boardwalk.

A woman with an iPad in her hand stepped out in front of her. "Ma'am, you have to—"

"I think my husband's on the ferry. He may be hurt."

"What was his name?"

The ferry blew its horn. Julia took a step toward the woman.

"I need to—"

"His name?"

She forced a breath out. "Michael . . . Michael Swann."

The woman tapped the name on the screen and shook her head. "Nope."

But then someone behind her spoke up. "Did you say 'Michael Swann'?"

She turned and saw a young man in a New York Water Taxi shirt. Julia's heart jumped.

"Yes."

"Holy crap! I just helped him aboard."

"Are you serious? On the boat?"

"Yes . . . but not this one. The one before it."

"The ferry before this?"

"Yeah. Let her through. Maybe you can catch him at Port Imperial."

Without a thought, Julia hugged the man. When he stiffened, it made her laugh. And she realized it was the first time she'd done that since everything started.

30

Surrounded by the throng of people from the ferry, I walked through the set of doors into the wide-open, glassed lobby of the terminal. People filled the space, pressing into the partitioned bar to the right and filling the corridor that ran under a large sign pointing the direction to parking and ground transportation. I let the traffic carry me straight through the building and out the other side.

As I stepped outside, we were once again ushered forward like cattle toward a line of people in bright orange pinnies that read *Volunteer*. They held up signs outside a line of shuttle buses. There had to be at least ten parked there. I stared at the signs, totally confused. When I didn't find any that said *Philadelphia*, my eye caught one that read *Newark Bus Station*. I moved toward that, thinking of the school bus that had driven us to the ferry terminal.

"Newark bus station," one of the volunteers said to me.

I just nodded and the woman helped me up the steps.

31

Julia shouldered her way off the ferry and along the slip as quickly as she could. Rushing into the terminal, she slowed, overwhelmed by the crowd.

"Michael!" she called out.

A few people turned but not her husband, so she continued to push through the mass of people, calling out his name, her head swiveling left and right. When she reached the far side of the station, she stepped outside. Even more people stood there, all being directed to a series of shuttles.

"Michael!" she screamed out. "Michael!"

Three shuttles pulled out, one after another. All Julia could do was stand there and watch them slip away.

32

When I stepped off the bus at Newark Station, I felt like I could breathe again. Compared to Port Imperial, it felt empty. I stood in the lobby, looking around. An employee at the station stopped and stared at me.

"You okay, man?"

"Yeah," I said.

He looked at the side of my head. His attention made me nervous, and I fought the urge to see if it was still bleeding.

"I'm just looking for the bus station."

"Down past the McDonald's." He paused. "You sure you're okay?"

I nodded and walked quickly away, heading in the direction he had pointed. When I reached the Greyhound ticketing window, I leaned over, my face close to the opening in the glass of the ticket booth. The woman working there watched me, clearly suspicious.

"Are you okay?"

"Yeah," I said.

The woman looked around, like she might call for assistance. Then I put the credit card on the ledge between us.

"I need to get a ticket."

"Destination?"

My head throbbed. Whenever I searched for an answer, the pain intensified. Maybe I hoped that in the moment, I might remember.

Instead, there was nothing. So I pulled my license out of the clip and placed it next to the credit card.

"To that address."

The woman looked at the license and up at me. She stared for a moment, like she was assessing me again.

"That address?"

"Yes."

Her eyes rolled. I remember thinking that she must deal with all types in a job like this. I wondered what type she pegged me for. Crazy and violent? Maybe I was. I had just stopped shaking from what happened in the apartment building. Maybe this woman was totally right.

She looked at the address again, then turned her attention to me. Her head tilted. I felt like she stared at my face, at the blood. I still had no idea how bad I looked. For some reason, I remember thinking that she looked at me like a stranger. I was, so the feeling made no sense at all.

She looked at the license again.

"Look, I have no idea where this is. It's crazy in here today." She paused, looking at her screen. "This is all crazy. They need more people down here helping you all. I don't know what they want me to do." Her frustration ebbed. "I can get you to Philadelphia. Is that close enough?"

I had no idea, really. But I nodded anyway. She ran the transaction without even looking at me. When she slid the ticket, my license, and the credit card at me, her eyes were lowered.

"Next."

I paused for a second, but another customer came up close behind me. I felt agitated, but I kept it in check. Instead, I wandered away from the window and looked at the ticket and up at the clock. I had a little over an hour. I somehow found my way to the gates and found a bench by the restrooms. I sat and closed my eyes, thinking that soon, at least, I'd be home . . . wherever that was.

33

Julia leaned against the wall inside the Port Imperial station, utterly defeated. She'd checked and rechecked every face. She listened as the PA system repeated her message for the fifth time.

"Michael Swann, please report to ticketing. Michael Swann, please report to ticketing."

She looked out at the crowd, willing him to appear. Instead, no one even noticed. Everyone continued to move, new faces on the same paths. Eventually, she closed her eyes, having no idea what to do next.

"Anything?" someone asked.

She opened her eyes. The woman from terminal security who had helped her with the PA announcement stood in front of her. She, too, looked defeated.

"Nothing," Julia said.

"I am so sorry."

Julia's head shook. She was about to say something—what, she had no idea—when her phone rang. The woman from security watched as Julia quickly answered the call.

"Hello."

"Mrs. Swann?"

"Yes."

"Um, hi, this is Joe from Visa. I spoke to you earlier."

Julia's eyes widened. So did the woman's from security.

"Yes," she said.

"Well, since you called, I kept checking your account. Um, your husband's card . . . it was just used."

"Where?" Julia barked out.

"He purchased a Greyhound ticket at Newark Penn Station."

Julia met eyes with the other woman and nodded, smiling. "Thank you so much."

"Is it him?" the woman asked before Julia could get a word out.

"He just used our credit card in Newark. At the bus station."

The woman grabbed her hand. "I'll drive you."

The two women sprinted from the station as if they had known each other for a lifetime.

34

My eyes opened. I think I might have fallen asleep. But the call woke me, somehow.

"Philadelphia Express service from Newark Penn Station boarding in twenty minutes."

I looked down at my ticket and then up at the gates. I stared at the numbers, trying to remember if I meant to choose that particular seat or if it happened by chance. When I tried to remember buying the ticket, I couldn't. The sensation, the emptiness in my head, brought with it an overwhelming sense of anxiety. Cold sweat beaded my forehead.

I closed my eyes, trying to picture the person who sold me the ticket. There was nothing. Nothing at all. When I opened them, I had to reread the ticket: *Philadelphia Express.*

I staggered as I stood up. The case remained locked in my grip as I made my way to the restroom. A dozen people filled the small space, but I found an open sink. I stood there, looking in the mirror, my head swimming and my stomach turning.

Dark blood plastered the short hair to my temple. A stripe ran down and disappeared into my ear. I couldn't take my eyes off of that for a second. Then I saw my face. The left half, the side with the blood, was swollen. Blood vessels around that eye had turned almost black. My lips were dry and cracked. To be honest, that face, my face, still seemed to belong to a stranger.

Still looking at myself, I turned on the faucet. The white porcelain sink turned red as I lowered my head and splashed water through my hair. The man next to me looked down and walked away. I worked harder, trying to get all the blood off, and noticed both sinks next to me remained unused. Water ran down my back and dotted my pants as I moved over and tore off about half a dozen paper towels. I heard people muttering, but I was still in such a fog that I barely noticed. Instead, I stepped back in front of a mirror and just looked at my reflection. And I had no memory of the man who stared back at me. None at all.

35

Julia had never been to Newark, New Jersey. And she noticed absolutely nothing of the city as they raced to the station. Once there, Julia bolted from the car, calling back her thanks this time before crashing through the doors. The crowd was thin, but it took her a minute to find the Greyhound ticket counter.

An agent sat at one window that was closed to customers. She bypassed the line at the other and went straight there. The man behind the counter spoke loudly to someone behind him.

"If you ask me, we need to bomb them to hell—"

"Excuse me," she interrupted.

He turned and looked at her. Dark stubble seemed to cover every inch of his face, and his eyes were small and set close together.

"I'm closed."

Julia ignored that, instead passing the picture of her and Michael across the counter. "Have you seen this man?"

The man wouldn't touch it.

"Ma'am, you need to—"

"No, please. He was at Penn Station. He's injured. My credit card company said he just used his card here."

To Julia, this should have been enough. This man should have been happy to help her. In fact, that's what she fully expected. All day, a wave of camaraderie had followed her through the city. Like what happened, the tragedy of so many lives being lost, had linked everyone nearby forever. This man must feel it as well. How could he not?

"I can't help you," he said.

He got up and walked away from the counter. Julia stared, her eyes wide with shock. She was about to yell after him when someone lightly touched her shoulder. She turned to see a woman in a head scarf. She wore the same transit uniform as the man behind the counter. A radio chirped at her belt.

"Down the concourse to the right," she said softly, pointing. "There's a police station there. We can't give you information on another passenger for security reasons. But maybe they can help."

Julia looked into the woman's eyes.

"He might still be here," she said.

The woman looked up at the big board of arrivals and departures. Julia's eyes followed hers. She saw the flashing *All Aboard* for a Philadelphia Express.

"That's it," Julia said.

The woman's voice rose. "That way! Past the McDonald's."

She ran.

36

Sitting in the back of the bus, I closed my eyes. I tried to picture the face I saw in the mirror. I tried to remember who it was. The harder I tried, though, the more diffuse the image became. The edges softened. The colors faded. Eyes turned gray. Hair turned drab. Skin turned to mist and floated away, leaving me with nothing but a shining silver mirror.

The axle rumbled softly below my feet as more passengers boarded. Many looked dressed for a night out, which surprised me. I looked down at my stained shirt and wondered what they must be thinking of me. The thought caused me to slink down deeper into the seat.

I dug the money clip out of my pocket. Slowly, I slipped the Pennsylvania driver's license out. I stared at the small picture on the front, willing something to connect, some light to go off. But again, a stranger stared back at me.

I remember thinking in that moment about what I was doing. In a way, even then, it didn't make much sense. Shouldn't I have gone to the police for help? Really, I should have stayed with the doctor, gotten the help I needed. Though the thought wasn't clear then, I think I knew, in a way, how serious head injuries could be. Yet all I wanted was for that bus to move. If I was being honest, it wasn't that I just wanted to get home. More than anything in my life, I needed to get farther away from the city.

———————

Julia flew. People parted before her and she sprinted to the gate for the Philadelphia Express. She was not twenty feet away from the bus when it lurched to a start, rolling away from the curbing.

"Stop!" Julia screamed.

———————

My eyes shot open when I heard the scream.

"Stop!"

I turned, looking out my window at a woman. She somehow looked different from everyone else there. She wore a white shirt and capris. Around my age, she looked fit and perfectly put together, except for her eyes. I saw desperation there.

Her arms waved. Her lips moved, but I couldn't hear anything else, for the engine roared and my bus lurched to a start. As it pulled out behind the one ahead, I remember staring at her. Although I had no idea who she was at the time, I can still close my eyes and see her there at the terminal, tears streaming down her cheeks. I'll never forget that moment. Never.

———————

Frantic, Julia tore her phone from her back pocket. She called Michael's cell. Again, it went straight to voicemail. She stared at the bus, listening to the recorded message, the woman's flat, robotic voice droning in her ear, as the Philadelphia Express rounded a corner and slipped from sight.

"No," she whispered.

Hopeless, she tried his old number, his work cell. It rang once. Her eyes closed. Then it rang a second time. She startled, her eyes shooting open. She took quick steps down the sidewalk, toward the direction in which the bus had disappeared. The phone rang a third time and she could barely breathe.

———————

I thought it was someone else's phone. The ring was soft, almost tentative, as if it feared the unknown. My head turned as I tried to orient on the sound. It rang a third time, and I realized, then, that it came from my case. The phone inside was ringing. My phone was ringing. Someone was calling *me*.

I fumbled. My fingers felt like giant bags of sand trying to keep back my flooding emotions. When I finally got the case open, the phone slid under a stack of papers. I dug through them as it continued to ring. Finally, my hand wrapped around the cool metal. I pulled it up, swiping the screen. I paused, fighting the irrational wave of fear that prevented me from speaking.

"Michael?" a woman's voice said.

My entire body seized up. The name came back to me like a heavenly vision appearing out of the darkness. *Julia*. It was Julia. Somehow, though the sound of her voice sparked no true memories, I knew it immediately. Yet the shock held me frozen for a second longer. I wanted to scream, to cry out my love for her. As I forced my mouth open, the word cracked and hissed before forming.

"Julia," I said.

———————

On the fifth ring, Julia heard a click. The line went silent.

"Michael," she said.

Static crackled. She heard another click, followed by a piercing whine. Instinctually, she pulled the phone away from her ear. When she put it back, the line was nothing but silence.

37

Julia stared at the screen. The call was lost, but for just a second, she was sure, it had connected. In fact, she was sure he had answered. With a rush of adrenaline, she tried again. That call failed. So did three more. Tears ran down her cheeks.

"Damn it," she hissed.

Before the word even got out, her phone rang. Her hope lasted nothing more than a split second before her home number appeared on the screen. The phone continued to ring. She stared at that number, and that briefest glimmer of hope faded away. She felt empty and alone. She felt utterly defeated. Yet she answered the call, thinking of Evan and Thomas.

"Julia," her mother said.

Hearing her mother's voice brought everything back. She spoke quickly.

"He's alive, Mom. Someone saw him. He used his credit card."

"Are you serious?"

"I called him. I think it connected. I think he answered . . . before the call died. He's on a bus going to Philadelphia."

"Are you going there?"

"My car is across town. I won't make it. I need to talk to the police, let them know."

Julia heard talking in the background. Then her mother relayed what she had said to someone else. She heard a shuffle and then Evelyn was on the line.

"Oh, my God," Evelyn said. "That's great!"

"You're still there?"

"I just brought the kids back. Tara's taking them to the movies in half an hour. Look, you go talk to the police. I'll head up to Philadelphia and be there when the bus arrives. What's the number?"

"Evelyn, I can't ask you to do that."

"Shut your mouth. I'm doing it."

Julia gave her the bus number. "You don't even know where the bus station is."

Evelyn laughed. "The Internet does."

Julia paused. She felt so overwhelmed. It was hard to believe her friends would do so much for her. How could she ever repay them?

"Thanks," she said. She meant so much more than that, but it was the only word that would come out.

———

Julia sat in a chair at a desk inside the police station at Newark Penn Station. A woman sat across from her, taking notes on a computer as Julia told her every detail.

"Are you okay?" the officer asked.

"Me?"

She nodded. "Have you slept?"

Julia shook her head.

"Eaten?"

"No."

"Wait here," the woman said.

She disappeared from the small office. Julia let out a breath. It left her feeling empty and exhausted. She had not thought about herself since the news broke the night before. That fact was not melodramatic. It was simply the truth. And the officer's questions brought her needs to the front. In a way, she wished the woman hadn't even opened that door.

Not five minutes later, the officer reappeared. She carried a cup of coffee and what looked like a cherry Danish. She placed it in front of Julia.

"I'm not sure if you like this sort of thing, but maybe you should eat."

Julia didn't, not before. But in that moment, it all looked like ambrosia to her. She dug in without even thinking about the fact that someone was watching her eat.

"We'll have an officer at the terminal in Philadelphia before the Express arrives. I've faxed the picture you gave me to them. They'll find your husband and get him home. I promise."

"Thank you so much."

"What about you?" she asked.

"Oh . . . I have to get my car. I think it's at the police station in Weehawken."

The officer smiled. Something about it seemed sad to Julia, and she didn't understand that.

"I'll drive you down there."

"Thank you," Julia said, and realized she'd said that a lot lately.

PICKET FENCE

The police officer returned Julia to her car. Within minutes, she was back on the highway, heading to Pennsylvania. As she drove to her children, feeling an overwhelming sense of relief, her mind wandered to the past, to a time when they were first making a home. She and Michael had been married for almost four years before they finally decided to try to start a family. Her schedule made it difficult. As promised, the governor hired her as his policy adviser on social issues. She spent long hours at work, capped off by nightly events. The only saving grace was that she worked in Delaware, a state that stretched a hundred miles long and fifty at its widest. Travel rarely involved anything beyond her Honda Civic.

Luckily, Michael had his dream job. He had grown more and more involved in the city's minor-league baseball team. Although his primary responsibility was ticket sales and marketing, he'd found a knack for putting on the countless contests and skits that ran between innings. He gave play-by-play over the sound system as middle-aged men scurried in tight circles with their foreheads resting on the end of bats, or as preteens tried to throw an oversized baseball through a hole in a sheet of plywood in the shape of a catcher's mitt. On special nights, he would introduce the paid acts, maybe a cowboy who trained a monkey to ride on the back of a dog or a man who danced with four puppets dressed as the many stages of Michael Jackson. In a way,

Michael Swann became a quasi celebrity in the city of Wilmington, and he ate it up like a slice of humble pie.

"It's now or never," Julia said one night, looking at her calendar.

"Huh?"

Michael sat in a recliner watching the Phillies. His team had road games for the rest of the week, and the governor was on his yearly vacation to Bethany Beach. Since it was one of the few nights in weeks that the two were home at the same time, it might have seemed like they should be out living it up at some bar downtown. In reality, due to their schedules, they both wanted nothing more than a quiet night at home. Together.

She looked at him, askew. "You're not getting any younger, Mr. Swann."

"Thanks."

"Stop being so thick," Julia said with a smile.

"Okay." Michael's eyebrows danced. "Tonight?"

Julia laughed. She moved to her husband and fell into his lap. "I love you."

"I love you, too."

They made love that night on the recliner while the Phillies game played on the television. To the best of their knowledge, it was a success all around.

———————

Four months later, Julia's pregnancy showed. She took to cradling her belly in her hand as she moved around their apartment, tidying up as she went. Each surface she dusted or sock she picked up off the floor left her more and more restless. Suddenly, everything felt too small. She cleaned, but it made no difference.

One Saturday afternoon, her husband came home from a meeting at the park to find her painting their bathroom.

"Really?" he asked.

Julia shook her head. "I felt claustrophobic."

"So you decided to paint the bathroom."

As had become habit, she touched her stomach. "I thought a lighter color . . ."

He put a hand out. "Come on."

She looked at her hands, speckled with beige paint. "But . . ."

His fingers wrapped around hers. "Come on."

She let him lead her out of the apartment and down to his car. As they pulled out of the complex, he glanced at Julia.

"I thought pregnant women weren't supposed to paint."

She scoffed. "Yeah, a man probably came up with that one. I opened all the windows. It was fine."

"Oh," he said.

"And where are we going, anyway?"

"For a drive."

"Where?"

"Around."

She laughed. "Fine."

He took her to a neighborhood north of the city. When he turned in, she grew suspicious.

"You know someone here?"

"Maybe," he said.

Squat brick houses with flat roofs and narrow windows peeked out from front yards lined with mature oaks and maples. She heard children's voices and noticed six or seven kids playing kickball at the adjacent public park. Their shrieks of excitement harmonized with the singing birds as they rolled toward the end of a cul-de-sac. That's when Julia noticed the open house sign and laughed.

She looked at Michael. "Really?"

He shrugged. "Why not?"

Hand in hand, they strolled up the walk and through the front door. Julia slowed, taking in the '70s slate floor and the olive-green paint. She squeezed his hand.

"Hello?" he called out.

She wanted to turn and run, but he was having too much fun.

"Hello?"

A woman in expensive clothes and sunglasses perfectly nestled atop her head in a mass of yellow-gold hair appeared from a hallway to the right. Her jewelry rattled as she hurried toward them.

"Hi, hello," she said, offering a hand. Michael shook it. Julia nodded. "My name's Emily. I'm the Realtor. You want to have a look around?"

"Sure," he said with a huge smile.

They moved together from room to room. The Realtor pointed out every selling point she could. They included running water and a large eat-in kitchen. Emily pretended not to notice the orange Formica counters or the banana-yellow powder room with flashing gold fixtures. When they reached the living room with its popcorn walls and purple shag carpet, Michael simply plopped down on the white leather couch.

"Much traffic today?" he asked the Realtor.

She nodded. "Quite a bit. A couple of families were very interested."

"I bet," he said.

She cleared her throat. Julia touched Michael's sleeve. "We need to go."

"Oh, okay," he said.

"Are you feeling okay?" the Realtor asked.

"Sure, yeah."

She rushed them from the house and back to the car. As they pulled away, Julia burst out laughing. "That place smelled like a zoo."

"Yup," he said.

After they visited a few more houses, much of the amusement faded away. Each one seemed less right than the last. Politely, she asked if they could stop looking. At first, Michael thought it was over. But he'd come home and catch her watching house-remodeling shows and searching the Internet for sales listings. Whenever he asked to help, Julia would just shake her head and change the subject.

One afternoon, while sitting in front of her computer looking through a particularly frustrating set of listings, she leaned back and rubbed her eyes. Checking her watch, she noticed the time. She had twenty minutes to make it to the lunch she had scheduled. It was with a woman whose husband worked with her father at DuLac. They had met years ago and had run into each other a half dozen times. During the last, they decided to meet up.

So, she shut down the computer and walked out of her office, stopping at the secretary's desk.

"Going to lunch. I should be back in an hour."

"Okay."

The place they had chosen was just two blocks from her building. She arrived in plenty of time to find the woman already seated. Walking up to the table, Julia had to remind herself that her name was Tara.

"Hi," Tara said, getting up and giving Julia a hug.

"How are you?"

"Great, great."

They both sat. After they ordered, the conversation lulled for a second, so Julia mentioned that she had been looking for a house.

"Oh, that can be crazy," Tara said.

"I know. At first, it was fun. Then it just turned . . . kinda awful."

She laughed. "I know what you mean. But keep at it. I remember when we were looking, I'd almost given up. Then we stumbled into GBA and I just fell in love."

"GBA?"

Tara laughed again. "Oh, sorry. Glen Brook Acres. It's our neighborhood."

"Oh."

"It's really amazing. So many kids. And the schools are great."

Julia leaned forward. "Where is it? North Wilmington?"

"No, Pennsylvania."

Tara went on and on about GBA. Julia listened, but once she heard "Pennsylvania," the conversation lost some weight. For her job, she had to live in Delaware, so they hadn't even considered something like that.

Lunch ended and Tara hugged Julia good-bye.

"Hey," she said. "If I hear of any houses going up for sale, I'll let you know."

"Thanks," Julia said. At the time, though, she thought nothing of it. But that night, before Michael got home, she searched the Internet for Glen Brook Acres. The houses had been built in the past ten years. They had vaulted ceilings and great open floor plans. Every yard she saw in the pictures looked immaculate. Like Tara had said, it just seemed perfect.

From there, her obsession grew. Julia took to investigating the house prices in the neighborhood. Then the taxes, and the school district. With everything she looked up, she hoped to find some silver bullet that might kill the idea. She couldn't move to Pennsylvania. It was that simple. Until her mind drifted again, and the proverbial picket fences called to her like a siren.

Things took a turn for the worse when, less than a month later, she got a call from Tara.

"There's a house going up this weekend. You have to see it. It's beautiful."

"Well," Julia said, "I'm not sure we'd want to move out of Delaware."

"Just come see it."

"Maybe," she said. "I'll let you know."

When Julia told her husband, he looked into her face. After a pause, he nodded. "Let's go see it."

"You sure?"

"Yup."

So that Saturday they crossed the line out of Delaware and came to a stop outside the house on Glen Meadow Drive. It sat on a slight hill with two young maples out front. The sun shined down on the peaked roofline and large, sparkling windows. Even the air seemed to smell fresher, crisper as they got out of the car.

When she stepped foot into the house, Julia already knew. And every room they looked at felt more and more perfect. At one point, Julia lost Michael as the Realtor talked to her about the Shaker cabinets in the kitchen. She turned and saw him standing on the back porch, hands on the railings, looking out at the fenced-in backyard.

"Excuse me," she said.

He didn't turn around when she opened the sliding door and approached from behind. So she sidled up next to him.

"You can't live in Pennsylvania," he said before she could say anything.

She couldn't, not and keep her job. She had known that all along. And so had he. They also knew that they couldn't afford to live there on Michael's salary with the baseball team. It's funny how so much is left unsaid when the biggest decisions are being made.

"And you love your job," she said.

He shrugged. "I love you and Junior more."

"Me, too," she said, rubbing her belly.

"Well, then it's decided. Mitch was talking to me about medical sales. Good money, and they love athletes. He thinks I'd be perfect."

She nodded. Though Julia felt a ping of sadness, she knew he was right. And so was she.

"So?" he added.

"Let's go for it," she said with a smile.

They put an offer on the house the next morning. It was negotiated and accepted within a day. Inspections followed, and before they could come up for air, Julia and Michael sat at the settlement table across from the owners of what would, in moments, be their new home. The nice couple in their fifties mentioned how much they loved the house and how great a childhood their kids had. Julia and Michael smiled as they signed their mortgage papers. A blink of an eye later, they stood on that same deck, looking out over their new neighborhood, their concerns for the future outweighed by a beautiful setting sun.

"We did it," Julia whispered.

And Michael seemed happy when he nodded and hugged his wife.

38

S tupid."

It all started with the move, she thought. Julia squeezed the steering wheel as she drove south on the Jersey Turnpike toward exit 6, back home toward Glen Brook Acres and her children. *Home.* It was perfect, but maybe for someone else. Maybe she, they, needed to redefine the word. The last year had been rocky for them. When Michael got home, they should talk things through. Those moments when she thought she had lost him changed everything. It shifted priorities. Julia knew that nothing would be the same, yet she was okay with that. Almost excited as she exited onto the Pennsylvania Turnpike.

Once she was home. Once they were both home . . . Julia's thoughts shifted. Michael should have tried to call her. But maybe he did. Why would he get on a bus to Philadelphia, though? Could he have lost his phone? The woman said he had been injured. Was it bad? How bad?

Any plans that had started to form in her head had completely vanished. Her grip on the wheel tightened again as her thoughts whirred. She grabbed her phone and, while traveling at over sixty miles per hour, found the number that Marci Simmons had given her. She dialed. When the dispatcher at the station answered, she asked for Marci.

"This is Dr. Simmons. How can I help you?"

"Uh . . . hi, this is Julia Swann. We spoke this . . . last night."

The therapist paused, like she might not remember who Julia was. "Mrs. Swann. How are you? Have you heard from your husband?"

"I did, well, I mean . . ."

Julia felt inordinately confused. For no discernible reason, something about the conversation itched her worries. Maybe the pauses, or something more.

"You heard from him?" Dr. Simmons asked.

"I called . . . and I think he answered."

"You spoke to him?"

"Not . . . The call dropped. I guess cell service is bad right now."

"Okay," Marci said, her tone sounding dismissive to Julia.

"No, listen. I went back to the city . . . and put up flyers. Someone called me. They said Michael was in their lobby."

Marci cut in. "Sometimes in situations like this, people do, or say, strange things. They—"

"No," Julia said. "She had my husband's name tag from his interview."

"His name was on it?" she asked, quickly.

"Yes. He—"

"Do you have the address of the building?"

"No," Julia said, somewhat frustrated. "I just . . . I wanted to know if you heard anything." She paused waiting for a response. When it didn't come, she continued. "And I just . . . He hasn't called me. I . . . wondered if that was normal?"

"Are you sure it was really your husband?"

"He used his credit card," Julia said.

"Really?"

"He bought a ticket on an express bus to Philadelphia. I've contacted the police."

"So you've talked to the authorities already?"

"Yes," she said, flustered. "I'm on my way back from New York, but my friend will be at the station when he gets there. I assume the bus will arrive any minute."

"Are you serious?"

"Yes!"

"And you said you called the authorities there?"

"Yes."

"Thank you for letting us know. I'll contact you if I hear anything else."

Julia's cheeks burned. "Wait. I called . . . I wanted to ask you what it means. That he just got on a bus . . ."

"After something like this, survivors can tend to be disoriented. Don't worry at all. I'm sure the police will handle it. Thank you for calling, Mrs. Swann."

Marci Simmons hung up. It wasn't until that instant that Julia thought she might have heard a strange tone in the woman's voice. It was easily explainable, though. Her station had to be swamped. So many people commuted across the river into New Jersey. Hundreds had to be in Penn Station. Julia knew that she had been one of what felt like countless people trying to find their loved ones. She also knew that, within the hour, she would.

Julia pictured Evelyn's car pulling into the driveway. She could almost see Michael climbing out, and how it would feel as she ran to him, taking him into her arms. So she let anything strange about her conversation with the therapist go. Now that she knew where Michael was, she suddenly craved more information about what happened.

She turned on the radio.

". . . large trucks still being stopped on the turnpike. The Department of Homeland Security recently confirmed earlier reports stating that no biological or chemical agents were used in the attack. It is believed that the initial bombing injured hundreds, but the subsequent rupture to the gas line near the station caused catastrophic damage to life and property. We go now to Jennifer Hart in Manhattan with a breaking report."

A woman with a strong but urgent voice took over. "This is Jennifer Hart reporting outside the mobile headquarters for Homeland Security, just a block from the corner of the heavily damaged Madison Square Garden. I've just spoken to an unofficial source inside the department. At this time, the FBI, CIA, and Homeland Security do not feel like this was an attack by *foreign* terrorists. Once again, this is by no means official, but according to multiple people I've spoken to, they are narrowing in on a suspect as we speak. And at this time, they believe that the attack was carried out by one or more American citizens."

Just as the original newscaster questioned Jennifer Hart, Julia's phone rang. It was Evelyn's number. She fumbled for the button on the wheel to answer the call through the car's Bluetooth. She found herself out of breath when she finally connected to the call.

"Hello, Evelyn?"

"He's not here," Evelyn said, her voice cracking.

"What?"

"The bus arrived. He's not on it. The police checked twice."

Julia's heart sank.

"No, he's on that bus!"

"He's not, Julia . . ."

"No . . . he has to be."

Michael, she thought. Her car slipped out of the right lane. When the front tire ran atop the rumble strip, Julia's body shook. She could barely breathe. A rasping whisper slipped out from between her thin lips.

"Something's horribly wrong."

The rumble shook the steering wheel hard enough to snap her out of it. She swerved back into the lane. It took her another mile, however, to realize she was still shaking.

NOT YOUR FATHER'S COMPANY

Not long after moving into Glen Brook Acres, Julia stood in her new kitchen arranging coffee cups in a half-filled cabinet. Evan slept in his car seat on the floor. The phone rang and she checked the number. It was Tara. Julia answered the call, thinking her new neighbor was just calling to say hi. Immediately, though, she knew something was wrong.

"Are you okay?" Tara asked.

"Um, yeah," Julia said. "Why?"

Tara paused. "Oh, I just . . ."

"What, Tara?"

"Nothing."

Another pause stretched out. Julia's tone grew sharp. "What?"

"I just heard . . . about the layoffs."

Julia's stomach flipped. Michael had just started his new job. They had everything riding on his salary at that point. If he got laid off . . .

"What layoffs?"

"At DuLac."

Julia didn't even think about her father. Not at first. Instead, all she could think about was Tara's husband. "Kevin?"

"Oh, no. He's fine. But I heard the composites division got hit hard . . . especially the chemists."

"Oh," Julia said. "Oh."

"You okay?"

"Yeah," she said, distractedly. "I better go."

"Okay."

As soon as she hung up, Julia called her mother. The phone rang seven or eight times without the machine picking up. So she tried a second time, though the results were the same. Then she called Michael.

"I think my dad just got laid off," she said to her husband.

"Are you serious?"

"I'm not sure. But, I mean, why would they lay off a fifty-eight-year-old chemist?"

"That's crazy. Did you call?"

"I tried, but no one answered. I think I'll run over and see if they're home."

"Okay, call me back."

"I will, I love you."

"Love you, too."

Julia hung up. She looked out the window, feeling disjointed. For just that moment, she felt strangely relieved. Michael was okay. His job was okay. She'd never admit that thought to anyone, but she would always remember it.

———————

Julia rang the door of her childhood home. She would have walked in, but the door was locked. Strangely, her mother's car was in the driveway. She took a step away from the door and checked out her father's front garden. As usual, it looked perfectly tended. When the door opened, it startled her.

"Julia, and my little Evan," her mother said, opening the screen and putting her hands out for the baby. "What are you doing here?"

"Hi," she said. "Just checking on you guys. Everything okay?"

Her mother's head tilted. "You heard?"

That's when it first hit Julia. As bad as it might sound, up until that moment, she'd thought only of herself and Michael. Seeing her mother's face, the concern so clear in the creases around her eyes, Julia realized that everything was not okay.

"Did he . . . ?"

Julia couldn't say the words, but her mother knew what she asked. She nodded.

"Crap," Julia said. "Are you guys going to be okay?"

"Why don't you come in?" her mom said.

Julia barked out an awkward laugh. She hadn't realized that they were having the conversation on the front porch. She walked through the door as her mother held it open with her foot, and the two women walked into the kitchen.

"Do you want some coffee?" her mom asked. "I just brewed a pot."

"Sure," Julia said. "Is Dad here?"

"No."

Julia waited, but her mother didn't add any more detail. So she left Kate cooing at Evan and poured herself a cup. She grabbed her mom's off the counter and brought it with her back to the table.

"Is he at work?"

Her mother shook her head. "No."

"Where is he?"

She shrugged. "Out."

"Oh."

They sipped their coffee in silence for a moment. Julia had no idea what to say. Her whole life, her father had been a workaholic. His brain worked like a chemist's, so his penchant to remain working 24/7 never seemed all that odd. To be honest, she'd had a few conversations with her mother already about how retirement might not work out for them. But they had just laughed it off, really.

"Is he okay?" Julia asked, breaking the stillness.

Her mother shrugged again. "I don't really know. He found out today. He had a sense it might be coming, but he wouldn't talk about it. This morning, they came into his office, handed him a folder, and told him he could leave right then. He called, but I haven't heard from him since."

"Should we look for him?" Julia asked.

"No," her mom said.

Julia blinked. Something seemed off. She'd never seen her mother like that before. She seemed detached. Or maybe resolved. It unnerved her.

"Should I stay until he gets home?"

"I'd love the visit," her mother said. "But I don't know when he'll be home."

"And you don't know where he is?" Julia asked.

"No," her mom said, looking at Evan. "I don't."

———————

An hour later, the front door opened. Julia stood, but her mother remained sitting, watching Evan in the bouncy seat she had found at their neighborhood garage sale. Her father walked into the kitchen, his cheeks a little rosy but otherwise looking like his normal self. He stood straight as the wall with his gray hair cut close and his broad shoulders belying the profession he'd held for over thirty years.

"Jules, how are you?"

She hugged him. "Good. Are you okay?"

He looked into her eyes for a second, and then turned away. "Of course I am."

Her father poured himself a cup of coffee and left the room. Julia watched him go. Then she looked at her mother, who said nothing, though the smell of alcohol had been so strong that Julia was sure she had noticed as well. Glancing back in the direction that her father had gone, Julia sensed something far bigger than she expected. And when she turned back around, she found her mother silently crying.

39

The rest of the drive passed as if Julia floated through a thick haze. She had spoken to the police, who verified that her husband had bought a ticket for that bus. They told Julia that they would work with Greyhound and the transit police to find out what happened. There would be surveillance video, eye witnesses. All she could do after that was wait and drive.

She turned onto her street and, for a second, thought she had taken a wrong turn. Six cars lined the curb in front of her house. As she pulled up, Tara walked out the front door and down the walk to the driveway. When she saw Julia, she hesitated, but then rushed to meet her. Her friend's hug wrapped Julia up before she could fully get herself out of the car.

"Are you okay?" Tara asked.

Julia nodded.

Tara seemed agitated. "Did you hear? The CEO of DuLac is dead. She was in the station. They found her body."

"What?"

"My husband called and . . ."

Julia stared at her. Tara went silent. She began to fidget.

"Is Evelyn here?" Julia asked.

"Oh . . . ," Tara said, stepping away. "She just got back. Lyndsey and Sara May are here, too."

Julia felt like crying. "Thank you so much."

Tara shook her off. "No. Just focus on you." Her friend smiled, sheepishly. "We'll take care of the rest."

Evelyn rushed out of the house next. She, too, hugged Julia.

"It'll be okay. They'll find him. He's out there, Julia. They know that. There's no doubt. Okay?"

Julia nodded. This time, the tears came freely. She couldn't even wipe them away, she felt so overwhelmed. Evelyn cried, too.

"There were six police officers at the station, Jules. Six! They are doing everything they can."

Julia blinked. "Six?"

"Yeah. Can you believe it?"

"Why?" Julia whispered.

Evelyn looked confused. "What, sweetie?"

"Why six? That doesn't make sense."

Her friend shook her head. "You stop. Trust me. They are doing everything they can to find Michael."

Julia couldn't stop thinking, *But why so many?*

40

My eyes opened. I closed them quickly, the shocking brightness sending a jolt of pain from my forehead to my neck.

"Sir?"

I opened one eye. A woman in a blue uniform looked down at me. Her hair smelled just slightly of mothballs. When I blinked, I noticed the phone still clutched in my hand. *Julia*, I thought, remembering the voice perfectly, like I could actually hear it repeating over and over again inside my skull.

"Sir?"

I looked up at the woman again. She stared down at me, waiting. When I finally answered, it came out more like a croak. "Yes?"

"You have to exit the bus," she said.

That's when I noticed all the other passengers were gone. I must have fallen asleep the second I sat down because I remembered nothing of the drive. Honestly, for those first few seconds after the woman woke me up, I didn't remember anything but the phone ringing. Not the explosion. Not the man in the lobby. Not the bus ride. The strangest part was that I didn't even remember that I'd forgotten everything. It just didn't seem to matter. *I* didn't seem to matter.

I exited the bus carrying the phone and my case. Outside, the first thing I noticed was the humidity. The air clung to my face like a wet, hot hand. Instantly, I had a hard time catching my breath. I took a few steps and found a bench by the sidewalk. I sat, heavily, and knew already that something wasn't right.

That's when I noticed the outlets. I saw signs for Nautica and Ralph Lauren. I stood back up and moved a few feet away from the station. There were stores for Tommy Hilfiger and Calvin Klein.

Understand, I still felt confused. But even I knew this could not be Philadelphia. In a way, I didn't even truly understand what I saw. But somehow I'd expected tall buildings, city streets. And what I saw didn't match up.

As I took a deep breath, I swear I could smell the ocean.

"What?" I said.

Someone passing by paused. It was a woman, dressed in a short skirt and flip-flops that looked like plastic flowers. She stared at me through oversized sunglasses.

"Are you okay?"

I took a step away from her. And the world started to spin. I staggered back again and then doubled over.

"Oh, God," the woman said.

The corners of my vision turned dark. I think I sat down on the pavement. Then I heard her calling for help. The next thing I can remember was sitting back in the station. A Greyhound employee leaned over in front of me.

"You drunk?"

"What?"

"I'm asking if you're drunk?"

"Stop," I heard the woman say.

She stood beside the man, her sunglasses off. Thick bangs of hair covered one of her large brown eyes. The rest was braided into pigtails.

"Something's wrong," the man said, clearly suspicious.

"Where am I?" I asked.

He snorted. "At the bus station."

"In Philadelphia?"

"What?"

"Am I in Philadelphia?"

The man laughed outright at this. "No, you're in Atlantic City."

"Are you trying to get to Philadelphia?" the woman asked, her kind words a stark contrast to the man's.

"I thought I did." My eyes stayed on the man. "Someone is waiting for me."

"Your wife?" she asked.

"Yes."

The woman's eyes might have watered. She moved closer, sort of pushing the man away.

"We'll get you there."

She took my hand and led me to a ticket window.

"He needs to get to Philadelphia."

"Fifteen dollars."

The woman reached down to the frayed bag she wore on her shoulder. I put my hand out.

"No, it's okay. I'm okay."

I pulled out my money clip. My fingertip touched the credit card and I paused, looking at the woman out of the corner of my eye. I tapped the edge of the plastic, lightly. Then I slipped a twenty out instead. Maybe some of my memories were returning. Maybe, like a fog melting away from a mirror, I couldn't see the truth yet, but a shadow had come back. I really don't know. It was just that something told me to pay in cash.

"When does the bus leave?" the woman asked.

"Five minutes."

I turned to her and looked the woman dead in the eye.

"Thank you so much," I said. I think I teared up a bit, but I'm not sure exactly why. Maybe it was her kindness.

She definitely cried. As I watched her walk away, my heart yearned. Not for her, though. I slipped my phone out and hit the home button. The screen was empty, but when I closed my eyes, I saw her name. *Julia*, I yearned for Julia.

41

The police called not long after Julia returned home. She stood in her kitchen between Evelyn and her mother, who had fixed her a glass of white wine. Julia hadn't touched it yet. She had been looking out the window watching the kids, hers and half the neighborhood's, play in the backyard again. The sight felt so different from the day before.

The call startled her, even though she had been on the edge of her seat waiting for it since she stepped in the house. Julia grabbed her phone off the quartz counter and looked at the screen. She did not recognize the extension on her caller ID.

"Hello?"

"Mrs. Swann? This is Agent Longacre. I'm just calling to follow up on your contact with the New Jersey State Police. How are you, ma'am?"

Her stomach dropped. For some reason, she felt utterly off balance. So she said nothing. Seconds passed in silence before the officer, or whoever it was, finally spoke again.

"Ma'am, are you there?"

Everyone around her kitchen counter stared. She felt a cold sweat touch the skin on her forearms. When she spun and walked away, Julia accidently bumped her mother. She didn't slow, though, until she was halfway up the stairs.

"Yes," she whispered.

Julia shut herself in her bedroom. Her back leaned against the closed door, and her chest felt like someone large was standing on it.

"Are you okay?" the man asked.

"Have you found him?"

The man cleared his throat, softly. "We are doing everything we can, I promise you that, Mrs. Swann. I wondered if I could ask you a couple of questions."

The air poured out before she realized she had been holding her breath. "Of course. Sure."

"Your husband is Michael Swann, correct?"

Her brow furrowed. "Uh, yes."

"And he was at Penn Station at the time of the explosion?"

"I don't . . ."

"Please, ma'am, just bear with me for a moment." He repeated his previous question and waited for an answer.

"Yes, but—"

"Have you heard from Michael Swann directly?"

"No, but he used his credit card."

"Has he called or texted your cell phone?"

Her hand started to shake. "No. But I called him. I can't get through. Once I might have, but . . . Please, why are you . . . ?"

"Have any strangers been to your house in the past few months? Men or women that you didn't know?"

"No," she snapped.

"Has he traveled out of the country recently?"

"Why are you asking?"

"Does he have any known association to religious extremists?"

"Stop!"

The man paused. "I'm sorry, Mrs. Swann. Understand that hundreds of people have died. Our first priority is to help survivors, but our second is to prevent anything like this from happening again. I hope you understand."

"I don't," she said.

"I'm sorry about that. Let me give you my number. Please call me back if you hear from your husband."

Speaking very slowly, the agent gave his full name and phone number. Julia did not write it down. Instead, she stared at nothing while the entire weight of her body pressed against her bedroom door.

Religious extremists?

42

A few of her friends huddled around the television set. Julia stood at the edge of the family room, looking at the screen. It showed a close-up of a smoldering debris pile while a report talked about the challenges rescue workers faced in trying to find survivors.

"Multiple gas lines are thought to be ruptured, though the city acted quickly in shutting off service to the area. We are being told that some of the areas where power has been recently restored may have additional outages in the coming hours as heavy machinery begins the process of clearing debris below the main stairwell down to the station."

After that, the reporter moved among pedestrians, asking them questions about their memory of the blast and its continued aftermath. Julia watched until, in the background, she saw a flash of blue that looked exactly the same shade as one of her flyers. For some reason, that was too much. She moved back to the kitchen and picked up her wine. The phone call haunted her, but she told no one at first.

Evelyn was there talking softly to Julia's mother. Two other women, more acquaintances than meaningful friends, spoke loudly by the sink, each holding a glass of wine in their right hand.

"They're saying that it's not the Muslims," one woman said.

"I doubt that," the other answered.

"No, seriously. I mean, if it was and they knew it, the president would be bombing someone already."

"Thank God she didn't win."

"Yeah, then maybe we'd go over there and hug someone."

They laughed. Julia felt sick to her stomach. It had nothing to do with what the ladies said. She barely even heard them. And she had no idea what she would be saying if Michael were someone else's husband. But he wasn't. He was hers. He was Evan's and Thomas's dad. In a weird way, she wished she could have opinions like that, ones that floated away on the air that birthed them, having no more of an effect than a soft breeze. Instead, her mind stormed with so many thoughts that they failed to form with any true meaning. It felt like some ravenous tiger was stalking her. It was so close she could feel it, but it might as well have been invisible because no one else seemed to know it was there.

"You okay?" Evelyn asked.

Julia nodded. And then shook her head. She started to cry again.

"The police . . . God, I can't believe this." She covered her eyes for a second, then pressed in on her temples. "This just can't be happening."

"He'll get home," her mother said. "I promise."

Julia nodded, but her mother's words seemed to hold little weight. How could she promise? She knew less than Julia did.

"Have you talked to Michael's parents?"

Julia shook her head, feeling even more overwhelmed. They lived in Florida. And they had no idea Michael had been in New York the day before. Evelyn smiled and handed her the glass of wine. She finished most of it in one swallow.

It was in that instant, just as she lowered her glass to the counter, that everything changed. The first thing she noticed was the phone. It rang in her front pocket. At the same time, she heard the intake of a half dozen breaths at once. Someone whispered, "Oh, God," or "Oh, Julia." She couldn't tell which.

There was an instant that occurred, one that would stick with Julia forever. Over the years, she would go back to it, wish it back into existence. If she ever could, she would hold on to it forever. She would live in that instant, never moving past it. It would be her own Groundhog Day.

In it, her hand held the phone. Her brain, a second behind reality, truly expected it to be a call from the police officers in Philadelphia, telling her that they had found Michael, confused but okay. She would nurse her husband back to a full recovery. She knew that this would still change their lives forever. They would never be the same. But in that instant, she saw some good in it.

Then that moment, that unbelievable nirvana, passed. Her eyes focused on the television screen before she had time to answer the call. That is where she saw his name in white, written across a large blood-red banner.

MICHAEL SWANN, the banner read. She stared at it, like it might be some surreal and unexplainable piece of pop art. Then six faces turned to look at her. Six pale circles, like full moons. And like full moons, they changed her. She became the beast reflected in those eyes. She knew it, somehow, before she could even understand it.

For the banner said more than her husband's name. It read:

MICHAEL SWANN SUSPECT IN PENN STATION ATTACK.

PART

TWO

BEING HOME

When Thomas was an infant and Evan a toddler, Michael traveled for work every week. Just before Evan was born, he had taken a job with a medical device company doing sales. And Julia had regretfully yet excitedly submitted her resignation to the governor to be a stay-at-home mom. They moved into a new and bucolic neighborhood, Glen Brook Acres. After their second son was born, she had walked the hilly streets of her neighborhood twice a day, like clockwork, the baby in the stroller and Evan doing his best to push it. Once in the morning by themselves. The second time at 2:00 p.m. with four of the other moms in the neighborhood.

"I don't know how you do it with your husband traveling as much as he does," a friend said one day as they crested Barberry Road and turned onto Glen Meadow Drive.

Julia laughed it off. "Sometimes it's easier."

The other moms laughed and chimed in with their own stories. They all matched, thematically. Even the well-meaning husbands got lumped into a single diffuse category of buffoonery.

"Oh, my God," a mom said. "Last week, I went to Darcie's Cabi party and I left Bobby at home with Jilly and Caiden. I told him to get them into bed by eight. When I got home, it was almost eleven, he was sitting on the floor in the family room trying to teach them *both* to catch a little football. I mean, Cai isn't even a year old yet."

"Did they sleep in the next morning?"

"Of course *not*. They were a mess. No nap, either. It took me two days to get them back on track."

A mom looked at Julia. "Speaking of napping, how are yours doing?"

"Still a battle. Evan just wants to stay awake so he can hang out with me. I think he's adjusting to being a big brother."

The mom shook her head. "It'll get there. I remember when I had my second. I used Dr. Jenson's method to regulate their sleeping time. Worked like a charm. You should try it."

Julia nodded. "Maybe I will."

"I just bought flash cards from him," another mom, the group's organizer, said. "Jilly's already reading all her sight words."

The conversation turned to early-childhood enrichment. Julia smiled. She turned slightly to see the newest member of the group. The mother had moved in earlier that year but had come out for the first time. Julia didn't know it yet, but her name was Evelyn and she would become her best friend in the neighborhood.

"Does your husband travel?" Evelyn asked her as a side conversation to the rest of the group.

"He does," Julia said.

"Is it hard?"

"Kind of. But you find a rhythm. How about yours?"

"No. He's an accountant, though, so I don't see him much from January through April. He pretty much eats, sleeps, adds, and subtracts."

Julia laughed. It felt odd, new in a way. Like it might have been the first adult laugh she'd had since having children. Feeling strangely happy, she introduced herself. They spoke for a moment more before being assimilated into the group. After the walk, they stopped outside one of the other moms' houses.

"I'll add you to the text chain, Evelyn. I'm so happy you came out," the mother said.

"Thanks for inviting me," Evelyn said.

They broke up, heading their separate ways back home. Julia glanced over her shoulder once and watched the newcomer head up into one of the cul-de-sacs. The emotion she felt made her uncomfortable. It was creepy, in a way, like she might follow this relative stranger home. At the same time, some connections formed just that quickly. It was like those moments in life that seem ordained. Not surprisingly, Julia likened it to the day she met Michael.

———————

Later that night, Julia got a text. She sat on one of their new counter stools. Evan had been secured in a booster seat, and Thomas sat buckled into his car seat, which rested atop the kitchen table. She cut up boiled carrots and baked chicken breast into perfect little choke-proof cubes. She put the plate and a stubby, blunt fork with a green rubber handle on Evan's tray.

"You do," Evan said.

"Not tonight."

Evan's lower lip popped out like he'd been stung by a bee.

"Ev, you're a big boy now. You can do it."

A single, comically large tear ejected from his left eye. Julia shook her head and picked up the fork. While feeding her four-year-old, she read the text. It was her walking chain. Their leader had decided to cancel the next day's meet-up due to a nor'easter heading their way. Her phone lit up as other moms replied, acknowledging the cancellation and thanking the head mom for organizing everything. She stopped on a response from a number not in her contacts.

```
Thanx
```

She saved that number as *Evelyn*. Absently forking more food into Evan's open mouth, Julia stared at the number for a second and then, on a whim, texted it.

```
Hey, this is Julia. Are you around for a glass of
wine tonight? Maybe 8:30?
```

Julia put her phone down.

"You do one, okay?"

Evan started to protest again, but Julia held her ground. She had to bribe him with an M&M, but he fed himself one cube of chicken. Julia decided to celebrate the small victory by letting Evan push his new orange rider around on the kitchen floor. After dinner, she even put Thomas's car seat on the floor and swore he had his first smile while he listened to his big brother's belly laugh. She almost forgot about texting Evelyn until her response came in.

```
Awesome! Hubby will be home around then. I'll
walk up.
```

Smiling, she decided to call Michael, who was in Indianapolis for a sales meeting.

"Hey," she said.

"What's up? Everything okay?" he asked.

She paused. "Everything's great. How about you?"

"You would have loved this place we went to today. Best cocktail sauce I've ever had."

"Awesome," she said. "How was the sales meeting?"

He had sounded happy, like the trip was going well. If he hadn't, she wouldn't have asked. When he paused before saying anything, she knew she shouldn't have.

"Fine . . . Fine."

"Great, I—"

Michael kept talking. "Hugh is being a little jerk. Our numbers are down a little, I guess. But come on. All they care about is squeezing every dollar. It's like they can't see the big picture, you know."

"Yeah," she said, carefully.

"God." He laughed. "Sometimes I totally agree with your dad."

Julia froze. Her chest tightened. Somehow, even through the phone line, he sensed her reaction.

"Geez, Jules . . . I'm sorry. I just . . . Sometimes when I'm around corporate too much I just get—"

"It's okay," Julia said. "It's good. And I get it."

"No, I shouldn't have said that. Sorry."

A silence stretched between them. Finally, Julia spoke.

"Maybe we should start thinking about options . . . you know?"

"No, no, it's all okay. Seriously. Hugh's just annoying. Everything's great. I promise. But look, I need to head down to the reception. Can I call you later?"

"What time?"

"Not sure," he said.

She heard other voices, which meant he was walking with his co-workers.

"Text first to see if I'm awake."

"Perfect. I'll text you later then."

He hung up. Julia held the phone for a minute before placing it lightly on the counter. Without meaning to, she thought about how Michael used to talk about his job. He loved working at the ballpark. He would have bad days, sure. But it had been different. Very different.

Evan slammed his rider into the wall and started to scream. It startled Thomas, who also started to scream. The sound tore through the house like a siren, and Julia's head started to ache. Her lips tight, she went through the motions of calming both of them, then got back on her routine. By 8:00 P.M. sharp, they were in bed and she had poured her first glass of wine.

———————

Julia had no idea what time it was. Crickets sang in the trees above, a soft medley with the faint buzz of her baby monitor. A sliver of a moon cast almost no shadows across her back lawn. Evelyn sat beside her on a matching Adirondack chair. The jewelry dangling from her wineglass hung off the thin stem as she lifted it up for a sip of chardonnay.

Their conversation paused for a moment. They'd danced as new friends tend to do, parrying soft questions about the past and complimenting each other's children and homes. Julia had no idea the kind of day Evelyn had, but she looked tired. Not in a sleepy way. More in the way that Julia saw on her own face most days. Maybe it was the precursor to aging. More likely it came from keeping little, helpless humans alive day after day.

Since leaving her job, Julia had adjusted to not saying much. She spoke every day, yet the conversations that passed between the other moms sometimes felt more like the conversation she had with the person checking her out at the grocery store. More of real life was left unsaid than said.

She would never understand what opened her up that night. Maybe it was that spark she'd felt when watching Evelyn walk away, like they had known each other in some past, exotic lifetime. Maybe it was the second glass of wine. Or maybe it was something more, a tectonic plate of parenthood that shifted when least expected, exposing some part of the psyche that had been lost since dedicating everything to their children. Julia felt like talking about herself for a change. When Evelyn asked if her parents were local, the dam broke and she let out news she had been hiding from the neighborhood for months.

"My father passed," she said.

"Oh, I'm sorry."

"It was a few months ago. He didn't take retirement too well. I guess he had been drinking even before that, but it turned bad real fast. It was really hard on my mother. She had to watch him slowly kill himself."

"Oh, God," Evelyn said.

"Yeah. Eventually, his liver failed. It was rough. But enough about that. How about you? Are your parents local?"

Evelyn shook her head. "Yeah. But I'm not following that story."

Julia laughed. It surprised her, really, as her father remained a very raw subject in her family. But Evelyn had a way about her that felt so liberating.

"What did you do before having kids?" Julia asked, softly.

This subject was almost taboo, at least among the stay-at-home moms. Sometimes, on girls' night or at neighborhood mixers, when the working moms were there, too, it came up and was met with awkward titters and a barely veiled change of subject. Instead, employment hung between women like some unsightly birthmark, unavoidable yet unspoken.

Evelyn leaned back and sighed. "I was a middle school teacher."

"Really," Julia said. "That's a tough age."

"You can say that again. How about you?"

Julia paused. She felt sheepish, but she answered anyway.

"I worked for the government."

Evelyn looked at her. "Yeah, me, too. More specific."

In the short time she knew her, Julia had already noticed Evelyn's penchant to put it on the table. It was somewhat refreshing, at least when properly directed.

"I worked for the governor of Delaware as a policy adviser."

"Wow, that's cool."

"Not really," Julia said.

"Shut up."

A laugh burst out of her then. She took a drink before speaking again, but it was as if Evelyn's bluntness freed her to say the things she mostly thought otherwise.

"I miss it," Julia admitted, looking out at the dark night.

"Working?"

"Yeah," she said. "I know I'm not supposed to. But I do."

"I get that," Evelyn said.

Julia could tell from the response that her new friend did not see it the same way. Usually, that would divert the conversation down a new path. Not that night.

"I love my kids to death. I just . . . Do you ever feel like everyone's doing it better than you?"

Evelyn snorted. "Only every freaking day."

"I know, right. I can't keep up. I try sometimes. Like that Dr. Jenson thing. I read it . . . some of it. But then I forget to even try what he says. You know what? I bribed my son with candy so he'd feed himself tonight."

Julia turned to see Evelyn's response. It did not shock her.

"So what? Do you really think you'll be feeding him at sixteen?"

"No." She laughed. "But if the other moms knew, I'd be so embarrassed."

"Yeah, I get it."

Julia looked up at the stars. "I was really good at what I did. And

I really liked it. And I shouldn't feel so guilty about that. But I do. I feel like I'm not supposed to talk about it. Like I shouldn't even think about it." She closed her eyes. "The other day . . . when the kids were napping, I actually put on one of my favorite work outfits."

Evelyn laughed. It didn't bother Julia. She knew how weird that had been. For a second, she wondered if admitting it was such a great idea. But she couldn't stop.

"Some days, I'm afraid." Julia looked at her wine. "Of becoming him . . . my dad. I mean, if I get depressed or something like that. My mom used to tell me all the time that I inherited my father's workaholic gene."

"Why'd you stop working?" Evelyn asked.

"Because . . . I don't really know. I felt like Michael and I could afford to do it without day care. But I bet Evan would have learned to feed himself there!"

They clinked glasses and laughed together.

"I think there's no right way. Just the way that feels right."

"That's deep," Julia said. It was a joke, but she'd remember that phrase.

Their conversation eased forward, but Julia knew the moment was over. She didn't open up again. In fact, she let Evelyn do most of the talking from then on. When they realized it was after eleven, Evelyn headed home. Julia stood at her kitchen counter rinsing out the empty bottle of white. Her head went through the night's conversation and she worried that she'd said too much. At the same time, it didn't really matter. What was done was done, and she'd have to get up in four hours to feed Thomas. So she slipped into bed and fell quickly to sleep. It wasn't until the morning that she noticed Michael never even texted.

1

N o, that's not right," Julia whispered.

No one in the room heard her words. They escaped barely louder than a breath. At the same time, the room was utterly silent except for the television. Everyone's eyes locked onto the screen and what it said.

A second later and the picture flashed like a sudden lightning strike. Julia looked at a younger version of herself on the screen, standing next to Michael. It was the same picture she had used on the flyers, but it appeared in high-definition color on whatever news channel her neighbors had been watching while she'd been gone.

"That isn't right," she said, louder this time.

Julia didn't move. But she looked at her friends, a slow, furtive scan around the room. No one made eye contact. No one moved. The television might as well have been muted because no one heard a word that the anchor read from the teleprompter offscreen. Instead, the picture mesmerized every one of them. They swayed like charmed snakes.

Neurons exploded in Julia's head. It was like a flash of blinding light, and it tore her feet off the tile floor in the kitchen. She moved in a swift but stiff walk, passing among her friends like they might be bystanders gathering around a train wreck. She never thought about her actions, what she would do. She might have looked around quickly, trying to find the remote. If so, that action was barely noticeable. What she did next, however, could never be missed.

Without slowing, Julia reached the television, where it rested atop a black wood stand. Her thighs struck the edge and her arms shot out, stiff and straight. Palms open, she struck the side of the flat screen. The television spun once and then flew off the stand, striking the wall before hitting the ground at an awkward angle. A blue spark shot out a vent in the back, and there was a sharp squeal before it went silent.

Julia stood, her side to her neighbors and her mother, facing the television. A thin wisp of silver smoke rose up as if from a burning cigarette. A miniature mockery of the smoke she'd seen in the city. Her arms lowered and her hands, hot and damp, hung limp by her side.

"It's not right!" she said, again.

Julia would never know just how long everyone simply stood there, staring, mouths hanging open, eyes wide. Time shrunk to its most basic meaning, a rhythmic ticking of the passage of their days. Those seconds became years peeling away from her life like dead skin after a bad sunburn. It left her raw and hot and unbelievably tired.

"No," she said. "It's . . ."

She didn't finish it that time. The dangling sentence started the clock for everyone else in the room. Neighbors, friends, they moved toward her. Hands reached for her. Soft words were spoken for her. Then Evelyn was there, standing before her, holding Julia's face in her hands. Eyes finding hers.

"Listen to me," her friend said. "It's a mistake. You know it's a mistake."

Julia blinked. She knew that. Without a doubt. In that instant, she knew that for certain. A strange laugh escaped Julia. It struck those around her. Their purpose shifted. Bodies inched away from her, just slightly, as her lips clamped shut.

Undeniable, the laugh burst out again. Evelyn grabbed her, pressing into her tightly. The sound Julia made morphed. At some point, it switched over to a racking sob.

"He's coming home," Evelyn kept whispering. "It'll all be okay."

But often words are empty.

2

I dreamed that I stood in a long, shadowy hallway. The floor below me swayed like I was a passenger on a boat. Off in the distance, a woman stood in the darkness. I couldn't see her face. Her hand reached out for me, but she was yards and yards away. Then she said my name. Over and over again, she said it. At first, she called for me like a lost love. But each time her tone changed. I became a stranger. Then a villain. *Michael Swann*, she swooned. *Michael Swann*, she sneered.

My eyes opened, and I was back on the bus heading from Atlantic City to Philadelphia. I had trouble focusing, my vision wavering. Then I heard my name again. It sent a shock through my chest. I sat up, my head following the sound, and I saw a passenger across the aisle from me watching television on his phone. Although the afternoon sun glared the screen, I could just barely hear the volume.

". . . Michael Swann of West Chester, Pennsylvania, thought to be behind the bombing at Penn Station. At this time, authorities have not *officially* released any information, including a suspected motive, but in a post on Twitter, a terrorist group with ties to ISIL has taken responsibility. At this time, Homeland Security warns that there is no evidence supporting their claim, but they are working around the clock to identify any others responsible for this cowardly act of hatred. We are receiving word that the president of the United States will be addressing the country at 5:00 P.M. this evening. We will broadcast his remarks live. Once again, anonymous sources within Homeland Security state that a manhunt is underway in Philadelphia and the surrounding suburbs for Michael Swann. He was thought to have arrived there two hours ago aboard a bus. Police were able to track the use of his credit card at a transit station in northern New Jersey . . ."

The man shifted in his seat, his body moving between me and the phone. The sound muffled enough that I could no longer make out the words. I'd heard enough, though my understanding of it was odd. I recognized the name, but for a second forgot that it was mine. The strangest part, though, was that I reached into my pocket and pulled out the money clip. Turning it, I reread the name, my name—*Michael Swann*. And my heart began to race.

Jamming the clip back in my pocket, I hunched over and turned away from the aisle. Although I couldn't see the screen, I was sure they must be showing my picture over the airways. After what had happened, everyone in the country had to be watching the news. They would all hear my name, see my face. And they would think that I did that horrible thing.

Did I? That was the worst of it. Maybe I did. How could I know for sure? I couldn't remember anything. It wasn't that I didn't know what I did or didn't do. It was that I had no idea what I *could* or *couldn't* do.

3

Evelyn sat her down at the kitchen table. Oddly, for the moment at least, no one else existed in that kitchen. Julia could not even hear the murmur of soft voices that milled around her. None of the others, except for Julia's mother and Tara, came any closer than arm's length as Evelyn rubbed her back.

Nothing made any sense. That was all Julia could think. Michael was alive. The father of her children, beyond all hope, was alive. He had almost made it home. Then he vanished. And now this. It just didn't make any sense.

"There's no proof," Julia said to no one.

Evelyn's head tilted, as if she found her words odd, out of place. Julia just stared at her, confused. The moment stretched awkwardly until Evelyn moved to make room for Julia's mother—yet the older, wiser woman had no idea what to do, either. She sat close to her daughter. She wanted to engulf her, protect her from whatever it was that just happened, but it made no sense. She had no idea how to react to something like that. Nothing had prepared her. She could bandage a wound, make a killer chicken soup, and drop everything to watch her grandchildren. But she sat powerless, impotent, before what had just unfolded.

Tara did not sit. She stood near them, just behind a high-backed kitchen chair. She, too, said nothing. Nor would she. There was nothing to say. Or so much that if a single word slipped out, the world would shudder under its weight.

"It's okay," Evelyn kept saying. "It's just a mistake."

"It has to be," Julia whispered. "Where is he?"

At first, none of the three noticed. One at a time, neighbors moved away. Like planets slowly breaking free from their orbits, their milling drew them farther and farther away from Julia. Patricia Welles, 445 Barberry Road, was the first. She slipped into the bathroom and then, without anyone really noticing, slipped out the front door. She wandered around the side yard and got the attention of her two kids, Francis and Bella. When the second neighbor, Georgia McShea, five doors down on Glen Meadow Drive, stepped out of the house, she saw Patricia walking her kids around the corner. She, too, slipped through the side yard and gathered her children. She was gone before the next to leave saw her.

Julia never looked up until the back door opened. Tara, holding the handle, caught her eye. She looked guilty, and Julia noticed her son in tow.

"I have to get him home. I'll call you, okay?"

Evelyn shot her a look. Tara shrugged, but her hangdog expression softened when Julia managed a strained smile. Tara shuttled her child through the foyer and out the front door without looking back. That's when Julia turned her head, slowly, taking in her not-so-suddenly empty house. They had all gone. Everyone but Evelyn and her mother.

Truthfully, nothing about that fazed Julia in those first moments. It wasn't until the back door opened once again and Thomas stood in the threshold, his knees grass-stained and his hair matted down with sweat that Julia's heart truly broke. She looked into the still innocent face of her younger son, and it felt like her chest went empty, like this truth had become a dark talon that ripped clean her soul.

"Everybody's leaving," he said.

Julia broke down. She shuddered. Before she could hide her face, she saw Thomas's eyes widen. She knew that her reaction, that moment of weakness, took some of his innocence away. But it no longer mattered. For life was about to take its due, and the Swann family suddenly owed more than they could possibly pay.

4

As I stared at the floor of the moving bus, I swore I felt every eye boring into me. I imagined the other passengers on the bus slowly realizing who I was. Ironic, considering I still felt unable to answer that question myself. Sweat dampened my hair and dripped off the tip of my nose, the droplet flattening when it hit the rubber matting at my feet.

I'm a killer.

I was afraid to even lift my head. I couldn't let anyone see me. So I sat, sweating and almost hyperventilating, trying to come up with a way off the bus. I heard voices rising further toward the front of the cabin. I tried to ignore them, yet they grew louder and louder.

"Why don't you just go back to where you came from?"

That was a man's voice. Even from a distance, it was almost as if I could taste the hatred that dripped from every word. No one responded at first. Then a woman spoke. Her tone was soft and nonconfrontational.

"Just leave her alone."

"What, are you some kind of Muslim lover?" the man shouted. "Are all you a bunch of *MOOO-slim* lovers?"

I looked up and saw who was speaking. He was a middle-aged man wearing an Under Armour shirt beneath a fleece vest even though it was almost ninety degrees outside. He had a tight goatee and black hair. His eyes were narrow but sharp. In all, he looked like a recreational soccer coach.

Across from him and up three seats sat a woman wearing a head scarf. Her complexion was dark and her back straight. She sat with her hands on her lap, staring forward. Her body language seemed, at least to me, to say that she'd experienced something like this before.

As I watched, forgetting everything for a second, lost in the un-folding drama, the guy with the phone stood up.

"Hey, idiot," he called out to the guy with the goatee. "It was an American."

The man near the front ignored him. He stood up and stepped into the aisle, moving so close to the woman in the head scarf that his head tilted downward to look at her.

"Go home," he said. "No one wants you here."

She did not flinch. I stared, utterly lost in the confrontation. Maybe it was the injury, but everything that had happened slipped away, and I was left sitting on that bus, watching a man tower over a woman. And I couldn't understand.

Killer, I thought. *Am I a killer?*

Who was I? I heard the man in the vest. I heard his hatred. I felt the fear. It radiated out like heat from some angry star. Did it come from the woman, sitting so stoically in her seat as the man spit vitriol over her? Shouldn't she be afraid?

But it wasn't right. That's not where it came from. Instead, I sud-denly realized it came from me. I was afraid. Although I couldn't re-ally understand it, I was afraid of that woman. She was the source. And in a way, I understood that was what the man in the vest felt, too.

My head throbbed. It made no sense. Nothing did. The man was so full of aggression. He towered over her, threatening her with every word, every movement he made. She should be afraid. Maybe she was. But why would he fear her? Why would I?

I sat frozen as the man with the phone beside me moved closer to the guy in the vest. He moved to protect the woman with her head covered. Yet I felt an overwhelming urge to strike *him* down.

At that exact moment, the phone in my hand received a text. I looked at it, read it.

Hey, call me. I'm worried

I stared at the screen. At the name above the message: *Julia*.

The notifications rang in a staccato series, one after another, as more texts pinged the phone.

Michael where R U
Call me please
Answer

I read the rest, but they floated away on the emptiness of my lost memories. It didn't seem to matter, either. For my eyes returned to that name. I stared at it as it repeated within me over and over again.

Julia, Julia, Julia . . .

It vibrated against my skull. Something changed. I changed. I thought of her. What she would want me to do. I couldn't even picture her face, but somehow I knew what she would expect of me. I knew.

Julia, I thought. And I stood. It's strange. A moment before, all I could think to do was run. I knew they were looking for me. And the last thing I should have wanted to do was draw attention. But I walked up the aisle, eyes locked on the man with the vest.

The man with the phone didn't notice me until I shouldered him back into a seat. The other guy, however, did. He turned slowly, his attention focusing on me. I didn't say a word. My mind was empty but for a single impulse.

"What the fuck do you want?" the man said. "You got a problem?"

Never worry about the guy who talks. Maybe I knew that lesson before my mind went blank. I've definitely learned it over and over again since. But it is an undeniable truth. If a guy is running his mouth, he's not going to start anything. If, however, a guy is silent, then it means trouble. I was that guy on the bus. I took three more steps and my fist shot out. I caught him just below his larynx.

I hit him hard, but fights aren't like the ones on television or in movies. It's not easy to knock someone out with one punch, especially someone who's aware he's going to be hit. The man did take a step back. He coughed, sputtering to take a breath. So I dipped my shoulder and ran into him. My foot caught on a seat and I lost my balance. We fell to the aisle, together.

The man struggled under me. I could hear him wheezing. At the same time, my head spun. All thoughts turned blank, then. Like nothing existed inside my head. Like a dull white light. But strangely, I have one memory that is so clear. As the man pushed against me, I turned my head, looking for a handhold to regain my feet. That's when I saw the woman. She was right next to me. She sat exactly as she had before, hands on her lap, eyes straight forward. Her face was a mask of ice. Sharp and cold. There was no reaction. No relief. No shock. Nothing but a wall of some emotion that I may never understand.

The aggression left me as I looked at her. A hand grabbed my arm. I rose, with someone's help. That's when I realized the bus had stopped. I half expected the driver to be the one holding my arm, but it was the guy with the phone. The driver, an aging man with unwashed hair and a tattoo of what looked like a turtle on his forearm, sat in his seat, talking on his radio to dispatch.

Someone else helped the goatee man up. They sat him on a seat as he continued to gasp for breath. I wondered, for just an instant, if I had really hurt him.

"Dude," the guy with the phone said.

I looked at him, then, and remembered the report on his phone. He stared at me. He knew. I was sure of it. With a snap, I freed my arm and walked down the aisle toward my seat. I grabbed the case and turned. Before I took two steps back up the aisle, though, I heard the phone notification. This time, though, it was a different tone from the texts. Spinning, I lunged backwards and found it sitting on the seat. When I looked at the screen, it said I had missed another call from Julia.

Inside, I raged. Jamming the phone into my front pocket, I moved through the bus, shouldering people as I passed. Others took one look and moved out of my way. When I reached the driver, I did not even look at him.

"Open the door," I said.

The driver did. He said nothing as I walked off the bus. He had pulled up close to the guardrail, so I had to sidle along it. The metal felt cool as I vaulted it and took my first step down the embankment.

That's when I took a breath and smelled Christmas, of all things. I pictured children unwrapping presents. And, strangely, a vague emptiness, full of unmet expectations and deep disappointment. I felt an overwhelming sadness. Yet I didn't know why.

In reality, that smell came from the towering pines that lined the highway. It was the first association my mind had been able to make since coming to. I should have been excited, but I wasn't. Instead, in a way, I wished it hadn't happened at all. I wished I could just disappear into the forest, forever.

5

'll come back later tonight. Are you sure you don't want me to take the kids?"

Evelyn held the front door open as she spoke. Julia, who had regained composure, answered in a toneless voice.

"It's okay. I think . . . I need to talk to them."

"Are you sure?"

Julia wasn't. Not at all. Yet she knew that everyone in the country suddenly thought her husband, their father, was a vile murderer. She could no more hide that from them than wish it out of existence.

"Mom?"

She turned. Evan stood at the back door, the late sun elongating his shadowed body, making him appear taller than he was. For a second, Julia saw Michael instead. Their older son was growing to look more and more like his father, with darker hair and a long face. His voice, though still higher, shared a tone with his dad as well. She swallowed down the emotions that vision brought up inside her.

Evan wouldn't say anything else. He hadn't spoken much since he woke up. She could see his accusation clearly on his young face. *Liar*, it seemed to scream at Julia. As she watched him, he pointed at the front window.

"What?" Julia asked.

He didn't answer, so Julia walked slowly to the window, glancing back at her son once. Then she parted the curtain just as a white van with the colorful logo of the local network affiliate slowed to a stop at the base of her winding drive. She ducked, looking under the low-hanging branches of the two sugar maples in her front yard. She saw the other cars and vans making a jagged line down the street.

"Oh, God," Evelyn said behind her.

Thomas appeared. He moved closer to her, touching her. Nothing was said, but his childish intuition picked up on the tension. Julia turned to see if Evan sensed it, too, but he was gone. His footsteps echoed down the stairs to the basement. Julia pressed Thomas close to her.

"Go out the back," Julia said to Evelyn.

Evelyn turned. Julia let the curtain fall closed as her friend gathered her son and headed into the backyard. A white fence ran the perimeter. Evelyn moved to the gate at the side yard but stopped.

"They have cameras out," she said, stepping back behind the house.

Evelyn looked around, moving like a trapped animal. Grabbing her son's hand, she pulled him across the yard to the back corner. Without a word, she picked him up and placed him on the other side of the fence. His foot caught on the way down, and he fell to the ground. Although it didn't seem like the impact could have hurt him seriously, he shouted in pain.

Evelyn's stress became a spreading thundercloud. As her son wailed, Evelyn followed him. The leg of her shorts looped one of the posts. As she went over, it tore and a deep red mark sprang up on the back of her thigh. She didn't make a sound, though. Instead, she pulled her crying boy off the ground and hurried across the neighbor's yard, her strides long and stiff.

Julia stood on the porch, watching the entire thing. So did Thomas. They might have stood there forever, caught up in the web of that unnerving display, but one even worse occurred next. A head appeared, craning around the side of the house. It was a man with scruffy facial hair and hipster glasses. He swung one arm over the fence. A television camera hung from his hand.

Thomas froze. He stared at the stranger, every muscle in his body rigid and still. Julia, on the other hand, moved quickly. She thrust herself between the cameraman and her son, blocking him from view. The motion seemed to turn her son's once rigid body to liquid. His legs wobbled, and he looked like he might lift off in the breeze and sail away.

Julia saw this. She felt it. Her arms wrapped around him. She picked him up as she once had, as she stopped doing when he turned seven. In a way, it mirrored what Evelyn had done moments before. Yet she had seemed to act out of a panicked fear, whereas Julia's stance hinted more at a lioness protecting her young.

Thomas's arms clung to Julia's neck. He buried his head in her shoulder. Barely noticing his weight, she spun and walked back into the house. Using her foot, she swung the door closed. It slammed so hard that the glasses in the kitchen cupboard rattled.

Immediately, she felt eyes on her back. Slowly, she put Thomas on the ground and turned. Evan stood in the family room, his face as pale as the whites of his eyes. Julia's chest tightened.

"Oh, sweetie," she whispered.

His mouth opened, but it took time for the words to come out. When they did, they sounded as thin as the air between them.

"What happened to the TV?"

6

Julia left the kids in the basement. Evan had gone back to giving her the silent treatment, and Thomas calmed when she turned on the Xbox. As she walked up the stairs, she heard the faint sounds of their video game coming through the partially opened pocket door that led to the media room. Her eyes closed as she focused on lifting her feet, one step at a time. They felt as heavy as if they had been cast in iron.

Her mother waited at the top of the steps, her reading glasses hanging from a silver chain around her neck, one she had not stopped tugging at since the report had come on the TV. The expression on her mother's face was undecipherable. It seemed at once protective and accusatory. But Julia failed to notice. Instead, she pushed past her and paced. She went from the kitchen through the dining room. Then from the foyer through the living room and back through the kitchen. She did this three times before her mother finally spoke.

"Did you tell them?"

She shook her head. "No. How could I? Evan won't speak to me."

"I thought . . ."

"No," Julia repeated.

She paced another lap. The physical effort was in vain, though. It cleared none of the cacophony of thoughts that rolled through her brain like some overplayed and torturous pop song. She needed to act.

She could not sit still. But she was trapped like an animal in the zoo, needing to hunt but instead walking in circles just waiting to be fed.

"The TV's broken," her mother said. Julia felt like she wasn't even talking to her, that her mom was just putting words out there into the ether. "I tried to put it on, but it's fried for sure."

Julia kept pacing until she reached the living room again. There, she parted the curtains. People were everywhere, so she quickly closed them again. Without saying anything, she turned and walked up the stairs. As if she somehow knew what Julia was thinking, her mother followed her into the master bedroom. Julia sat on the edge of their king-size mattress and, without asking, her mother put on the television.

The image on the screen was surreal. On the station that the television had last been set to, a live shot of the front of her house appeared. Julia sat on her bed and looked at the outside of her own bedroom window. The shade was partially open. Although it was most likely a trick of her mind, she swore she saw herself there, watching herself watch herself like she and her mother stood between fun-house mirrors.

"Change it," she snapped.

Her mother did. They found another station. It, too, was covering her husband.

"As we wait for confirmation of recent reports that Michael Swann is the lone suspect in the attack on Penn Station, new sources have come forward with some chilling news. According to those who knew Swann, he spoke often about the polarizing elections. In fact, someone claiming to be a family friend told a reporter for one of our affiliated stations that Swann often made racially insensitive remarks . . ."

Julia's cheeks burned. "That's bullshit!"

Her mother switched the channel again. For her part, Julia was reeling. *Knew Swann? Family friend?* She wasn't even sure an hour had passed since this new madness started. How could they be reporting things like that? It made no sense.

The next station provided factual accounts of the attack. Thousands injured. Hundreds dead. News that engineers had concluded that Madison Square Garden could not be saved. Due to structural-integrity issues, the iconic building would have to be utterly demolished. Cell service was returning in the tristate area.

Julia heard that. She grabbed her phone and tried to call Michael on the work phone again, the one that she thought he had picked up. It rang four times and went to voicemail. She listened to his voice, so calm and professional. It made her cry. Through the tears, she left a message.

"Please call me. I know this isn't true. Just call . . . We can figure it out."

Julia had never felt as empty as when she ended that call. The news continued to drone on. Julia heard none of it. Her mind could not leave the other report, the one about Michael. She buried her head in her hands. In that moment, she thought she might die. Julia could feel her lungs seizing up. Her body willing itself to quit on her. And maybe she wanted that. Maybe that was the only way out.

"Jules?" her mother said softly.

Through shaking hands, Julia said, "It's a mistake. He could never do something like that."

"I know, sweetie," Kate said.

Instead, Julia heard, *How do you know?*

STRIKING THE FUSE

The entire country had been smoldering like a lit stick of dynamite. Though the presidential primaries were still months away, rhetoric was ramping up with surprising fervor. It was midsummer, and the lines in the sand had been drawn. Some spit acid as they argued on Facebook over who the candidates should be. Others sat in upscale suburban neighborhoods listening to the first sounds of crickets and discussing the carnival with a mixture of humor and veiled panic, or what eventually would be revealed as closeted support.

On this particular night, Evelyn, Tara, and their husbands sat on the Swanns' back porch with three other couples, two from the neighborhood and one of Michael's friends from work and his wife. Julia, Evelyn, and the men drank LandSharks while the other women polished off their second bottle of white wine. Thunderstorms had rolled through that afternoon, breaking a weeklong hot spell.

Julia leaned back and let the relatively cool and considerably less humid breeze play across her face. It seemed to move along with the soft but lively discussion going on around her.

"Global warming sucks," one of the men said.

"That's random," Michael responded, then listened to others argue.

"The heat, man. It's crazy."

"It's summer."

"No, man, this is different. I don't remember it being this hot out."

"In the summer?"

"Yeah."

"You watch too much news."

"Are you one of those people that don't believe in global warming?"

"No, I'm one of those people that don't believe what I see on the news. Do you believe everything you see on a sitcom?"

The guy laughed. "No."

"Well, they're subject to the same ratings system. And that ratings system dictates how much the television station can sell their ad space for during the news. So the more people that watch, the more money the station can make. Hate to say it, bro, but I doubt that coexists with that fantasy of journalistic integrity . . ."

"Chill out," his wife interrupted.

Everyone laughed. But the door had been open. Tara's husband jumped in, targeting his question to the man with all the opinions.

"I bet you're voting for Trump, too," he said.

"I might," Michael blurted out.

Everyone from their neighborhood spun around to look at him, shocked.

"What?" Julia said with a chuckle.

"Seriously," he said.

She noticed his tone, and she was likely the only one to recognize it. It wasn't new, per se. The first time she had heard it was when they were still dating and they ran into an ex of hers out one night. Michael had been a gentleman about the whole thing until Julia decided it was a good idea to walk her old boyfriend out to his car. She was gone for only a minute, but when she came back, Michael didn't hesitate to address what happened.

"Look, I trust you. I know nothing happened. But don't make me a *goat*," he had said.

Julia hadn't understood it that night. Later she would, though. It wasn't about her walking the guy out. It was about what others might think about her walking him out. She thought about that night before saying anything else. But his comment had surprised her.

"Stop," Julia said. "They might believe you."

As she looked at her husband, afraid at what his response might be, she remembered the second time she heard his tone like that. It had been when he called from his trip to Indianapolis. And she corrected herself. She had heard that tone many times recently. Whenever he spoke about his job.

"You think I'm kidding," he said. "I mean, look around. Everything's so messed up. Everyone's turned soft. You can't say anything or do anything without offending people."

"You sound like Trump," Evelyn's husband said.

Their laughter echoed through the neighborhood, but Julia noticed. Her husband and Evelyn's were good friends. They golfed and played tennis at the club all the time. Michael was usually his most reliable audience. Not this time.

"He's going to win the primaries. You know that, right? You know who's voting for him? It's white men. They've become second-class citizens. They're losing their jobs. They're not getting into schools. And it has nothing to do with their ability. Their intelligence. It's just about the color of their skin. It's crazy."

"Um, aren't you a white man?" Evelyn's husband said, smiling.

Again, Michael didn't bite. Julia reached over, put a hand on his shoulder. He shrugged it off.

"Come on, let it go," she whispered.

Michael looked her dead in the eyes. "I mean, look what happened to my father-in-law. That fucking company of his killed him."

The party went silent. Julia couldn't breathe. The moment stretched out for what felt like an eternity, the only sound that of the insects singing in the silence.

———————

That night, as they lay in bed, Julia looked at her husband. The buzz he'd clearly built up on the back porch had faded away, replaced by a deep tiredness apparent under his eyes as he looked up at the slowly turning ceiling fan above their heads. She sensed his regret, but also knew him well. He'd never openly admit he had said anything stupid and out of character.

"You okay?" she asked.

"Yeah, why?"

Julia took a deep breath. "Something's up."

His eyes closed, but he told her. "I'm in trouble at work."

"Why? What happened?"

His statement had taken her unaware. His comment about her father hurt, badly, but she had never considered why he might have said it.

"Hugh came into my office. He closed the door and told me that he thinks our business is about to be sold to another company out of Germany. They have a similar product . . ." He let out a long breath. "Which means they have a similar sales force. And . . ." He paused again. When he continued, she had never heard him sound so low. "He said my numbers aren't good enough. That . . . I might be in trouble."

"What? When could this happen?"

"A few months, maybe. He thinks it's already pretty far along."

Julia's heart stuttered. She thought about the house, the kids, their life. And for the first time, she realized just how reliant she was on her husband. She'd known it, ever since she decided to stay home with the kids. But she hadn't realized how heavy that was until then.

"Maybe I'm just not cut out to be a salesman," he said.

"What? Why?"

He shook his head. "Nothing. I just need to fix things."

"What are you going to do?"

She had always taken care of herself, relied on herself. If things went south, she fixed them. She had acted. This time, she was helpless. Julia wanted to do something, to help him fix it. But as she made suggestions, the lines of his face grew deeper and his eyes took on a coldness she'd never seen before.

"Look," he interrupted as Julia was saying something about helping him update his résumé. "I just need to put in more hours. I can't keep covering for you with the kids, and going to all their stuff at school."

Julia flinched. "Really? Is that how you see it?"

"Look, that's why you're home, so someone can be there all the time. That's your job."

Julia shook her head. "Fine, Michael."

She got out of bed and left the room. Julia slept that night on the couch downstairs. By the next morning, they both acted as if nothing had happened.

7

The sun set as I moved through a thicket of bramble. Sweat stung my eyes as the barbs bit into the exposed skin of my forearms and face. I lashed out at the branches, and they returned with a vengeance.

"Who the hell am I?"

What happened on the bus had shaken me. Not the fight, but the conflict I felt right before it. In a way, I felt it every time I tried to think. Each thought became far more exhausting than trying to push through the underbrush.

It took me nearly an hour to reach the first exit off the highway. My legs started to cramp. That's when I realized I hadn't eaten or drank anything in almost twenty-four hours. Actually, it might have been longer. Obviously, at the time, I couldn't remember.

As I neared the embankment of the cloverleaf, I heard a siren. Dropping to the ground, I lurked in the shadow until it passed. Then I rose, barely aware of my own decisions, and moved down a grassy embankment. As my physical exhaustion caught up, my thinking slowed. With my head down, I walked along the smaller road toward a gas station a few hundred yards away.

My nerves picked up as I moved closer. People stood under the lights up ahead, pumping gas and slipping in and out of the convenience store. Car headlights turned on as the long shadows of the early evening fell over both sides of the road. But the growing darkness didn't put me at ease one bit. With every step, I expected to be found out. I imagined being swarmed by guns and dogs. My head on a swivel, I watched every direction, looking for the inevitable. Yet it never came.

So I continued, inching closer and closer. As I neared the parking lot, I shied away from the cars, moving along the perimeter. My head down, I neared the back and then came around, moving along the side of the building. As I passed, I tried the door to the men's room, but it was locked.

I had no idea what I was doing, much less what I should do next. I just moved like some rabid animal, like some primal instinct to survive against all odds was pushing me feverishly forward, ever forward. And I kept thinking about that dream I had on the bus. Hearing that voice calling out my name.

Michael Swann . . . Michael Swann . . .

I imagined pushing through the fog and the gloom to get closer and closer to her. I needed to reach her. She called to me, begging me on. And I moved, one step past another, inching along the wall, creeping through the shadows.

I think that I expected to ask for a ride. I know that didn't make any sense. The risk of someone recognizing me was far too high. At the same time, what else could I do? I didn't even know where I was. Who I was. I needed help or I'd never make it.

As I reached the corner of the store, though, a car pulled up. With the headlights still on, a young woman, maybe in her twenties, popped out of the driver's seat. Slamming the door, she walked quickly into the store as she typed away on her phone with two lightning-fast thumbs. I stood there, watching her, until the door closed. Then I heard her engine running.

There was no premeditation. There wasn't even a thought. I just acted—walking out, stepping off the curb, and climbing into her car. Without even knowing if I actually knew how to drive, I put the car in reverse and slowly, carefully backed out. Then I rolled out of the parking lot, turning right onto the two-lane road. I passed back under the highway and drove away.

8

The television was still on. Julia shook her head, clearing away the memory of Michael from that night so long ago, only to make room for more reporters to vilify him. She blinked, and the screen came into focus. A man with a morose yet canned expression looked into the camera and said, "The video you are about to watch may be disturbing for some audiences."

A grainy video played, clearly shot from above by a surveillance camera inside Penn Station. At first, it was a wide shot. In it, hundreds of people milled around what looked like the Acela lounge. In the distance, Julia could see out to the main part of the station. People stood shoulder to shoulder around the enormous board that showed arrivals and departures. There were so many that it looked more like some singularity, like the individuals had merged together in a primordial ooze of frustrated commuters.

After only a second or two of this shot, the camera zoomed in on one person in the lounge. For a second, Julia didn't recognize him. Instead, her mind, reeling from everything that had crashed around her, had a very mundane and rational thought. She decided that the zoom must have been done digitally, after the fact. Why else would the camera suddenly zoom in on one sole person? A clean-cut, middle-aged man in a nice suit. He stood among others, holding his phone to his ear. His movements were jerky and amorphous due to the pixelation, and the coloring transformed him into a specter.

Michael, she thought.

The image of her husband was too much. In a way, it numbed her, removing her from her own existence. It is, she would later think, possibly the human mind's defense mechanism. Maybe it is how people who endure horrendous torture somehow survive. They walk away from the tragedy looking normal. Yet they've changed. That numbness never truly leaves their eyes. They step through the days like the image she watched on the screen, like a soulless shell existing in a world that has lost all color.

She continued to watch, though, in a way, it was no longer her. His hand dropped suddenly to his side. His attention snapped to the right, as if some sound or motion startled him. She noticed a change in him, then. He looked on edge. He reached down and started to pick up his briefcase. As soon as the case lifted off the floor, he stopped, as if confused, and looked down. At that instant, the video stopped. An instant later, the somber reporter came back onto the screen. His flat eyes did not blink as he spoke.

"Once again, this video was obtained through an unnamed source close to the investigation. It purportedly shows the prime suspect in the Penn Station attack holding the case containing the explosives just moments before the bomb goes off, killing and wounding thousands."

Julia ripped herself away. Standing, she turned on her mother.

"No!" she screamed. "I'm not going to let them *fucking* do this!"

She stepped out of the room, pulling out her phone. Julia called Michael and the call failed. She texted him again.

```
Where are you
```

They were wrong, she thought. She continued down the stairs, staring at the text. It felt so futile, like screaming in an empty room. She felt helpless and hopeless, powerless to act in any way that seemed even remotely productive.

She started to cry again, staring at what seemed like an endless chain of unanswered texts. She had convinced herself that he never saw them, that they were lost in the service disruption following the bombing. With each minute that passed, though, that excuse pulled thinner and thinner. Through it, the truth became uncomfortably too clear.

At the bottom of the stairs, she dialed the number for the New Jersey State Police. She needed answers. And she'd get them. She had to.

On the third ring, the call was answered.

"Can I speak with Marci Simmons? This is . . ."

At that instant, someone pounded at her front door. Her heart leapt and the phone lowered to her side. Julia turned toward the sound, filling with an unrealistic hope. She pictured the door swinging open and Michael standing there, hurt but okay. It would all be okay. Everything would get cleared up. If . . .

The pounding started again. The door shook. Then she heard a man's voice.

"Homeland Security."

9

The man sitting across Julia's kitchen table from her looked as if he were still wearing sunglasses. Not that his eyes were deep-set or shadowed. His face just looked as if it were made to wear them. And without them, something seemed off.

His partner, on the other hand, was not what she expected. A thin man with a dark complexion and facial hair, he might pass for a Saudi Arabian prince or, to more than half of the United States at that moment in history, a well-dressed terrorist. He spoke with a slight British accent and in a manner that caused Julia to feel interrogated.

They began immediately, once they had shown their badges and introduced themselves. She showed them to the table, and the thinner agent, Bakhash, began the questions.

"How long have you and Mr. Swann been married?" and "How many children do you have?"

Julia answered, trying her best to hide her growing frustration. She slipped her own questions in between theirs. Yet every single one went essentially unanswered.

"Do you know where Michael is?" and "Are you saying he did this?"

Agent Bakhash smiled a good bit. His partner—Julia never remembered his name—did not, not even once. He sat staring at her. She would not say it was with open disgust. Nor was it with any noticeable suspicion. It was something else, something far more frightening. He looked at her like a butcher might look at a chicken.

"Have you heard anything from your husband?" Bakhash asked.

"No. But I spoke to someone that saw him in New York. And I was told he used his credit card to get a bus ticket. I think one call went through . . . but I don't know."

"Has any stranger contacted you recently, before or after the events yesterday?"

"No, nothing I can think of."

"Do any of these names sound familiar to you? Eugene Franklin? Daniel Schmidt? Eric Maney?"

"No. Why?"

He ignored her again. "Have you noticed any strange behaviors from your husband? Had he been speaking to anyone that was a stranger?"

"No, I answered that when the police called me earlier. He couldn't do something like this."

"Why was he visiting New York?"

Julia did not blink. Nor did she answer right away. The other agent leaned forward just a hair. She looked at him. He barely seemed to notice.

"Mrs. Swann, can you please answer my question?" Agent Bakhash said.

"No, I can't," Julia said, still staring at the other man.

The anger boiled up. Who the hell did this man think he was, coming into her house and threatening her? she thought. Julia fought the urge to get up from the table, to walk away. But she wouldn't do that. She was tired of all of this. And she was done being treated like a criminal, and letting people treat her husband like that, too. She . . .

"Do you know what your husband has done?" the other agent asked.

His voice was dry like a dead leaf. It burned in her ears. It cut through her, crashing up against her anger, fueling it while at the same time peeling away what felt like years of her life.

"How dare you—"

He cut her off. "He killed hundreds of innocent people."

Her voice rose. "You don't know that!"

His voice remained unchanged when he said, "We know he's involved, ma'am. We have zero doubt."

"Show me the proof," she demanded. "What? That video they're playing? So what? He was there. We all know that."

"We know that the bomb was in the case your husband was carrying."

"Show me, then. You can't, can you? Because you're lying!"

The agent shook his head, slowly. "No, I'm not."

Julia rose to her feet. "Show me then! Goddamn it! Show ME!"

The blood rose to Julia's head. Her cheeks felt ready to catch fire. She hated the tears that forced themselves from her eyes. Her teeth clicked together as she kept herself from saying more. Agent Bakhash's hand moved. It rested against the other agent's broad shoulder. His fingernails were perfectly, unnervingly manicured.

"Please, Mrs. Swann. Sit down. I know this has to be hard," he said, softly. "At this point, all we are trying to do is keep innocent Americans safe. We'd appreciate your help. But I understand. I have a wife. I have children. I can't imagine what you must be going through."

The look on his face carried more strength than his words. His dark eyes were soft and wide-open. The lines of his face, though not many, hinted at a life that was not always easy. The way his words left his lips changed the air in the room. The charge seemed to fade, and Julia just felt an overwhelming sense of fatigue. She fell back into the chair, like if she lowered her head to the tabletop it might never rise up again.

Over the agent's head, she saw her mother. She stood in the foyer, her back to the front door. They made eye contact and her mother gestured at something, like asking Julia a question that she didn't understand.

At that moment, the basement door opened. Evan, with Thomas close behind, stood on the top step. They looked frightened.

"Mom, is everything okay?" Thomas asked.

He sounded so young. Julia quickly wiped away the tears and stood.

"Sweetie, it's okay."

Julia's mother swept the kids up and moved them slowly back down the stairs.

"I'll be down in a second," Julia said.

Once the door closed, she turned to Agent Bakhash.

"I don't believe you. You don't know he did this!" she said, her back straight.

He shook his head, slowly. The look in his eyes seemed to share her pain.

"Yes, we do. We are sure of it. But there are holes, Mrs. Swann. And if we don't fill them soon, I'm afraid more people may be hurt. So, please, let me ask you just a couple more questions."

Julia stared at this stranger. She refused to look at the other one. But every instinct told her that this man, Agent Bakhash, lied. At the same time, she sensed something worse. Julia was sure that this man *knew* without a shade of doubt that her husband was involved in the bombing. Though her heart raged against what her eyes saw, her brain faltered. She sat back down.

"I can't believe it."

"I understand," the agent said, barely louder than a whisper. "Let me ask you, had your husband recently lost his job?"

Julia closed her eyes. But she nodded.

Agent Bakhash asked her details about Michael's job and his employer. He seemed to be searching for something. And Julia was not trying to be misleading by any means. Yet Bakhash eventually grew more serious. The look in his eyes changed into something different, something more intense.

"Now, please, really think before you answer. Did your husband have any ties with DuLac Chemicals?"

Julia's eyebrows lowered. "The company in Wilmington? No. I mean, my father worked for them. And a neighbor's husband. I mean, he might have been laid off."

Bakhash leaned forward, a hungry look in his eye. "Can I have his name?"

Julia told him and the agent jotted it on a small notepad.

"Your father's name, too?"

Julia froze. Bakhash acted like he didn't notice, like he never asked the question.

"Did your father and your husband ever talk about that? About the company?"

"No, not really. I mean, I don't think so."

Someone knocked. The other agent got up. Without a word, he walked to the front door. After a quiet exchange, he opened it. Two uniformed officers from the Pennsylvania State Police stood on the porch. The agent returned to the table, and Bakhash handed him the notepad. The other agent took it and returned to the front door. He and the uniformed officers continued to speak, softly. Then the agent closed the door and returned to the table again.

"Are you sure, Mrs. Swann? This is very important."

She shook her head. Suddenly, she felt overwhelmingly dizzy. Everything crashed down at once. She attempted to stand, but her hand slammed to the tabletop as she tried to keep her balance.

"Mrs. Swann, are you okay?" she heard someone say.

"I just need water . . . I think."

But the truth was, Julia needed far more than that.

10

The high beams spread out across the empty road. The light flashed against the straight tall trunks of oaks and pines that lined the way. I stared forward, in a daze really. My thoughts, more often than not, led to dead ends. So I acted instead. I moved forward, ever forward, with little premeditation.

I had no idea where I was going. Nothing looked even the slightest bit familiar. Oddly, I still had a sense of direction. I knew when I drove south or west or north. It just meant nothing at all in context.

It took me miles to realize that the radio was on. Although the station played pop music, every few minutes a news report broke in. I heard my name, *Michael Swann*, and it drew me in. As I listened to the woman talk about the bombing, however, I quickly turned it off. A part of me needed to know what happened. Even more, I should have wanted to know why they thought I was a suspect. At the same time, though, I physically could not force myself to listen, not even for a minute. Instead, I drove aimlessly through the night, oblivious to everything but my oblivion.

———

An hour or so later, I pulled into the parking lot of another gas station. What I was doing just would not work. I felt an overwhelming need to get home, back to the address on my driver's license that might as well have belonged to someone else. *I should know how to get home*, I thought. Yet I had no idea.

I needed help. Even if I walked in and purchased a map, which was what I was planning to do, I would have no idea where I currently was, let alone where I was going. I parked the car in the farthest space from the store and killed the engine. I sat there, with my hands on the wheel. I felt no emotion, really. Not even the panic someone might expect. To be honest, I just felt confused.

It was then that I remembered the phone. It would have a map app—all of them did. Somehow I knew it. I think. Or maybe . . . My thoughts were like water through spread fingers.

I moaned and pressed the knuckles of my hands into my eye sockets. The pain flared, but it focused me. I reached over to the passenger seat and pulled the case onto my lap. When I opened it, I found the phone right away. When I hit the home button, I saw all the texts for the first time. Or had they been there before? I couldn't remember.

Slowly, carefully, I read through them. They meant nothing at all. The words seemed to hold no weight, except for one. I stared at that name.

Julia, I thought.

That name became the beam of a lighthouse lantern cutting through the fog inside my brain. It was my beacon, and it called to me so loudly that I thought I could hear it out in the night.

So I turned to the only thing I had, the dream from the bus. Julia, just as she already was in my own head, became that woman in the shadows. She had the answers. I knew that. I also knew that she needed me. I could feel it in her words. Hear it in the way she called to me.

But why did I want the phone? Why did I look for it? I had no idea. I held it, staring at the texts, unable to unlock the phone and respond, and I knew nothing at all. Looking around the parking lot, I couldn't even remember how I got there, or whose car it was.

Map.

I needed a map. I needed to know where I was. That's why I stopped. That's why I grabbed the phone. But it would be no help. Bits and pieces cleared up. I was in trouble. I was being chased. If I went into the store and asked for help, surely someone would recognize me. At the same time, there was nothing else for me to do but drive without purpose until I ran out of gas somewhere on the side of the road. I looked at the display. The arrow was on *E*. I had no choice.

Hesitantly, I got out of the car and walked into the store. Looking up, I saw a surveillance camera pointed down at me. Quickly, I lowered my face and shuffled over to a rack of road maps by the window. I grabbed the one that had the most copies. It was a map of the Mid-Atlantic. Taking a deep breath, I took it to the counter.

"Can you help me?" I whispered, as if some microphone might hear my voice and bring the police swarming in on me.

"Sure," the young woman behind the counter said.

I pulled out the money clip and read the address on my license.

"Can you show me how to get to West Chester?"

"New York?" she asked.

I looked to the license again. Her eyes lowered and she saw it as well. A new expression came to her face. It was a mix of confusion and suspicion. She looked at the license and then back at my swollen face. And I knew she knew. But it was too late.

"Please, just help me," I said.

"Look, I can call—"

"No!" I snapped.

She took a step back. The frustration grew. And a tear came to my eye and rolled down a cheek. She saw it.

"Are you hurt?"

"I just need to get home," I whispered.

She moved closer. "West Chester, Pennsylvania?"

I nodded.

"You could get on 322. It's just down the road. That'll take you across the Commodore Barry Bridge. In fact, I think it goes right to West Chester."

"Down the road?"

"Yeah, go out and take a left. It's the next intersection. You can't miss the sign. Just go west."

"I think I came in that way," I said, scratching my arm. "Where am I?"

She laughed, but I just looked at her.

"Really?" she asked.

I didn't say anything.

"You're in New Jersey. Hamilton Township."

"Okay," I said.

I turned and walked toward the door. She called to me. "You forgot the map." But I never turned, I just kept walking. Outside, I almost drove off without getting gas. When I pulled up to the pump, I paid for that gas with my credit card. And then I drove back off into the night.

11

Agent Bakhash took a call. He listened, his face like it was cast in iron. When he hung up, he looked at Julia.

"He's coming here," the agent said.

Julia felt a rush. "What do you mean?"

Bakhash paused. When he spoke, he measured every word.

"Your husband's credit card was just used at a gas station in Hamilton Township, New Jersey. Police are at the scene. The woman working at the station claims that he asked for directions to West Chester."

"Directions? Why?"

Bakhash shook his head. "I don't know."

"I thought he was on a bus?"

"Our best guess is that he misdirected our efforts to locate him by boarding a different bus. We have been monitoring his credit card, and it hasn't been used again until now. But we do have blurry surveillance footage of him at the bus station in Atlantic City. Police stopped the bus he had allegedly boarded and were told by the driver that the suspect was in a physical altercation with another passenger and he fled on foot.

"An hour ago, we received a report of a stolen vehicle at a different gas station just off the Atlantic City Expressway. We believe he's driving that car somewhere on Route 322, heading in this direction."

"Michael stole a car?"

The agent blinked. "Yes."

Julia stood up. Her feet shuffled as she rounded the counter. She found her glass of wine by the refrigerator and finished it in one long drink. Grabbing the bottle, she refilled it and walked out of the kitchen toward the living room.

"Mrs. Swann," Agent Bakhash said.

"Please, I need a minute."

Julia moved to the window. With her free hand, she parted the curtain. Outside, flashing red and blue lights illuminated the street around her house. She could see four police cars outside, interspersed with the news vans and a few other cars and SUVs. In the surreal glow, she also saw people wandering among the chaos. One walked a dog on a leash, pulling the frightened animal closer and closer to the circus outside her house. She suddenly recognized the man as a neighbor. Some of the others, too. They haunted her yard, craning necks, trying to get a view of the freak show.

She tore the curtain closed and grabbed her phone. Bakhash moved as if he might try to stop her. Julia ignored him. She walked into the other room, redialing her credit card company. When she reached a live person, her heart beat so hard it almost hurt.

"What was the last transaction on the card?" she asked, her eyes closed.

"Looks like a gas station in New Jersey . . ."

That's all Julia heard.

THE NIGHT BEFORE

Everything boiled over the night before Michael left for his interview in New York. Julia had been out running through the neighborhood. Jogging in and out of every cul-de-sac and all the way out to the entrance, she could get just over three miles. This left the kids alone for about half an hour. Although she had been hesitant about it during the school year, once summer hit, leaving the boys alone for little bits of time had sounded like a better and better idea. She could use a breather away every once in a while, a chance to have adult thoughts without having to play Uno at the same time. She decided that they loved the slices of time she was away from them, too. They felt older, more responsible, and, more importantly, nagged less, especially her preteen, Evan.

She knew things were bad. Her first glimpse came that night on their back porch. Since then, her husband's disillusionment, his struggles, became more apparent the less he smiled.

He did not seem himself anymore. At first, she barely saw him. He was working all the time, away most weekends. Even when he was home, he wasn't *home*. He'd be on his computer most of the time. Every so often, she'd find him watching sports, particularly baseball, out in the family room. Julia missed him, so she thought she'd just snuggle up and watch with him. As soon as she walked in, though, he'd grab the laptop and start back up.

As time passed, a second suspicion battled the first. Julia started to take some of his standoffish behaviors personally. During one particularly bad span, she counted the days that he hadn't touched her, not even by accident, and that number reached fifteen. Though it angered her, she performed that test a half dozen more times over the months that followed. Each time, just as she reached her boiling point, something good would happen. They'd have a night out with friends and a glimpse of the old Michael might come out. Sure enough, though, after a few days, maybe a week, the ice would re-form.

As she rounded the last turn that day, having come from the back side of the neighborhood, Julia thought about all of this. *Twenty-four*, she repeated a few times in her head. It was the longest stretch yet. She vowed she'd talk to him about it that night. She couldn't keep going on like this.

That's when she saw his car in the driveway. The twist of her stomach was visceral. It could have been intuition or a product of her mind-set during the run. What popped into Julia's head in the moment, however, was that she hadn't told her husband that she was leaving the kids alone to run.

When she entered the house through the garage door, she found the boys sitting on the couch. The television was off and their heads turned in synchrony. With sheepish expressions, they watched her walk slowly into the house.

"Is Daddy home?" she asked.

They both nodded. She stopped a couple of paces in the house, looking from her kids to the hallway leading to the kitchen.

"Did something happen?"

Thomas lowered his head. Evan, on the other hand, looked a little angry.

"We got yelled at," he said.

"Why?"

"The TV."

Julia blinked. She had told them they could watch a show while she was out.

"Well, why don't you two go outside?"

"Mom," Evan moaned.

"Really? You haven't been out all day."

"There's nothing to do out there."

"Yeah," Thomas whispered without looking up.

Julia reached out an arm and pointed to the back door. They hesitated, but she didn't move. With an adolescent huff, Evan went first. He almost brushed against her arm as he stomped outside. Thomas got up, his head still lowered. As he passed, she grabbed him and brought him in for a hug.

"You okay?" she asked softly.

"I feel bad about Dad."

"It's okay, buddy. He probably had a bad day at work. No worries, okay?"

He nodded and she hugged him again, smiling.

She heard the crash as she reached the top step. It came from inside their bedroom. Through the closed door, her husband's voice rose.

"Fuck him," she heard, the words muffled but distinct.

Julia paused there. His footsteps were heavy. His mood, unquestionable. For a moment, she thought about slipping back down the stairs. She could grab the boys and take them to the old-fashioned hamburger place. She didn't like the food all that much, as she'd given up red meat almost seven years prior, but it would make them happy. And they wouldn't be gone too long. She could say she didn't even know he was home.

As nice as it sounded, that option, the ability to bury her head in the sand, had slipped away months ago. When she closed her eyes, she saw Thomas's soft brown eyes. She had to face this, and she had to do it that night. Her gut told her there was no other decision to be made. So she took the last few steps and knocked lightly on their door. The house went silent for a moment; then he said, "Come in."

When Julia opened the door, she found him sitting on the edge of the bed. His eyes were red-rimmed and cheeks red. He wore dark socks, boxer shorts, and a white undershirt. His elbows rested on his knees, supporting the weight that suddenly looked to be too heavy for either of them to bear any longer.

"Don't start," he said, the words like a terse hiss.

Julia stood in the doorway. She didn't move. She didn't back down. Nor did she speak. He finally turned and looked at her.

"It's official. Bastard probably knew I had an interview tomorrow. Probably just fucking with me."

Julia remained still. He didn't use words like that, not anymore. He rarely ever did even before the kids. They sounded raw and wrong coming from him that night.

"Goddamn it." He rolled a sock off his foot and threw it as hard as he could against the wall. It bounced off, harmless and without even the satisfaction of making a sound. "They just do whatever the hell they want. Think about it. We pay for everything. The poor get it free. The rich get it free. And the middle class just puts them all up on our backs. We're so fucking stupid. It's like we smile while they just screw us over and over again."

When he pulled off the second sock, his arm cocked back. It paused. As if remembering the futility of his first attempt, he simply let it fall to the carpeted floor. For some reason, that was worse, more frightening than his anger.

"What are you talking about, Michael?"

"Everything," he said, rubbing at his eyes. "Corporate America. These assholes in management, the ones that get the big bonuses in stock and then can't make their numbers. So what else do you expect them to do? They can't just admit they suck. They can't let the price fall. So they just start laying people off.

"And the politicians. They all say it'll change. That they're on our side. One of the *people*. How can we be so fucking dumb?"

"They did it?" she asked, whispering.

His voice rose. "Of course they did. I told you they would. None of this shit mattered. All the work I did since he talked to me. My numbers doubled. But it was all a fucking lie. He knew. They all knew. They just do whatever the hell they want to make a fucking dollar. No consequences. None at all. And if we say anything, well, that's just un-American, right? That's just liberal horseshit. That's *not* capitalism."

He barked out a laugh. It dripped with open hatred. In a way, though, Julia felt better. Maybe he didn't hate her. Maybe he hated everyone else. As sad as that sounded, maybe that was better.

"It's okay. You have your interview tomorrow." She took a step into the room. "I think it's for the best. You've been so stressed. I think you need a new start."

"I'll make half as much," he snapped.

"So what," she said, firmly. "I'll get a job. I want to. I need to. Staying home is making me crazy, if you want to know the truth. The boys will be fine. It's time."

He shook his head. Julia had thought what she said would help, that it would make him feel better, but it didn't. His cheeks grew a deeper shade of red.

"So, you'll just swoop in and save me, huh?" he asked.

Slowly, he turned back and looked at her again. The hatred was still there. Julia took a step back. His rage burned. It boiled up. It oozed out of him, filling the room with an unbearable tension. She actually felt afraid, like he might lunge at her, strike her. Or maybe he'd just leave them all. Run away, flee from the weight of adulthood in a world full of stunted, selfish children. Not Thomas and Evan, or any other true child. They were pure still. They were not yet fully lost. What she meant was the rest of the world. Everyone else. All the supposed adults who thought their desires were needs. That their wants were inalienable rights.

In a way, Julia understood. She saw it, too, in the parents who ignored the rules of the drop-off lane because they were running late. Or the coach who acted like he volunteered his time for altruistic reasons, but truly only wanted to prop up his own son or daughter in a vain attempt to repair some insecurity he had carried since childhood. Or in the person who walked through the door that her boys held open without even a nod or a thank-you.

These thoughts seemed small. They seemed petty. She dared not tell him what she thought. She could feel his anger. His fury.

"It'll be okay," she whispered.

He just looked at her and shook his head. He laughed again. And the sound might as well have poisoned her ears forever.

12

Julia was straining her ears, listening for sounds coming from the basement, where her mother sat watching television with the boys, so the knock on the front door startled her. As the other agent rose to answer it, Bakhash looked at her, openly assessing her state.

"I hope you understand what I'm trying to tell you," he said for the third time.

Julia rubbed at her face and turned to look as the door opened. Two uniformed police officers stood on the front porch again. The other agent motioned for Bakhash, who stood and joined them. Though they spoke softly, Julia could hear every word.

"Set the perimeter outside the neighborhood."

"They've already called in to the chief."

"This is a matter of national security. Push them back. I want every one of them out of this neighborhood within the hour. And I want soft blockades at the two access points. Sweep these streets and report back. Understood?"

More so than at any moment during the ordeal, Julia felt detached. Things were happening around her at breakneck speed. It was clear that events were moving as she remained locked away in her house. It was also clear that these events would shape, or misshape, her life from that day on. Yet she sat frozen in her chair.

It would be easy to judge her inactivity. As is always the case, people will look at others' misfortune and know that they would handle it better. They would take control. They would act with decisive vigor.

In truth, the human mind is a fragile thing. It can only allow in so many stimuli before the machine shuts down. At the same time, it is a resilient thing. Even in that moment, new pathways eased to life within her mind. New possibilities emerged, peeking out from the tidal wave of pain and fear she felt. Though Julia could not yet grasp them, not firmly, they were there, and they grew from a very simple seed. Her husband, the father of her children, the man she loved, was in danger.

Agent Bakhash rejoined her at the table. The other agent did not. He stepped out of the house, into the darkness. The door shut behind him and they were alone.

"It's for Michael's own good," the agent said. "It's the only way I can keep him safe."

She said nothing. Julia felt badgered, and the familiar use of her husband's name set off a vague alarm in her mind.

"We believe he has his phone. Text him. Tell him to come here. To come home."

He'd asked her to do that for the last half hour. Julia never said yes. The strangest thing, though, was she didn't quite know why. Something itched at her thoughts. Something sat in her gut, telling her to be careful. That everything wasn't as it seemed.

"Text him?" she asked, her eyebrows lowering. "Not *call*?"

Bakhash watched her. He assessed her. She could not know why or for what, but she saw the intensity masked behind his soft brown eyes.

"Mrs. Swann, this isn't a game anymore. He needs to come in. He needs *my* help. He's not well. He's not himself. As far as we can tell, he's injured, badly. We're worried that if he spoke to you, he may do something drastic . . . more drastic than he already has. We can't have him hurting anyone else." He touched her forearm. His eyes fairly dripped with earnestness. "But I won't let him hurt himself, either. He needs direction, not discussion. We need to make it simple and clear . . . no question. It's his only chance. I'm sorry, but it is."

Julia looked away, and he saw her waver. So Bakhash took a breath and spoke softly again.

"I need you to understand. The CEO of the DuLac Chemical Company was killed in the attack. At this time, we have reason to believe that she was the primary target of the attack. Three months ago, the company announced a merger with one of its largest competitors. Over two thousand jobs would be downsized. DuLac had moved their annual meeting to New York to avoid local backlash in Wilmington."

Julia looked at him. He paused, watching her. Her thoughts betrayed her. All she could think about was the night before all this happened. She could still picture the anger that had painted Michael's face in shades of red. And somehow Bakhash could see it, too, through her eyes. It was as if this man could read her mind.

"We know about what happened," he said. "We know that your husband lost his job. I understand what you're feeling. I really do. That must have hit close to home." He paused. "And when you saw everything that was happening at DuLac, it must have been difficult. You must have thought about your father, what happened to him."

Without a word, Julia stood. Bakhash reached out, his fingers gently wrapped around her forearm. They felt like iron.

"Mrs. Swann," he said.

Her face blank, she looked down at this stranger and thought about everything that had happened. They drove her into the city, past the blockade. All the calls to Marci Simmons, how she helped her. That gut feeling she had had all along. For the first time, a new pattern emerged. The game, as it was, had just changed.

Without a word, Julia brushed off his hand and walked away.

THERE IS A PRICE

Julia thought about that day, years before, when all she wished for was her father to come back to them. It was a year after he had been laid off from DuLac Chemicals. Twelve months since he had seemed himself. As she looked down, she had wanted to take his hand, but she couldn't, not right away. She had a lifetime of memories of him standing tall and straight, his broad shoulders seeming to hold up her world. On that day, he had rested in a hospital bed in her mother's living room.

"Dad," she whispered.

One eye fluttered open. It rolled, unfocused, and shut again. He muttered something about a seed and then slipped into a fitful silence.

"I love you, Dad," she said.

His hand slipped out from under the sheet. Next to the white fabric, the thin skin glowed a sickly orange and his long fingers curled into jagged hooks. He clawed at the air.

"Move it," he muttered, his voice a dry rasp.

"It's okay."

She reached out to touch his hand but stopped short. *It's not him.* The thought invaded her head. It made no sense. Looking down at him, this man who had been so strong for so long, she saw only a shrunken body and sunken cheeks. The alien coloring of his skin. Maybe this wasn't her father. Maybe it hadn't been since he lost his job.

Pushing through it, refusing to surrender to her fears, Julia's hand lowered. Her fingers touched the top of his hand. It felt like a fragile plastic bag filled with sticks. At the same time, he felt surprisingly warm to the touch, like his life was radiating out, reaching for some last chance at survival. It reminded her that he was alive. That he hadn't been taken from her yet.

Julia rose to her feet. Bending at the waist, she leaned forward. Her lips touched his forehead. It tasted bitter and wrong.

"I love you, Daddy," she whispered. "I'm so sorry."

————————

She met her mother in the kitchen. The year had aged her. Whereas before Julia had thought she looked young for her age, now life had caught up. Dark rings hung under her eyes, accentuated by an exhausted pallor.

"Was he awake?" she asked, flatly.

"For a second, I think," Julia said. "Are you okay?"

She nodded. "I am." Her mother paused before something changed. Her expression sharpened. The air in the room seemed charged. She looked into Julia's eyes. "It's almost over."

"Mom?" she said.

"No," her mom snapped. "It is. And it's okay. It's over. It's done."

Julia watched her mother, suddenly understanding. She reached out and touched the top of her mother's hand. It felt so different from her dad's.

"I watched him do it," her mother said.

"There was nothing you could do."

Her mother scoffed. "Maybe not." She shook her head. When she continued to speak, her words were raw. "The thing is, I was so mad at him. I still am. So what, he lost his job. We would have been fine. I thought we could travel. Take care of the kids."

Her mother began to shake. Julia got up and moved around the table, taking the older woman into her arms.

"It's okay, Mom."

"No, it's not. *He* did this. Why wasn't it enough? Why wasn't our life enough?"

"He was sick. Probably for a long time. He loved you. He loved all of us."

She barked out a cold laugh. "He loved his job."

Surprisingly, Julia laughed with her. "He did."

Her mother nodded. Their eyes met. Maybe tears should have flowed. Maybe they should have torn at their clothes or their hair. Someone watching might have expected some melodramatic moment of loss. But alcoholism isn't like that. It didn't shock or surprise. Instead, it sanded away at their love, rubbing it raw and bloody over a year that felt longer than a lifetime.

So, in the end, there was surprisingly little sadness. Instead, both her mother and Julia felt one thing. A deep and unforgettable anger.

Her mother was the first to look away. As she did, she whispered, "And his job killed him."

13

Julia stood at the window of her living room. The pain nearly buckled her knees. Her thoughts came in jagged shards, cutting at her until she bled from the inside out.

Outside, the crush of media had disappeared, leaving behind only the police. One by one, their spinning red and blue lights cut off, returning the night to stark normalcy. No neighbors could be seen any longer, and she wondered if the police had sent them home. A chill ran up her back.

In the glow from their headlights, she could see police officers moving around, returning to their cars. Engines started. Red brake lights flashed. The cars rolled slowly up and down her street. As they moved out of sight, she noticed one kill its lamps. The darkness returned, and with it came a horrible sense of dread.

They were planning something, like a hunter using a snare. As this dawned on her, a hand touched her shoulder.

"Send the text," Agent Bakhash whispered.

His voice sounded like the hiss of a snake. She cringed, her body tensing.

"Tell him to come home. It's the only way I can guarantee his safety."

That's when she was sure. It was a trap. And she was the bait.

"No!"

Julia wrenched away from him and ran up the stairs, slamming the bedroom door behind her.

14

Julia sat alone in the master bath. Once the door closed behind her, she slid down it, sitting on the cold tile. Her body racked with sobs as she let it out. She couldn't breathe. She couldn't think. All she could do was cry.

Her phone rang. Julia pulled it from her back pocket quickly, still feeling a particle of hope that it might be her husband calling. It was Evelyn instead. She almost didn't answer. She had nothing to say. And nothing that she wanted to hear.

"Jules, are you there?" Evelyn asked after Julia connected the call but said nothing.

"Yeah."

"Are you okay?"

She barked out a laugh. "No."

"Sorry. I know. I—"

"Homeland Security is here. They think . . ."

Julia stopped, suddenly. *Could they be listening in on my cell phone?* The thought tasted sour in the back of her throat.

"Julia?" Evelyn said. "I don't want to tell you this, but . . ."

Julia felt so tired. "What?"

"The press is everywhere out there. Knocking on everyone's door. But I . . . I heard that Tara talked to them. That she told them about that night on your porch, when your husband and mine were joking about the election. She made it sound serious. I can't believe she did that."

Julia could barely breathe. "Tara?"

"Yeah. I'm so sorry. Look, anything you need, I'm here. I'd take the kids . . ." Evelyn paused. "But maybe we should wait until all these people are gone. I mean, then . . ."

Julia said nothing. She let the quiet grow between them. Her friend would help, Julia thought, once no one could see her do it.

"I have to go. I'll call you, okay. It'll be all right. I'm sure."

Julia still said nothing.

"Jules, are you . . . ?"

She heard none of the rest, for Julia simply put her phone facedown on the tile floor. Her body shook but no tears came. Instead, it was a different pain. One that made her question if there was a path forward. Was there any way that tomorrow could dawn? Was there a point?

Her throat tightened. Suddenly, she had trouble pulling in a breath. Her chest heaved as she panted out of control. The very walls of the bathroom pressed in on her. Julia covered her mouth with her hands.

Impossible.

It was the one thought she couldn't have. And it simply repeated itself over and over in her head. Her fingers pried at the skin of her face. She pulled her hair. Her body rattled and she threw her head back into the door. She hit it hard enough that a bright white light flashed and then she lost focus.

———————

"Mom?"

The voice was soft, careful. It seemed to slip under the bathroom door and just barely touch her ears. Julia's eyes opened and she wondered if she had even heard anything at all.

"Mom?"

A light tap followed. It was one of the boys. She was suddenly sure of that. Her head hurt, but she could not let him see her like that. So she stood. With her hand on her chest, Julia composed herself. When she opened the door, though, and saw Evan, his big brown eyes glistening with unshed tears, Julia broke.

In that torturous minute, Julia forgot the past, forgot her mistake, and saw the future. She saw her family left raw and alone. She saw everyone slipping away. She saw the way people would look at them, at her kids. This would follow them. It would devour them, leaving them empty shells cast into the dark corner of society. It was already happening. Tara had already talked to the press. Evelyn was already pulling away. She would be the last. But the scourge that swallowed her family would be too much. And in a way, Julia wasn't sure she could blame Evelyn. If the roles were reversed, would it be any different?

Evan's sharply lined face, so much like Michael's, brought her back. Over the years his face had changed and matured. He tiptoed toward manhood with each passing day. But in that moment, she didn't see twelve-year-old Evan; she saw Evan's face when he was a baby. That face had not seen pain. It had not seen betrayal, or been lied to. Nor had it seen loss. Instead, with glowing bright eyes, it had taken in the world as it could be, not as it was. Those eyes had looked at them, at Julia and Michael, and had seen perfection. They saw goodness and strength and loyalty. They trusted without question, loved without condition, and needed them without guilt. She saw those eyes looking back at her and nothing more.

The tears came. She had thought to hide them. To protect him. But that was no more possible than wishing everything away. She cried, sweeping him into a hug, pulling him to her and pressing him into her, like she might become the shield he would need every day going forward.

For a second, he resisted. Then Evan gave himself over to her. He forgave her without uttering a word, the way only a child can. A slight weight lifted off of both of them in that moment, yet it couldn't be enough. Evan broke down, becoming a twelve-year-old once again.

"Baby, it's okay. It's okay."

He wouldn't look up at her. He just cried.

"Where's Grandma?" she said through her tears.

He still would not talk. But the crying suddenly stopped. So did the shakes. In her arms, his body, feeling bigger than it had any right to, stiffened.

"Dad didn't do what they said."

She'd never heard defiance like that from her boy. She'd never heard that grit. It shocked her. Julia pushed him away, gently, holding him at arm's length. Evan still wouldn't look at his mother. She let go with one hand and lovingly lifted his chin. His eyes shot closed.

"Evan?"

"No," he shouted.

His bright, young lips thinned. He grabbed his mother's arm with unexpected strength.

"He didn't!" Evan said. "Daddy's a good person!"

His words cut through her like a sharpened blade. They pierced the noise, the heartbreak, and they touched something inside her that had been pushed so far down just a moment before. Her son's words rekindled the very core of her, that part of Julia that burned white-hot, the part that had carried her through life, skyrocketed her through college and her career. Being home with the kids blanketed that part of her, but could never extinguish it. This part of her was action, strength, grit. It was Julia.

What was it about Evan's words that changed everything? Was it his claim? No. Julia still saw the eyes of the agents downstairs. They carried with them truth, as painful as it might be. It was not Evan's words at all, in fact. Instead, it was the way he said them, the stiffness with which he stood. In that, Julia saw herself. She remembered who she was.

That's when she let the clues break through as well. She thought about what the agents had said. She thought about how they'd cleared the streets and moved their cars out of sight. She thought about the text they wanted her to send, pleading with Michael to come home. They were luring him to her. To a trap.

She thought about their questions. About her father and about DuLac. About Michael losing his job. She realized that Michael was not the only suspect, just the only one that they didn't have in their hands already.

"I'm going to find him," she said.

Evan opened his eyes. She saw a prayer. She felt it. She needed to say something to him, to assure him but not give him the kind of false hope that would crush them all in the end.

Everything will be okay.

Daddy didn't do it.

He'll be home soon.

All the things that a mother would want to say, she couldn't. But Julia knew not to fall into that trap again. Evan watched her, waiting. Julia put her hands on his cheeks. One thumb gently brushing away a tear.

"Daddy is a good person," she told Evan.

And he nodded back at her.

"And I'm going to find him."

———

"Mom?"

Julia stood at the top of the stairs. Evan held her hand. She waited, but her mother didn't answer.

"I'll get them," Evan said.

She wanted to say no. She didn't want him near those agents. But he looked up at her with those eyes. Not the baby ones, but the ones that he'd own for the rest of his life, cool and blue. So she nodded and he ran down the stairs, returning a minute later with Thomas in tow. Julia's mother was not far behind. Julia nodded toward her bedroom. The three of them followed her in and she closed the door.

"I need you to take them to your house," Julia said to her mother.

"No, we want to stay," Thomas said.

It was Evan who quieted his little brother. Watching him, Julia smiled, a thin thing filled with pride and hopeless resolve.

"I'm going after him," she said.

And Evan nodded in agreement.

NOT AS IT APPEARS

Poison? Julia thought.

Memory is a funny thing. So often, the present alters the past, fits it onto a more comfortable shelf. Not necessarily good, not necessarily bad. Just in a place with less uncertainty, fewer questions, and more dust. It nestles reality between books that have already been read, ones with no mystery left to them. Yet like those books, memories are often fiction.

Everything that had happened, everything that Agent Bakhash had said, burrowed into her mind. She picked her life apart like she might try to dig a worm out of an apple. She had left the good on the counter, battered and forgotten.

Evan's words lifted the veil. She remembered the night before Michael traveled to New York in a new light. It was not pleasant, not at first. He did rage. Worse, Julia had seen the defeat in her husband's eyes.

"I tried," Michael had whispered.

"What do you mean?" she asked.

"To support us. I did." He ran his hands through his hair. His voice trailed even lower when he said, "Maybe you should have . . ."

"I can," she said, moving to her husband. "I'll call Susan tomorrow. It's okay. Everything's going to be okay."

His shoulders slumped by the time Julia reached him. Her hand touched him, lightly. But he didn't look up.

"I feel it, too, you know," she said.

The muscles of his back tensed. His head slowly turned.

"I remember how happy you were," she said. "And I know how it's been since. The worst part is that I knew it then. I knew you wouldn't like being a salesman. Not like this. And I knew how much you loved working for the team, how much you love baseball. And I . . . I took that from you."

Julia teared up. Her husband stood and took her into his arms. They wrapped around her, pressing her close, fending off everything outside their space. The sound of the boys downstairs faded. The light from the lamp by the door dimmed. The air went still. It was just Julia and Michael then. Nothing else.

"You didn't," he said.

"I did," she said.

In a relationship, moments of potential honesty flash by. They are fleetingly brief and hidden under the weight of life's challenges. But they come and go, and so often they are missed. Yet that night, both Julia and Michael seized that moment. They pulled back the layers and exposed the raw truths that are usually weighed down by fear.

"We did it together," he said. "Not just you. And I thought I could do it. Better than I did, at least. But . . . every day, I do something that feels . . . wrong. I do something that has no other meaning than . . . money."

"We don't need all this," she said. "This house, the cars, all this stuff. It's suffocating us, Michael. I've been feeling it for so long, but I didn't know how to say it. I didn't know how to put it into words."

"What about the kids?" he asked.

She paused. "They love it here."

"I know. We can't move them."

"We could."

He pulled back, looked into his wife's eyes. Their entire relationship seemed open to them in that moment. Every up and every down. And in every one of those moments, he remembered the love he felt for her. And she for him.

"No matter what," she said, "it'll work. We don't have to move. Not right now. But maybe what we need to do is think about what will make us happy. I want . . ."

"What?" he asked.

"I want to go back to work," she said.

And the air thinned. The light returned, as did the sound of the boys. With it said, with it out there, everything might change. But at least that truth could no longer haunt her. With those words, the water flowed.

"I need to," she said. "I don't even know who I am anymore. I love the kids so much. And I love spending time with them. But . . . being home, it . . . I don't even know." She laughed. "I mean, the other day, I was reading and out of the corner of my eye, someone walked by outside. I actually jumped off the couch to see who it was.

"At the end of the school year, I spent hours . . . literally hours writing and rewriting an email asking all the moms if they wanted to contribute to an end-of-the-year gift for the boys' bus driver." She shook her head. "I've already planned out how I'm going to try to get Thomas in Dr. Swisher's class next year. And it's *July*!"

Michael laughed with her. They looked into each other's eyes.

"And you know what," she continued, "I am freaking sick of going to the gym . . . and walk-jogging. And wearing these freaking yoga pants!"

"Whoa," he said. "Isn't that going a little far?"

She smacked him on the arm. "But seriously. What kind of mother am I? I mean, I can't believe I said that. I can't believe I feel it."

"But you do," he said. "And that's okay. I feel like at some point, we took a turn and jumped into someone else's life."

"Me, too." She paused. "But we can fix it. We can!"

"We can . . ." He smiled. "I think we can."

"I love you, Michael Swann."

"I love you, Julia Swann."

Laughing, they kissed. Their bodies moved like years shed away with every passing second. They felt young and alive as his hands moved along the slick fabric of her athletic wear. Julia still giggled as she pulled off Michael's T-shirt. He kicked the bedroom door closed. And just as husband and wife were about to make love on the bedroom floor, footsteps pounded up the stairs.

"Mom?" Thomas called out. "Dad?"

Red-faced and wide-eyed, they struggled back into their clothes as their son knocked on the door. With a final kiss and the widest smile she'd had in quite some time, Julia opened the door.

"Were you exercising?" Thomas asked.

And they couldn't help but burst into laughter again.

15

Bakhash called up from the foyer. "Mrs. Swann?"

With a quick look to Evan as he led Thomas toward their bedrooms, Julia grabbed her mother by the forearm. She pulled her into the bathroom, flicking on the ceiling fan.

"What are you . . . ?"

Julia cut her mother off, speaking softly but quickly. "They're trying to lure him here. It's a trap."

"What?"

Julia blinked. "You think he did it, don't you?"

Her mother didn't respond.

"They asked me about Dad."

Her mother's eyes widened in shock. "What?"

"They're not on our side, Mom. And they're calling all the shots. I need to change that."

"Julia," she said. "You—"

"I have to, Mom."

They stared at each other for a moment. Then her mother nodded.

"They won't let you leave," her mother said.

At the same moment, she heard footsteps coming up the stairs.

Julia shook her head. "No, they won't. But I have a plan."

———————

Julia met Bakhash at the top of the stairs and whisked past him. He spun, following her back toward the kitchen. As she passed the living room, she paused at the window again. When she pulled back the curtain, all she saw was darkness. She stood, staring. On any other night, it would have been expected, the normal tranquility of a suburban evening. That night, however, the stillness carried with it a foreboding that only Julia could understand. A pressure built behind her breastbone, and she had to touch the wall before her legs gave way beneath her. The trap was set. And her body tingled with the danger.

"Mrs. Swann?"

She turned and found Bakhash beside her. His eyes met hers and took Julia's measure. For an instant, she thought to hide her true thoughts from him. But something told her that such a decision would be futile. He would see right through her. So, instead, she let her emotions out, let them show, and just hoped he wouldn't see the reality behind it all.

"He's closer?" she asked, her voice crackling with emotion.

"We hope so," he said. "It's the only way. If they find him out there, something awful might happen. You need to understand that."

"I do," she whispered.

"Will you text him?"

She nodded. "Can I have my mother take the kids to her house first? I don't want them here for this. I can't."

He nodded, slowly. "I understand."

"Thank you," she whispered.

Julia walked her mother and the boys out to the garage. She hugged them. Thomas cried, but Evan was there for his brother. Julia hugged them both and then turned to find Bakhash watching her. As she closed the door, tears came, more from nerves than anything else. But she let him think otherwise.

"I need a second," she said, her voice breaking.

Julia hurried through the kitchen and up to her bedroom. Once again, she shut the door to the master bath but this time she didn't crumble to the floor. Instead, she acted with purpose. Slipping on her shoes, she moved to the toilet and flushed it. As the water ran, she opened the window between the two sinks and pulled the screen into the house. A stubby roof sat just below, a cutout for the breakfast nook in the kitchen. She swung one leg out, then the other. Holding on to the sill, she lowered herself onto the shingles.

She moved as quietly but as quickly as she could. Agent Bakhash could be directly below her. He could hear her at any second. So she slipped through the night like a cat, reaching the edge of the roofline and lowering herself to the railing of their back deck.

In her mind, when she planned her escape, she moved like some mystical ninja. In reality, lowering herself from a roof was not so easy. As she dangled, her foot swinging as she reached for the ground, the gutter tore away from the fascia. She dropped, hitting the wood hard. At the same time, the gutter swung inward, grazing the window before clattering off the side of the deck.

Pain shot down her shin and around her ankle. As she tried to push herself off the deck, the slider from the family room opened. She froze, and then heard footsteps coming out onto the far side of the porch.

Julia only had time to scurry along the damp boards toward one of the large planters by the stairs to the yard. Ignoring the splinters that cut into her hands, she balled up in the shadow of the large stone pot, holding her breath.

The footsteps approached, slowly. As her entire body shook, Julia opened one eye. She saw Bakhash's silhouette darker across the deep blue of the night sky. He stood no more than ten feet away. Although she could not see him clearly, his head seemed to turn, slowly. He paused when he faced the torn edge of the gutter. And Julia knew she had failed.

Oddly, in that moment when she knew her escape would not succeed, the shaking stopped. She let out a breath and, in a strange way, felt ready to face Bakhash again. She would stand up to him, tell him that she knew his game. She would never cooperate, not now. And she would find a way to help Michael.

Julia shifted her weight to her hands, ready to push herself up. Just as she made to rise up, Bakhash turned. Quickly, he walked across the deck and back into the house, leaving Julia squatting in the darkness. A soft, nervous laugh escaped her as she rose up and slipped off the deck into the backyard.

Adrenaline from the close call pumped through her body, giving her strength and speed. She moved more quickly, ducking behind a shrub and rushing in a crouch to the side door of the garage. It was open already and her mother stood in the shadows.

Breathing heavily, Julia brushed past her and slid into the backseat beside Thomas. He looked at her, his eyes wide, and she put a finger to her lips. Her mother got into the driver's seat. Taking a deep breath, she opened the garage door and started the engine.

The tension crackled through the car as they backed down the driveway. Julia could feel the fear surrounding her boys. She reached out and touched Evan's and Thomas's arms. They each flinched but otherwise remained still.

The car rolled down their street toward the front of the neighborhood. Her mother's hands tightened on the wheel.

"I can see the police cars," she said.

Julia realized that without Bakhash's plan, him clearing out the police, hers would never have worked. That irony tasted beguilingly sweet.

"Just keep moving."

Everyone held their breath. Julia, ducked down in the backseat, couldn't see out the windows, but she could feel her mother taking the turn onto Route 52. The engine struggled as her foot pressed the pedal to the floor. With a jerk, her mother's car accelerated. Unable to take it any longer, Julia popped up and turned her body, looking out the rear window. The entrance to her neighborhood grew smaller and smaller as her mother sped away. And no one followed them. Not at first.

16

At her mother's house, they all got out of the car. Julia dropped to a knee and hugged the boys.

"I love you both," she whispered.

She knelt before them, one soft face on each side of hers. Tears were shared between them and Thomas shook slightly.

"Will Dad be okay?" Evan asked.

Julia didn't answer right away. She wanted to say, *Of course!* But she didn't. For she knew that wasn't true. Although that might make it easier to drive away and leave her sons behind, she knew better now. So she closed her eyes and spoke from the heart.

"I don't know." She felt them tense and it broke her heart. "I don't know."

Her mother laid a hand on Evan's shoulder. The older boy let go, standing straight, his hands in his pockets. He tried to be strong, to be the man of the family. But he was twelve, and scared out of his mind. Thomas, on the other hand, clung to his mother.

"Let me come with you," he cried.

"I can't, sweetie. I need to do this. Grandma will take care of you. You can watch all the television you want. And sleep in the family room." His head shook. She could barely get the words out as she continued. "I'll be back soon. Okay? Sweetie. Okay."

In the end, she had to pry herself away. Thomas sobbed. Worse,

Evan turned his back and walked to his grandmother's front door. Julia moved toward her mom's car. She backed into it and put a hand up.

"Take care of them," she said, through tears.

"Be careful," her mom whispered, and Thomas's cries grew louder.

Julia had to force herself to get in the car. Once behind the wheel, she looked away. She had to. So she left without looking back. At the first light, she stopped. Her hands shaking, Julia pulled out her phone. She thought about trying to call Michael, but Bakhash's words returned. He'd stolen a car. And more. Though she trusted little that the agent had said, Julia knew something was wrong with Michael. And she also knew she could not make any mistakes. They would figure out she had left soon enough. She had to act quickly, and clearly. So, fighting back more tears, she texted her husband instead.

DON'T COME HOME. POLICE. IM COMING
FOR YOU

Staring at it, Julia had no idea if he would ever see her words or not. Maybe, she thought with a frightening numbness, it was already too late. But she had to try. So Julia put Hamilton Township, New Jersey, into her GPS app and drove like their lives depended on it.

PART

—

THREE

1

I stared at the name. *Julia.* My eyes pressed together, tightly enough for a tear to squeeze out and run down my cheek. I tried, as hard as I could, to picture a face, to paint it on the blank canvas of my memories. A splash of color appeared, maybe a strong jawline or wide, beautiful eyes. Just as quickly, the image faded like some distant mirage. *Julia,* I thought over and over again. The tires of the car ran across a rumble strip, and my eyes shot open. Swerving, I moved back onto the road.

Do I love this woman?

The thought came out of nowhere. I didn't ask for it. But once it came, it wouldn't leave. I pulled the car off the road and into a neighborhood. Driving slowly, I passed among the homes, small ranches, some dark, others with warm light glowing through bay windows. I saw the blue flashes of televisions playing in darkened bedrooms. I imagined families sleeping soundly, together, safe from the night. Finally, I had to pull over, the tires running up onto the rounded curb. I didn't move, but I gripped the wheel as tightly as I could, like if I let go I might simply float away.

I had lost my anchor. I had lost myself. But as I stared at the name again, maybe I found it. She knew who I was. She knew me. She knew how I was supposed to feel, how I was supposed to act, what I was supposed to care about. She sat in a home, somewhere, maybe like the ones around me, waiting, looking. Suddenly, it all came easily. I knew who I was. Not through my memories, but through hers.

Out of the blue, a five-digit number appeared in my head. It was like a neon billboard sprang out of nowhere. But when I saw it, I knew what it was immediately. The passcode to my phone. I could text back if I unlocked the phone. I could call! My heart thumped against my chest as I quickly entered it. I hovered over the last digit, all my hopes resting on its accuracy. Closing my eyes, I hit it.

Did the phone vibrate? I thought it had. It must have worked, I thought. But when I opened my eyes, it remained locked. Frantic, I decided that I'd entered the last number incorrectly when I closed my eyes. I tried again. It didn't work. My fingers just kept pressing the numbers as they appeared in my head. Locked, locked, locked. I growled, my teeth clicking together. I needed it to work.

iPhone is disabled

The message appeared in red on the screen. It stopped me. My fingers froze over the screen. I stared at it, realizing I could no longer see the texts.

"No . . . no, no, no."

Then I saw the second part of the message: *Try again in 1 minute.* I held my breath, letting that sink in, letting it calm me down. I had to calm down.

As I sat there, that number wouldn't leave my head: *91101.* I just kept seeing it in my head. It screamed out to me, no matter how much I tried to clear it away. I glanced at the case sitting on the passenger seat. *That's it!* The thought was so clear. The number was a combination for the case. But when I looked closer, I realized it didn't even have a lock.

I put the phone on my lap and rubbed at my eyes. Obviously, it was not the passcode or a combination. My head was swimming. I felt dizzy as hell. So I opened the door and got out. The humid air hit me like a mugging, but I stepped away from the car and looked up at the stars.

What's happening to me?

My hand went to my temple again. I could feel the clump of hair and dried blood. I had a head injury. Suddenly, as the number had done a moment before, an understanding of that fact just seemed to bloom within my skull. I had a head injury. That's what happened.

I stood in the night and smiled. It made sense. Everything made sense. But the longer I tried to convince myself of that, the further it slipped away. Nothing made sense. I couldn't remember anything. And what I could remember—the apartment building, the buses— felt like they had happened to someone else. Maybe they never happened at all. Maybe none of this did. Maybe I was in a car accident and I was just waking up.

My head lifted and I screamed up at the sky. It came out a horrible sound, feral and ragged at the same time. A light went on in a house at the corner. I froze, staring at it, feeling the need to run. Slowly, I backed toward the car. That's when I heard the phone vibrate.

Spinning, I dove into the front seat. The phone sat on the floor. I scooped it up. The warning was gone and in its place a new text appeared.

DON'T COME HOME. POLICE. IM COMING
FOR YOU

It was her. It was from her. I stared at it. In my mind, those letters spread out into the night like a towline. I started the engine and a dog barked. Then I drove away, following that imaginary line. And where it led, I had no idea. But I knew, somehow, that I would follow it to the end of the earth.

2

In the last hour, authorities in New York City seized a truck parked two blocks from the Lincoln Tunnel entrance. According to sources, it is the same vehicle seen in footage from a traffic camera on the New Jersey Turnpike in the area where the brush fire was started. This same source told us that, considering how the coordinated strike maximized casualties, the attack was clearly planned in advance."

Julia gripped the wheel. The radio tortured her, piercing every aspect of her life. At the same time, she had to listen. She had to know what was happening. They were ahead of her, she knew that. They would find him, whether he came home or not. That's how these things worked.

"In the search for the primary suspect, Michael Swann, police have narrowed their efforts to a stretch of Route 322 in New Jersey from Atlantic City to Glassboro. Residents in that area are asked to stay at home and off the road. If anyone sees anything suspicious, please call 9-1-1 immediately."

"Shit," she hissed.

Ahead of her, traffic came to a stop. It was after 9:00 P.M. now, but on that stretch of Route 322 heading toward Interstate 95, there was always traffic. She knew that. She'd sat in it a thousand times.

Julia slowed. As she neared the car in front of her, something snapped. All the pressure, all her fears, they exploded out of her. And her foot pressed down on the gas pedal. Her car accelerated as she drifted onto the shoulder. Horns blared. People inched out to try to block her. To avoid one particularly angry and aggressive driver, she hit a curb, hard. On the recoil her head hit the side window. Yet she kept going. Kept pushing past the stopped vehicles.

Julia only slowed when she reached a traffic light. It was red, but she didn't stop. Instead, she inched out, forcing others to her will. She could hear shouts of anger at that point, but she would not stop, coming within inches of other cars. And when the way opened up ahead of her, she took it, hitting sixty miles per hour as she neared the interstate.

On the straightaway just before the exit ramp, she pulled her phone out. A strange laugh escaped Julia then. As she texted Michael's phone while speeding down the highway, she could only think of the wrath she would have endured if her boys were in the car. At twelve and eight, they were the morality police, and texting and driving had become almost as awful as smoking cigarettes.

Get off 322. Drive northeast away

Oh, they'd be so mad, she thought, and her laughter transformed into uncontrollable sobs. Julia could barely see through the tears as she passed the I-95 exit and headed toward the bridge over the Delaware River.

"Michael," she whispered.

And she drove.

3

The phone vibrated on my lap. I read the text. I still couldn't focus. I still didn't understand. I didn't know if I was on Route 322 anymore or not. But as I looked up, I saw a sign for Route 54 East. Swerving, I banked onto the ramp and merged onto another highway.

That's when I looked at the dash of the car and remembered the radio. Fumbling, I turned it on and listened to the reports. I heard them say where I was, where they thought I was. In a way, it was more than I knew myself. But my nerves fired and my hands shook. I was being chased. I needed to run. But I still had no idea where.

Then I saw the first helicopter. It was off in the distance, to my left. It looked to be following above the road I had just exited.

"God," I said.

My teeth actually chattered. I couldn't stop them. I felt like my body was on fire beneath the skin, like I might explode out. My neck craned as I watched the helicopter getting closer behind me.

Another exit appeared ahead of me. I took it onto another road with a number. Five hundred and something. I barely saw it. I just knew it merged onto a smaller road. Less conspicuous. I was the only car in sight. I tried to breathe. I tried to stay calm. But I was being hunted. And I couldn't remember exactly why.

4

J ulia crossed the bridge. High over the Delaware River, she heard
the report on the radio. The police had identified the car he drove.
She had to warn him.

`Get rid of car`

As she drove, she kept looking from her phone to the road and
back again. She read her texts to him. All in a line, one atop the other.
No response at all. She waited to see the three dots that meant he was
responding to her. But there was nothing. He was there. He was reading her texts. She had to believe that.

For the hundredth time since she had left her mother's house, Julia
thought about calling him. Each time, though, she heard Bakhash in
her head. And she pictured Michael, alone, injured, somehow caught
up in all of this. Her finger would hover over his name in her contacts.
She would hold her breath. Then a more insidious thought would
spring to life. Vaguely, with no specifics, she thought of Michael losing all hope. Learning she was putting herself in danger. Deciding
that he needed to do something drastic to protect her and protect the
kids. So she stopped herself.

Her heart rose in her chest and her fingers moved like lightning as,
instead, she poured herself out one note at a time.

5

```
Get rid of car
```

I heard the report before the text vibrated my phone. I read it, but was already looking for a place to stop. Outside, the landscape had changed. The mature oaks and maples surrounding suburban towns had become a long, tall line of straight-trunked pines. I reached an intersection and took a right onto a road with *Pleasant* in the name. I passed creeks and a pond on my right. But my eyes remained on those trees.

Then I saw the small outbuilding, maybe a pump station. I pulled onto the gravel drive and killed the car's headlights. Carefully, I rolled around and came to a stop behind the squat redbrick building.

The phone on my lap vibrated over and over again. I picked it up and read.

```
I love you
No matter what. Itll be ok
Well figure it out
```

I sat in the dark car and closed my eyes. It was like she sat next to me, speaking softly, lovingly in my ear. Funny, through all of this, through the fog that still clings to me, I can never forget that

moment. I felt alive. It felt real. Her words entered me, in a way became me.

I know you

"I don't," I whispered in reply.

Think about the boys they need you I need u

That feeling was like nothing I could understand. I felt like a child,
an infant who discovers he can smile for the first time. Everything
seemed brighter. Clearer. Before, I had run aimlessly, without purpose, but now I had one. I had to reach her. I had to find her, be with
her . . . and the boys . . . my boys.

I looked up from the phone, out the window at the line of sentinel
trees. My eyes burned. I felt like I no longer needed to breathe. I had
to be with her. To be with . . . My head snapped down. I looked at the
screen, at the name above each text . . .

"Julia," I read.

I had to be with *Julia*.

THE REAL MICHAEL SWANN

Julia almost closed her eyes. If she had, maybe she would have careened off the highway. Maybe that would have been better. For her, at least, not the kids. For it was the thought of them that caused her to falter. Even with her eyes open, she saw it.

———————

The scream came from Thomas as he was brought forth into this world by the hands of relative strangers. Evan was at home with her mother. Julia felt the pull, the need to reach out and snatch away her newborn son. He needed her. He was calling out for her. But she was in a bed, numb from her midriff down as it felt like her doctor and a resident were placing organs back into her abdomen.

"Michael," she said, her voice weak from the epidural.

"I'm here," he whispered.

She opened her eyes and looked up. His face hovered above hers. She felt his hand gently stroke the hair from her forehead.

"Is he okay?" she whispered.

His smile pushed away her fear, the pain, everything. It called his happiness out to the world. It embraced her, protected her, and let her know that their baby was more than fine. He was perfect, and loved, always.

"He's awesome," Michael said.

Julia barely heard a conversation about her incision and the minimal scar it would leave. For as the doctor spoke to her, a nurse spoke to Michael.

"Do you want to hold him?"

Michael paused, looking at her. The C-section had not been planned. Evan had been a natural birth. Immediately after the birth, they had put him on her bare skin. It was like his pink little fingers had reached in and held her soul. They were one from that moment on. No matter what.

Her husband paused because it wouldn't be that way with Thomas. She could not hold him yet. And with his eyes, Michael was asking if it was okay. Could he do it? Should he do it? And she had never loved him more than that moment.

With barely a nod and a smile that could never match his, Julia gave him that gift. He turned, and the nurse put Thomas in his arms. The screaming stopped, and four wide-open eyes looked down at her. And she cried that day, but those tears were so different from the ones that owned her as she raced toward the ocean.

6

I was shaking when I got out of the car. I couldn't put the phone down. I couldn't stop looking at the screen. It was like a lifeline, keeping me awake and alive. In that moment, her words felt like the only reality. Like everything else was a dream. But Julia was real. She was everything.

Off in the distance, I heard silence. I moved toward the tree line. The pressure surrounded me. Even then, I could feel it. But I couldn't turn off the screen. I knew the light might draw them to me, but I just couldn't.

The ground under my feet grew softer, damper, as I moved toward the forest. It smelled of evergreen the closer I came to the trees. But every few steps, a hint of sulfur touched the air, swampy and humid.

I could still hear the sirens. They moved closer and closer, it seemed. At the same time, the low thumping of a helicopter caught my ear. I looked up and saw dim lights flashing in the distance. Then I stepped into the woods, into the darkness. And disappeared.

7

Why doesn't he text back?

The question gnawed at Julia as she raced eastward. She was sure that he read them. Why would he not answer? It made no sense.

As that thought rolled through her mind for the millionth time, her phone rang. Julia's heart missed a beat. She hit the answer button on her steering wheel before the caller ID could appear on her dash display screen.

"Michael?"

"It's me," her mother said. "Where are you?"

"In Jersey, heading toward Atlantic City. Are the kids okay?"

"Yes," her mom said. "But they know you're gone."

"The kids?"

"No, the police. That weird agent guy was here. Looking for you. I told him I didn't know anything. He threatened me. Can you believe that? Said if I lied—"

"The Middle Eastern one?"

"No, that quiet one. He—"

Julia interrupted, her voice shrill. "Don't worry about it. It won't matter. I'll find him and it just won't matter."

"Maybe this is a bad idea," her mother said, tentatively.

"No, Mom. I have to."

"But . . . the kids. You can't let anything happen to you."

Her palm slammed the steering wheel. "I can't let anything happen to Michael."

"But . . ."

"No," Julia snapped. "I won't. Tell the boys I love them . . . And I'll be home soon."

She hung up.

8

I walked in the darkness among the trees. Everything around me felt old, timeless, like it had existed before us and would long after we were all forgotten. And the silence. It clung like the damp briny air, feeling heavy and foreign. The ground beneath my feet felt soft, almost like sand. But I pushed on, deeper and deeper. Further away from everything.

Every few minutes, I would check the phone. Nothing new would be there, so I would reread the others over and over again. She was coming to me. She was getting nearer every moment.

I heard the first creek before I came upon it. The soft rumble of water over rocks echoed through the night until the forest floor dropped off ahead of me. I stopped on the bank, looking down at the stream as it moved without thought, ever forward. I understood that. I was that. And it held me for a minute, entranced.

Then the thump of the helicopter rose above the babble of water. It got louder, quickly. As it neared, I heard the sirens, too. It sounded as if they surrounded me. But that might have been a trick of the forest, the high-pitched wail bouncing through the trunks like a pinball.

I jumped down, my feet splashing in the water. And I climbed up the far side. Ever forward. Like the water.

9

Julia's phone rang again, just as she passed a sign for Williamstown Township. Thinking it was her mother, she almost didn't answer. But it could have been about her boys, so she hit the button.

"Yes," she said, coolly.

"Mrs. Swann?"

The voice grabbed her. She instantly felt sick to her stomach. It was Agent Bakhash.

"What?" she snapped.

"I understand," he said, softly. Not, she thought, out of caring, but out of calculation.

Her rage burst out in words. "What do you understand?"

"What you're trying to do? I really do. But you're putting yourself in danger. You know that, right?"

She said nothing.

"Mrs. Swann? You understand that you are putting yourself in danger, right?"

"I need to do something. I can't let you hurt him."

"It doesn't have to come to that," he said. "He could give himself up. You could tell him to do that."

"I can't tell him anything. I don't even know where he is."

"Are you saying you haven't talked to him?"

"No, I haven't." She shook with a mixture of anger and stress and fear. "Have you? Has anyone?"

"No, we haven't. But I need to hear you say it, Mrs. Swann. You understand, right. That you are putting yourself in serious jeopardy by your course of action."

"I don't care," she said, loudly.

"But you understand?"

"Yes! Jesus! Yes, I understand. And I understand that you all want him dead for what you think he did. Everyone does. The whole goddamn country does. So I just don't *fucking* care."

Bakhash paused. The silence crackled between them, like it might suddenly burst into flame. Julia, overwhelmed but out of tears, looked through her windshield. She saw the sign just as Bakhash said the words.

"We found the car just outside the Pine Barrens. We think he's on foot now."

Julia never once thought about why he might be telling her that. Why he would help her. She simply hung up and accelerated.

After a mile, she glanced at her phone, sitting on the passenger seat. The police had found his car. They had to be so close to finding him. She had to try.

With a quick snatch, she grabbed it off the seat and dialed Michael's number.

10

The helicopter was almost on top of me. Somehow, I knew it would find me. That they would have an infrared camera. Once I was on their screen, my shadow would glow like the sun. They would be on me in seconds. And I couldn't let that happen.

I think it was instinct. Or maybe it was some deep, buried memory that was there, but just out of reach for me to really recall it. Whatever it was, I turned and broke into a run. Not fifty yards back, I had crossed another stream, this one bigger and deeper. As I neared it, I looked up. I saw light among the trunks, not far away. It flashed and moved, and the thumping sound grew louder and louder.

I reached the stream and carefully placed the phone and the case on the ground. Then I jumped from the bank, landing a few feet into the water. Quickly, I waded out until the depth reached my waist. The light was almost on me. I could see the helicopter through the thick patches of needles above and to the west. So I held my breath and dove. The cold water swallowed me, but I could only hope it was cold enough.

It was an effort, but I clung to the rocky bottom and forced my body to stay under. I swear the spotlight passed directly over me. The water seemed to pulse in time with the whirling blades. Then the sound faded. The light disappeared. I stood, gasping in air.

That's when I heard the phone ringing. Lurching up out of the water, I tried to high-step to the bank. A wet rock gave way beneath my foot. As my ankle twisted, I lost balance, falling back into the water. By the time I finally crawled out onto the grassy bank, the ringing had stopped.

My hand hovered over the phone before I picked it up. When I did, I saw the prompt.

```
Julia
Missed Call
```

I stared at it for only a second, knowing that I had to move. With the phone still in my hand, I continued deeper into the forest, a single thought in my head.

She has to find me first. Julia has to find me first.

11

Julia only drove a few miles down County Route 542 before she saw the blockade. Slowly, she pulled to the side of the road and stared as officers dragged a long orange barrier across the road. Police cars sat before it and beyond, and as she watched, a large black van passed her.

Even with the engine running, she could hear the helicopters. Leaning forward for a better look, she saw three darting across the night sky, spotlights shining down onto what she thought must be the Pine Barrens.

Julia had no idea what to do. She needed to keep going. To find him.

A tap on the window startled her. She turned to see an officer standing outside the car. He motioned for her to lower her window, which she did, slowly.

"Can I help you, ma'am?"

"Just trying to get home," she said.

"I can't let you pass. You can—"

"Okay, thanks," she said.

Without rolling the window up, she let go of her brake and rolled slowly past the man. Her hands shaking, she made a three-point turn that felt like it took hours. She tried not to screech her tires as she sped away.

Julia was so concerned that they'd stop her that she never once looked in the mirror. If she had, she might have seen the black sedan follow her back the way she came.

———————

Julia wasn't even sure she was out of the officer's sight when she reached the intersection. A narrow road made a sharp left. Without a thought, she killed her lights and took it. Speeding up, she went maybe a quarter of a mile and stopped, careful to take her foot off the brake once the car stopped so the taillights wouldn't give her away.

Im close, she texted.

Julia stared at the screen, once again waiting for those three dots. Knowing they would not appear. Since she tried to call Michael and there was no answer, she had lost hope that he was even seeing the messages. Yet she sent one, nonetheless, for there was simply nothing else she could do.

Shaking her head, she opened Google Maps. Using the arrow, she found her location. Immediately, she noticed the road she had just turned onto crossed a road that could take her back to 542 and maybe in behind the blockade. She had to try.

Putting the car in drive, she followed her map, turning onto a narrow road. Out her window, she saw moonlight sparkling off the ripples of a pond. To her right, the tall trees of the Pine Barrens rose up toward the stars. She saw a small brick building up ahead. Oddly, a bright light shined behind it, casting the pump house in an otherworldly glow.

Julia squinted. In the shadow cast by the building, she saw a car. As she got closer, light reflected off blue and red lights atop the hood. Her breath caught, but she kept moving forward. When the door opened and an officer stepped out, she knew it was over. Julia knew she had failed.

12

The memories hit like an endless avalanche. They rolled over her with crushing weight and bitter longing. One after another, they struck. She saw his face, with his long chin and wide cheekbones. His red-blond hair and blue eyes. The stubble of a Sunday morning. The strength, the love, the passion.

They came in snippets, almost meaningless snapshots of her life with him. Michael sitting low on a beach chair, gazing off into the Atlantic as dolphins moved along with the endless horizon. Walking up the ramp at the baseball stadium, a boy's hand in each of his, Thomas's Phillies hat on backwards. His silhouette on a dark winter morning as he crept through their room, dressing for work, so careful not to make a sound and wake her. Opening her eyes to find him looking into hers as they kissed.

Like a ghost, he came to her. They stood facing each other. Gray fog clung to their legs as he reached out and lightly touched her hand. The contact sent a crackle of energy running up her arm and into her body. She reached out to him, cupped his face, and smiled as the stubble tickled her skin.

"I'm coming," she whispered.

———————

She opened her eyes and realized the car had stopped. The police officer stood by the side of the road. Although the lighting was dim, she thought he looked directly at her. But he did not move. And for a second, she didn't, either, other than the shaking. Her head reeled from whatever had just happened, whatever journey had taken her out of that moment. Whatever it was, it sparked something in her. Her eyes narrowed. Slowly, her foot lowered onto the gas pedal again and she started to drive.

The officer did not move. He only watched. Julia gained speed. Fifty yards away from him, she ground her teeth together. The pedal hit the floorboard and the car lurched forward. She stared at the man in the dark uniform, daring him to stop her. Daring him to try. Yet he did not move. He only watched.

In a flash, she was past. Julia didn't slow. Speeding down the narrow road, she almost missed the T-intersection. Her tires screamed as she cut right. Then she was off again, heading for the rising forest ahead. Heading for her husband.

13

The spotlight shined down on her car. Julia hissed like a feral animal, caged and left with no option but to strike out. When a one-lane road appeared, she turned onto it and sped up. The helicopter followed above her.

"Stop!" she screamed.

It had appeared not a minute after she passed the officer on the road. And no matter how hard she tried, she could not shake it.

"Leave me alone!"

Her car continued to speed up. It rattled and shook like the wheels might rip from their axles. Yet the helicopter followed, the sound of its propellers driving her mad.

"Reports on the ground in New Jersey confirm that the search area for Michael Swann is tightening. At this time, the suspect is believed to be on foot in the Pine Barrens, a one-million-acre forest near the coast of New Jersey. It is believed that all access into the area is block-aded and, once again, authorities are asking that people stay in their homes."

Reality hit her then. The car slowed. Julia's muscles went slack. She realized that she could not even touch a happy ending. The presence of the helicopter. The sirens in the background. The soft baying of dogs she heard through the closed windows of her car. It all painted a grim picture, a visceral reminder of the truth. Michael was gone to her.

For the first time, she pictured their reunion. The first instant that she saw him. Running to him, launching herself into him. All the pain, all the loss, would vanish as they held each other. But then what?

That question was the final straw. Then what? Her foot came off the accelerator. The car slowed and eventually stopped. Her head lowered, resting on the steering wheel. And then what?

There was no escape. Every way out of that place was blocked. But that didn't even matter. This was no action movie. She and Michael couldn't win their way loose of this stranglehold, run off into the setting sun, live on some beautiful island, millions of dollars stashed in an offshore account. Even if that sort of thing happened, it wouldn't matter. This was her life, not someone's made-up story.

Evan and Thomas waited at home with her mother. No matter what, she couldn't leave them. She'd never do that. Now she also knew that Michael could never return to her. She pictured a new future, one where the boys drove to some awful prison one Sunday a month to talk to their father through shatterproof glass. Or worse. Julia's mind almost took her to that unfathomable place, seeing her Michael strapped to a table, an IV drip . . .

"God," she moaned. "Please."

The sound of the helicopter pounded in her ear. It was so close that her car shook. The spotlight burned her eyes, sending a shock wave from temple to temple. Julia pressed her palms into her eyes, hard.

"NO!!!" she screamed.

It was over. There was no hope. There was no way to win, no peace. All she did was lead the helicopter to him. She was powerless, helpless, at the mercy of a world that would have no mercy for her husband.

"No," she whispered.

And it all left her in that moment. She had nothing remaining. Julia sat in a motionless car and knew she would give . . .

Darkness.

At first, Julia thought she still had her hands over her eyes. But they had fallen to her lap. She blinked, but the darkness remained.

"What?" she said aloud.

She noticed the car no longer shook. The horrible sound, one that had vibrated her bones just an instant before, grew softer. It grew distant. More and more distant. Slowly, surprisingly, she found herself in silence.

With that sound, that light, came a crushing oppression. As it left her, Julia stirred again. She stared up at the stars and the helicopter was gone. A glimmer of hope returned.

"He didn't do it," she said.

If she could save him, if she could keep him alive, they'd figure it out. In time, they'd learn. They'd know that he couldn't have done it. Maybe she couldn't whisk him away to freedom. But maybe, in time, she wouldn't have to.

Once again, Julia found resolve. Her foot lowered. The car moved. And still, she never saw the other one, the black sedan, follow as she drove away.

14

The dogs. I heard them getting closer. As my head reemerged from the cold creek water, I knew that between the two, those dogs and the helicopters, they would find me. At the time, if I had known where I was, how big the forest was, maybe I would have thought I could slip free. But I felt that net closing in on me. And all I could do was keep going.

I waded back to the bank and grabbed the phone. Instead of climbing out, I stayed in the water this time, where it was shallow, and followed it. I hit the home button and looked at the texts. I read them all.

Eventually, I reached a fork in the river. The way north and east grew wider, the water rumbling over the rocks. Without a thought, I followed it. I went barely a quarter of a mile before I heard voices mingle with the braying of the dogs. I looked up and saw one helicopter not far off hovering over a spot. I hoped, for a second, that maybe they thought I was there, that it would draw them away. But as I watched, it flew quickly away to the north.

I ran.

15

Julia drove deeper into the forest. Each foot she traveled fueled her panic. She needed to do something. She heard the dogs, too. Though no car passed her, she thought she heard engines nearby. She was running out of time.

Nothing but trees surrounded her. She knew she would never find him this way. But then something appeared out of the darkness, a faint ray of light through the trees. She stared at it, almost missing the long dirt road. It led to a large house. The light came from a lamp on the porch and another in a good-sized parking area. Without knowing why, she turned and headed up to the house, to the light. In the parking lot, she stopped her car.

Julia knew she couldn't keep driving around aimlessly. She knew she needed to do something. And the idea hit her. She snatched the phone from her lap and opened her message app. She paused, looking at all the texts. She doubted if any of them had even been seen. But Julia pushed that feeling down and sent a new one.

Follow to car horn. Its me

She sent it and laid a hand on the horn. Over and over again she pressed it. The sound was jarring and otherworldly in that still darkness. But she could not stop. She would not. Not until Michael was safe.

16

heard it. Just when the phone vibrated, I heard the horn. And it was close, very close. I read the message and I sprinted, coming out of the water so I could run even faster. I forgot about the dogs and the helicopters, and everything else. All I thought about was her.

17

She sounded that horn, over and over again, almost forgetting that the radio was still on. When she heard her husband's name, she didn't stop, not right away. But something in the tone caught her attention. The words between each shrill blast started to make sense. They started to piece together. And a chill ran up her body. Her hand hovered over the horn. And she listened.

"Although unconfirmed, multiple sources within the investigation of the Penn Station bombing are now saying that earlier reports that Michael Swann was a suspect in the attack were not accurate. This shocking news comes as police have confirmed that he is close to capture. Once again, we are now reporting that Michael Swann is not the man responsible for the Penn Station bombing."

Julia sprang from the car. She staggered across the pavement, feeling like her legs might give out.

Innocent.

The word surrounded her. It at once threatened to throw her to the ground and kept her on her feet. The tears ran down her face, but they were different now. They were so, so different.

"Michael!" she called out. "I'm here. Michael."

Slowly, she moved closer to the tree line that ran right along the back side of the parking lot. She called out, over and over again.

"MICHAEL, MICHAEL, MICHAEL."

———

"MICHAEL, MICHAEL, MICHAEL."

I heard her voice. Amazingly, I heard it. It called out to me through the night like some guardian angel. My heart beat so hard against my chest that I thought I might die. But I heard it. I heard her. I heard Julia.

———

Between her calls to him, she heard tires rolling atop gravel. She stopped about twenty yards from the forest and listened. She heard cicadas surrounding her, and the first hint of crickets. The smell of pine and marsh hung heavy in the air. Her head lifted and she looked again at the stars. It was so dark there in the middle of the Pine Barrens that she could make out the soft glow of distant galaxies behind the bright constellations.

For a moment, she heard nothing else. Just as she was going to say his name again, though, there it was. That same sound. Julia spun and saw the shadow of a car turning into the parking lot. Its headlights were off, but the sliver of moonlight flashed off its windshield.

"No," she whispered. "Nonono."

Julia turned, her voice rising, her words frantic.

"Hurry! They're coming. MICHAEL! Hurry!"

———

Off in the distance, I saw the light. It was faint at first, but like the hand of God, it drew me closer and closer. After a few more steps, I could see the outline of a large building taking form behind the tall trunks that surrounded me.

She called out again. Her voice was so close. She sounded urgent. Telling me to hurry. I did. I tried. I ran through the forest, almost losing my footing in the soft sugar sand of the barrens.

A hundred yards, seventy, forty. I got closer and closer. Then I saw her for the first time. It was so dark, but I could see the darker lines of her body against the lightly lit building behind her. It was Julia. I was sure of it. My heart reached for her as I stumbled toward those last trees between us. All I wanted to do was see her face. Feel her touch. Hear her soft words. So much so, I never heard the helicopter approaching quickly behind me.

———————

Julia spun around to face the black sedan. The door opened and from the inside light she saw Agent Bakhash. His eyes remained locked on hers, but he didn't get out of the car right away. They remained still, staring at each other.

"Get out of here," she yelled at him. "Didn't you hear? He's innocent! He didn't do it."

Bakhash didn't seem to move. He just stared.

———————

My hand came to rest on the last of the pine trees. The bark felt surprisingly cool against my skin, and as I pulled away, the sap clung. My foot left the forest. Slowly, carefully, it touched the asphalt of the parking lot. All the while, I was fixated, my eyes locked on her.

As my other foot followed, though, I stopped. Even in the darkness, I noticed that she had her back to me. Why wouldn't she look at me? What was wrong?

"Julia," I said.

I don't know if I whispered or shouted. But she heard me. She turned and we saw each other.

———

Her eyes burned. She couldn't see anything. She was about to scream when she heard her name. Julia turned and she saw him. Saw his darker shadow standing just outside the trees. He looked tall and straight, but he wouldn't move. Her heart beat so hard in that moment, like her chest might explode outward. Julia glanced over her shoulder once and then put her hands up.

"Don't run," she said. "It's okay. They know. Everything's okay."

———

I wanted to laugh. What did they know? I still knew nothing but one simple truth. And I was almost there. I'd almost reached her. My Julia. I took a step closer and my soul sang. It was almost over.

———

He moved toward her. Julia soared. He'd come. Somehow, she'd found him. And it wasn't too late. It would all be okay. She took a tentative step forward, and then another. But then she heard it again. More tires rolling on gravel. She turned and saw them racing up the driveway. A half dozen police cars, lights flashing but no sirens. She turned to Bakhash, who now stood beside his car.

"No!" she yelled. "Stop them. He didn't do it."

Agent Bakhash spoke calmly. "Get on the ground."

"What?"

He reached into his jacket. As the first headlights from the patrol cars swept across the parking lot, she saw the gun as he drew it out.

"On the ground," he repeated.

"No!" she screamed.

———

I saw the police. I even saw the man with the gun. I didn't care, though. Because what I really saw was her. When Julia turned and ran toward me, I went to meet her.

———

The beat of the helicopter washed over the scene like a striking storm. Julia ran from Bakhash and the other police. If she had a coherent thought in that moment, it was to throw herself between them and Michael. After everything, she couldn't let it end like this.

Above the thumping blades overhead, she heard car doors slam. Men shouted, repeating words like *POLICE* and *DOWN*. She ignored them all. All Julia could do was get to him, protect him, and everything would be okay.

Suddenly, the spotlight from the helicopter flashed on. A circle of light appeared on the pavement near the building. It swept quickly toward the two as they raced into each other's arms.

———————

The light touched Julia and it was a dream. Like I said at the beginning, she appeared out of that darkness, a brightness that I simply didn't deserve. I can still picture her on that day. She wore a white tank top and capri pants, although it took me months to remember that is what they are called. She stood in the light, its beams touching the soft skin of her cheeks and the heart-stopping strength in her eyes. Her dark hair was pulled back, highlighting the lines of her face and classically long neck. She looked like a runner and a leader, a mother and a timeless beauty, at least to me. And I saw the ring on her finger, silver and simple. Her name was Julia, Julia Swann.

I ran to her, ready to take her into my arms. Hold on to her forever. But then . . . she stopped.

———————

Julia heard footsteps behind her as the spotlight neared. She ran as hard as she could, her chest burning and her eyes tearing. She had to reach him.

The light swung toward them. He was close, so close. She reached a hand out, willing the space between them to simply vanish. She would wrap him up. Take him to the ground. Hold him tight until this was all over.

And then the light shined down and everything was wrong. He was *wrong*. She saw blunt features, dark hair, black eyes. She saw a face that shocked her, frightened her, but not in a way that she could ever have expected. An instant before the light shined down on them, she saw her husband. She saw Michael's loving eyes, his ready smile. She saw the father of her children, the man that she dreamed of growing old with. In a flash of light, all that was stripped away. And Julia was left staring in horror at an utter stranger. For the man standing before her was not Michael Swann.

She dropped to her knees. The screams that burst from her froze everyone there in place. It tore from her heart and ripped through the air like lightning strikes.

"No," she wailed. "Noooooooo."

18

I didn't understand. I still don't, really. I stood there and watched Julia fall to her knees. The scream, the sound of it, it hit me like the winds of a tornado, throwing me back. I should have spoken. I should have said something. But I couldn't. That sound. It took my words away. All I could do was stand there and listen.

As she knelt there, her face changed. In the shining light from above, I saw her change. What had been the face of an angel darkened. I saw hatred there, visceral and raw, as she stared at me. Her hand rose, and she pointed a long, thin finger at me, at my face.

"Where's Michael?" she screamed. "What did you do to him?"

Her voice rose higher and higher. Her words were frantic and savage. She sprang to her feet, lunging at me, grabbing at my throat.

"What did you do to him? What did you do!?"

Fingernails cut at my skin. Pain flared and her momentum took us to the ground. But I never moved. I know that. I'm sure of it. I never fought back. I never defended myself. I never moved. I know I didn't.

19

Agent Bakhash arrived first. He grabbed Julia as the other officers reached them. They pried the two apart as Bakhash knelt beside her, holding her shoulder as she sat on the pavement. She looked down at the blood on her fingertips and then absently rubbed them on her shirt. Her eyes were wide-open, vacant, like she'd left already.

"Are you okay, Mrs. Swann?" Bakhash asked.

Julia said nothing. She started to rock. She never turned to watch what happened, yet there was no struggle to speak of. The arrest occurred quickly and without resistance. Two cars raced out of the parking lot and back onto the road. A moment later, an ambulance appeared as if it had been waiting all along.

"Mrs. Swann, I think it's best if you let the paramedics take you to the hospital. You've been through a lot tonight."

A stranger appeared and put a blanket on her shoulders. She still didn't move. She said nothing. She just sat on the pavement, staring off into the Pine Barrens, rocking back and forth.

Agent Bakhash was about to leave her when she reached out and gently grabbed his arm. Her words burned as she forced them out.

"Who was he?"

"Daniel Schmidt," Bakhash said. "He set a fire beside the Amtrak rails south of New York. When Penn Station filled to capacity with innocent people, he set off an explosion, killing hundreds. He is a terrorist, Mrs. Swann. And we had to stop him before he hurt anyone else."

Her eyes closed. "But why?"

"We're still figuring that out. We believe he intended to kill executives at—"

"No," Julia snapped. "Why did he do that? Why did he act like Michael?"

His voice softened. "We believe he has a head injury. That's all we know right now."

Julia cried, softly. Bakhash made to leave, but she stopped him again.

"You knew it wasn't Michael," she said, softly, emotionlessly. "You let me leave my house. You let me come after him. All the roadblocks, the police, they let me pass." Her last two words came out like the hiss of a deadly snake. "You knew."

He watched her for a moment, as if he weighed every word he might say in response.

"I'm sorry, Mrs. Swann. Your husband is dead. He was killed in the initial blast."

"You knew," she repeated.

"Not at first," he said. "But eventually, yes."

"Why?"

He looked at her the entire time he spoke.

"That man killed hundreds of people. We had no idea what he would do next. What we knew, though, was that your contact with him changed his course. This was a matter of national security. People were at risk. We couldn't take any chances. We needed to see if he would come to you. And as you can see, it was a calculated risk, but one that paid off."

"That call . . . when I was driving. You wanted me to say that I knew I was putting myself at risk. You wanted a *waiver*."

She blinked, slowly. And a barely noticeable quiver shook her body under the blanket. Julia had never before felt so tired. In a voice that sounded nothing like hers, she asked, "How was I contacting him?"

"He had one of your husband's phones."

"What? Why?"

"I'm sorry."

She shook. "You knew all this?"

He said nothing.

"Bastard," she whispered.

"Mrs. Swann. We did what we had to do."

"But you could have told me." Her voice rose. "You could have asked me. I would have helped. If I knew, I would have."

He stood. His face was utterly emotionless.

"Mrs. Swann, in cases like this, things progress quickly. We needed to find the suspect before he could hurt anyone else. It was our only priority. To that end, I did what I felt was best. At first, we could not be completely sure as to how involved your husband was in the attack. For that matter, yourself as well. I couldn't take that chance."

"Me?" Julia asked, though his words simply confirmed her own suspicions. "You thought I had something to do with it?"

Bakhash shook his head, slowly. "With your father's history with DuLac. Your family's recent financial issues. Your husband's job. We had a report from a New Jersey State police officer who said that you took responsibility. You said it was 'all your fault.'"

"My fault?" She could not fully remember saying that, exactly. Yet she knew why she would. "I was talking about Michael . . . It was all about Michael. How could they tell you that?"

"He was looking out for this country, Mrs. Swann. We all were."
He paused, as if expecting her to suddenly and simply understand
what they had done to her and her family. When that did not happen,
he nodded. "They'll take you to the hospital now and everything will
be sorted out after that. Good night, Mrs. Swann."

He nodded to the paramedic. As that man, with his kind face and
strong hands, helped her to her feet, Agent Bakhash turned and
walked away. After they loaded her into the back, a uniformed officer
climbed aboard. He sat across from her as they drove to the hospital,
never once looking away.

20

Julia sat up in the hospital bed, holding her phone against her chest. She could hear people whispering outside her door. She heard it all the time. They whispered. But no one spoke to her. They offered pleasantries. Nurses and doctors asked her how she felt. No one, however, mentioned anything. No one asked her anything real.

Julia's phone rang, startling her. It was Evelyn.

"Hello?"

"Are you okay?" Evelyn asked.

She went back to staring out the window. "No."

"Have you seen it?"

"What?"

"It's . . . I can't. Go to CNN dot com."

"What is it, Evelyn?"

"It's . . . He didn't do anything. He . . ."

She could hear Evelyn crying on the other end of the line. It brought back the pain, the emptiness.

"I have to go," she said, quickly, and hung up.

Phone in hand, Julia went back to staring out the window. Evelyn's words teased at her thoughts. She wanted to ignore them. Block them out. She wanted to block everything out, at least until she was home, with the kids. Then she would have to face it.

Yet she couldn't, no matter how hard she tried. Eventually, she turned and looked at her phone. She went to the website. Michael's name was everywhere. She shook a little, and cried. She even looked away. But then she tried again. Her eyes went to the red banner across the top.

MICHAEL SWANN INNOCENT VICTIM

Crying even harder, she opened the article and read.

Investigators recently uncovered new footage from security cameras inside Penn Station taken moments before the bombing. Originally thought destroyed in the blast, data from the additional camera was backed up digitally at an off-site facility in New Jersey. The new footage may help clarify the involvement of Michael Swann, the man initially named a suspect in the bombing.

Originally, a video taken at the same time by a different camera was leaked showing Swann holding a briefcase while standing in Penn Station. Forensic analysis had isolated that case as the most likely source of the explosion.

Hours ago, a second video was officially released by Homeland Security. The ten-second clip shows the man now accused of orchestrating and carrying out the bombing, Daniel Schmidt, switching cases with Swann just minutes before the blast. Schmidt exits quickly from the shot, moving toward the subway platforms.

Minutes later, Swann is seen picking up the case off the ground. At that time, he seems to react to something amiss. After opening the case and viewing the contents, he can be seen slamming it shut and running out of the picture, toward the station exit.

Julia had to read the last paragraph over again. The words lost meaning as she tried to see them through her tears. When she was done, she paused, staring at the video link. Knowing she shouldn't, sure that she didn't have the strength, she touched the arrow and the clip played.

The first thing Julia saw was her husband. He sat in a chair, talking on his phone. Though his face was a mask of pixelation and shades of gray-green, she pictured his smile. She imagined him talking to her over the line. They were discussing his interview. And the boys. Maybe dinner plans. Or maybe she had slipped into a quiet corner of the house and they were talking about their future plans. Maybe they shared a sense of adventure. A new beginning.

Then he appeared. The man from the parking lot. That face she saw under the harsh spotlight. Since that moment, it had morphed in her memory into the face of a monster. Julia wanted to look away. But she didn't. She couldn't.

He slipped in behind Michael. Her husband never noticed. Michael leaned forward and the man moved quickly. She could see Michael's case disappear and another take its place. The man turned and rushed away.

Julia dropped the phone. It bounced off her mattress and fell to the floor. It slid under the bed and the video played over and over again as she wept.

21

Julia sat in the passenger seat as her mother drove them home. She stared out the side window at the trees lining Route 322. Sunlight cut beams through the trunks. It triggered the memory. The darkness, a spotlight, that face that was wrong. At first, she had tried to convince herself. It had to be Michael. But everything was wrong. His eyes were too wide-set, too dead. His chin too square and dull. He could never be her Michael. Yet he had come out of the trees. He had answered her calls. And she hated him for it.

He's gone.

It just kept repeating. The thought tore her down and left her in the kind of emptiness that feels like it will last forever, like nothing could fill the gaping wound inside her. The rational side of her mind grasped at her memory of the boys. Certainly, they needed her. They would be devastated, beyond that really. Her entire being would be focused on their survival, not hers. She knew without a doubt that was her future. But that did nothing for the pain, either. If anything, it made it worse.

They had made a plan. Just the night before all of this started, they had lain in bed talking long into the night about how their lives would change. They laughed off their past mistakes and painted every step in shades of gold like sunshine. Julia could still feel those tears; there had been exactly two, running down her cheek. How many had fallen since then?

Michael.

Anger flared up, pushing back the grief for a moment. She had allowed herself to hope. Even worse than that, when the report broke that he was innocent, just before she saw that face, Julia had *known* it would be okay. She'd opened herself fully. She let it own her life, even the lives of their children. Michael was alive. That's what she thought. And she would never let anyone take him away from her again.

But somehow *he* had. He had ripped Michael from her like some cruel torture. He had appeared, run to her, and showed his face for the foul lie it was. It broke her, and she felt that break might last forever.

"Are you okay?" her mother asked.

Julia couldn't turn to look at her. "Are the boys okay?"

"They are," she said. "But they know some. They need to hear the rest."

"I need to tell them," she said.

"Are you . . ."

They said nothing else for a while. Julia continued to look out the window.

"Why?" she whispered.

Her mother took a breath "There's no answer to that. At least not one that we can understand. I wish there was, though. I wish we could just explain it. Maybe that would help."

"I thought it was him," Julia said, her words barely more than air.

Her mother felt those words deep in her chest. "I am so sorry."

After fifteen minutes of silence, Julia blinked. The scenery around her took focus as they crossed the Delaware River, which meant she would be home with Evan and Thomas in less than an hour. The thought scared her to death, in a way. She needed to see them, to have them close, fold them under her wing. But at the same time, she had no idea what to say or how to make them feel better, ever.

Her agitation grew, layering a shakiness over the crushing grief of it all. Absently, she turned on the radio. Maybe she wanted some breaking news to change everything, to paint a new picture. Some reporter could open her mouth and put words out that altered the truth. That could bring him back.

Instead, they spoke of the other one now. Everyone did. His name, *Schmidt*, seemed a language unto itself. *Schmidt, Schmidt, Schmidt.* It rattled against her ears.

"A coward. That's what I'd call him. At least those other fanatics blow themselves up. This guy left the bomb and ran. He got out. The craven."

She changed the station.

"What do you expect when the political climate of this country is so full of divisive rhetoric? This man, Schmidt, was on the edge. He'd lost his job. His marriage had recently ended. He had a gambling problem. They say he watched those Sunday programs religiously. Talk radio all the time. What did we expect, really? If Schmidt is some monster, then let's face it, folks. We are all Dr. Frankenstein."

Her finger moved again, though she barely noticed.

"If the president had done what he said, this never would have happened . . ."

"Twenty-four/seven coverage of the investigation . . ."

"An anonymous caller caused the evacuation of the Federal Building in Oklahoma City."

". . . bomb the shit out of . . ."

Endless . . . Click.

The car pulled into her driveway. Kate looked at her daughter, but Julia felt paralyzed. She had to get out. She had to face it. But she felt so heavy.

I can't.

She closed her eyes. And she pictured his face, his sharp chin and his bright eyes. She felt his hands, so strong, touching her, lifting her up. Julia knew she couldn't open her eyes. If she did, he would be gone. But oh, how she wanted to see him again.

I miss you, she said.

I'm so sorry, he whispered back, silently.

The boys need you, she said.

No, he said. *They need you. Just know you can't take their pain away. Just like us, they have to feel it. It has to embrace them so that, over time, they can slowly let it go.*

I don't know if I can watch them cry, Michael.

It is the same for them. But no matter how much you try, you will cry, too. Know that you'll do your best. And that's all you can do. Trust your heart and be there.

I thought I still had you.

"What?" her mother said.

Julia's eyes shot open. And he was gone. She opened the car door.

"Do you want me to . . . ?"

She shook her head. "No. I just want to be with them."

Julia walked out of the car, her mother watching silently. As she neared the front door, it opened. Evelyn was there. They hugged, but briefly. When Julia pulled away, Evelyn seemed to understand. She stepped onto the front porch, out of the way.

"If you need me . . . ," she said.

Julia nodded, but didn't say anything. She wanted to. Even in that moment, she saw how the woman standing beside her was a real friend, one who had stood by her through it all. Later, it would mean even more to her. She would put herself in Evelyn's shoes and wonder, often, whether she could have been as true. Would she have stood by someone whose husband had been accused of such a heinous crime? Some days, she doubted. But that thought was too hard to face.

As she stepped into the house, Julia heard their footsteps rising from the basement. Evan appeared, his eyes red and the tears fresh on his face. He stopped, not getting too close.

"I'm sorry, Mom," he said, his voice breaking.

"Oh, buddy, you shouldn't—"

"I was wrong," he said. "I got so mad at you, but I was wrong."

"No, I shouldn't have—"

"I get it," he said. "It was for Thomas. He's still a little kid."

Julia's heart broke. She could barely breathe. But Evan continued.

"And I'm sorry for telling you to go after Dad."

"You were right," she said, taking him into her arms. "For just a second, I thought he might have . . . I . . . And you reminded me, Evan. You did that."

She cried. He rubbed her back.

"It's okay," Evan said. "But I knew. I knew he couldn't do that."

"I know," she said.

Thomas came next. He still looked frightened, and far too young to lose his father.

"It's not fair," he said. "It's not . . ."

They surrounded him, taking him in. Together, the emotion poured out, as if an electrical current coursed from son to mother to son. Their faces pressed together. The world around them seemed to vanish. And for just a second, all three closed their eyes. And they saw him one last time. Their father, the *real* Michael Swann, smiled down at them as they wept together.

22

She had no idea how much time had passed. Her family remained locked together, their knees on the cool tile of the foyer floor. They spoke some. Words that could never be enough. Prayers that could never be answered. Fears that only time could slowly soften. In time, though, maybe weeks, or months, or maybe years, they would realize that only two things could help them lift up from their grief. The first they could never control. Instead, it would march forward one way or another. They might perceive it as seconds or years, but eventually time would heal, given the chance.

The second thing, the more important one, they had already. They were together. They had each other. And though one was missing, his absence would never come between them. On the contrary, it would bind them even deeper.

Yet life, as Julia had just learned, did not exist in a bubble. For, before the sun dipped toward that afternoon, as the Swanns held each other with all the strength they had left, a knock came to their front door.

Julia stirred. At first, she thought it would be a well-meaning neighbor. As word of Michael's innocence spread, they would return, needing to assuage their own perceived guilt. Yet even before she stood, she sensed this was different. Voices rose, two, three, maybe four. And another knock rattled the door.

She rose. Evan touched her hand, as if asking her to stop. But she couldn't. She had to know.

Julia walked across the foyer. Her hand touched the handle. She turned it, taking in what felt like a final breath. As the door opened, she saw people, maybe half a dozen, maybe more. Every face was a stranger to her. Some looked polished and vacant. Others looked rough and disheveled. They stared at her with unabashed obsession and a strange ownership. Like she and her family now belonged, in some heartbreaking way, to them.

"Mrs. Swann, Mrs. Swann."

She didn't answer. Over their shoulders, she saw the same news vans that had surrounded her house just the day before. They were back.

"Mrs. Swann, how does it feel?"

Her legs felt weak. Why would they ask a question like that? She stared into their hungry eyes as they thrust microphones in her face.

"Have you seen it? The video. How does it feel knowing your husband is a hero?"

It made no sense. As she stood there, aghast, more vans approached. They surrounded her house. Waves of people pushed in on Julia and her family, feet scurrying as if they raced to see who could touch her first.

"The video," another said. "It's gone viral. Everyone's seen it. He found the bomb. He tried to get it out of the station. He's a hero, Mrs. Swann. A hero."

The first thing Julia did was blink. It was a slow close of her eyes, as if she hoped that maybe, as they reopened, all this would be gone. But it wasn't. Instead, even more people approached.

Slowly, carefully, Julia stepped back. Her fingers touched the edge of the front door.

"Don't you have a comment? It's amazing. Everyone wants—"

Julia simply closed the door.

EPILOGUE

1

The backdrop reminded her of the sky that night in the Pine Barrens. Glowing blue panels rose like flames from both sides of the stage, adding depth to the huge image of a distant galaxy with clouds and pinprick stars. Just to the right of center, red block letters over six feet tall spelled out *TED30*.

A woman stepped on stage, microphone in hand, walking casually to a circular platform jutting out into the first dozen rows of seating. She moved about as if the fear of public speaking never once occurred to her. Dressed in sleek black pants and a perfectly cut white sleeveless top, she looked the juxtaposition of a 1950s mother and a millennial CrossFit trainer. Her tone was informal yet trained, and she peppered witty tales of motherhood in her introduction for the event's keynote speaker.

"If it came with a glass of wine, I'd sign up for anything," she said to uproarious laughter. "But seriously, folks, we all know why we're here. For me, this is something so special. Maybe you don't know this, but the first blog post I wrote, the very first one, was about our guest today. Can you believe it, people? That was fifteen years ago . . . I was three at the time."

More laughter.

"But seriously, like all of you, I saw the video. I mean, over three billion views. Most ever. Record-breaking. And what I found so amazing, what I wrote about that day, was that it was something *good*. Do you know what I mean?"

The audience nodded, a strangely practiced response that looked planned. Yet it wasn't.

"Do you remember what it felt like seeing it the first time?" Her tone grew somber. "Let's face it. We were all the same that day. We were told that Michael Swann had just killed hundreds of people. We believed it! I mean, it was all over the television. Every news program reported it as fact. Am I right?

"I remember it so well. I sat on my bed and watched it on my iPhone. I'd already heard that it was all a mistake. I didn't yet know about everything else . . . the rest of the story. But I still wondered. I still felt . . . I don't know . . . suspicious. Then I watched him."

She pauses. The audience is silent. No one even looks at each other. They have traveled back to relive their own experience of the day.

"I swear I could see his face. I swear I could. I know, the video is so blurry. But when he drops the phone and opens the case and sees it. He sees the bomb! Can you imagine? I remember wondering what the heck I would do. I mean, the me now, since kids, I'd probably dive on top of it, right? Protective mama bear!"

The crowd cheered again, sharing what was obviously an inside joke among fans.

"But then, before kids, I said to myself, I said, 'Nope, I would have dropped it and ran.' Not because I was a coward or anything like that. I just think, in the moment, it would have freaked me out. But anyway. Not him, right? What does he do? He takes off, with the case. He knew he wouldn't make it. There was no way he would. The only reason to do that is to save other people. Only reason. Only one.

"But that face. I watched it over and over. And every time, I swear I knew what he was thinking. It was like I could see his life there in his eyes. And I know, for sure, who he was thinking about. We all do.

And friends, we are so lucky, because today we all get to finally meet her together.

"Let's put our hands together for Julia Swann, author of *The real Michael Swann.*"

The crowd erupted. People stood. The speaker turned and, clapping her hands, waited for Julia. She walked out, her hair up in a tight bun. She dressed so much like her mother now, sharp, in shades of black. She wore glasses, something new for her, something she'd realized she needed while writing her book. As she took the microphone, the audience realized immediately that her talk would be very different from the first. She did not meander, and she spoke with a formality that was accessible, yet not quite the expectation any longer.

"Thank you, thank you," she said, looking abashed at the response.

It was her first event, ever. And she looked out at the faces of thousands of strangers and wondered, *Can I do this?* Then she saw them, Thomas and Evan. Grown men, now. Handsome. They shared the tired eyes of new fathers. They'd each had their first child, her first grandchildren, days apart in June. The fact that they had made it to her talk filled her with an almost overwhelming emotion. It was at once pride and nostalgia. Yet below that, the loss still lingered. It never truly disappeared. She knew that now. But it was better. Every day, it got better for all of them.

Julia smiled at her boys. Thomas gave her the littlest of waves, and it choked her up. The audience, sensing her emotion, simply cheered louder.

"Thank you."

It came out like a croak. Julia cleared her throat. She had to do this. She had a lot to say.

"Thank you. I can't believe I'm up here. It feels like a dream." She paused. "But in reality, it is the opposite. In a way, I've woken up. That's why I wrote my story. Up until recently, I kept it trapped inside me. Sharing it only with my sons. I shut the door on everything else. I never gave an interview. I never mentioned any of it to friends or coworkers. No matter how many people told me I should sue the government for what they did, I stayed quiet. For some reason, when we lost . . . lost Michael, I just couldn't do it.

"I was asked to read a passage from the book today. Instead, I've decided to just tell you a little story that's in it. It might not come out in exactly the same words. I don't know, really. But it's mine. And for the first time, I'm willing to share.

"Someone once asked me, what did it feel like, the moment I realized that it wasn't Michael. 'You must have hated that man.' And truly, I did. For a long time. In fact, I have never said his name, not once. Nor, I think, have my children.

"When the spotlight fell on us that night, it hit me from the inside out. I think I fell to the ground at first. I . . . I really thought it was . . . him."

She paused again, trying to hold it all together. When she continued, her voice broke, but she didn't cry.

"I don't remember this, but I . . . I attacked him. I clawed at his throat like an animal. I drew blood . . . I tried to hurt that man. Honestly, though I've never said it before, I wanted to kill him.

"A few weeks ago, though, something happened. Something fabulous and something frightening. I became a grandmother, not once but twice."

The audience clapped. It gave her a chance to take a breath. Every word she spoke brought up long forgotten pain. Yet she had to continue.

"Frightening? Maybe you think it was frightening because there is nothing that ages you faster than being called a grandmother. That's not it, though. In fact, I wear that label with more pride than I wear any other.

"No, what frightens me is . . . all of us, including me."

A hush fell over the crowd. She could sense the tension. But she went on, regardless.

"I am told that nearly everyone in this building watched the video of my husband. You all saw his reaction. You saw what he did. In that station, there were men and woman. People of all races and all religions. They might have been married. They might not have been. They might be labeled based on their sexual orientation or their gender identity. Some may have had a mental illness, and maybe some were truly gifted. Maybe there were artists and"—her voice broke—"hardworking, loving parents just trying to get home to their families.

"I guarantee you that there were people who felt our country was spiraling down into oblivion. Maybe they blamed corporate greed. Maybe they blamed immigrants, or the rich. Maybe, like my husband, they felt like the entire burden of our society rested square on their shoulders and they were running out of hope.

"Maybe they hated the president and prayed for the next one. Maybe it was the other way around. Regardless, I fear one word that likely burned inside far too many of them. It was the same word that burned inside of me when I saw that man's face instead of my husband's. That word is *hate*.

"I have no doubt that hate led to what happened. Anger drove the man that did it. I will never understand that. Nor will I try. Instead, I will always think about the one person I truly knew. The man I lost. My husband.

"And I can wonder. If I was there, how different it would have been. Would I have taken his hand? Begged him to run away? But like you, I can see what he did. Whether it saved lives or not, in the end, he tried to help people. He tried to make a difference. And I ask you, all of you, why? Why would he do that?

"Michael was a great father. He was a great husband." Julia closes her eyes for a second, thinking back to the night before he left for New York. "He wasn't perfect. We weren't perfect. We regretted things. And we struggled just like everyone else. To be honest, the weeks before that horrible day had been . . . well . . . horrible. He was in trouble at work. We were fighting about money. And my husband felt the pressure of our lives like it crushed every last breath out of his lungs.

"But none of that mattered in the end. It all means nothing. And I would take a lifetime of bad days if the kids and I could spend them with him. Instead, what I have are memories, and that video. And what I have is the real Michael Swann.

"Maybe next time we feel that anger building up. We feel that rage. That fear . . . that hatred, we can all see him again. Because the one thing I know is that he didn't act out of hate. He didn't cast judgment on the people around him. He didn't dehumanize those that were different. In the moment, when chaos ruled, he simply acted. His heart, his true heart, the one that is free of all this, it guided him in that moment.

"The more hatred that spreads between us. The more we hear it on the radio and see it on the television and the Internet. The more we let people spew it into our ears, into our children's ears, day in and day out, the deeper we fall.

"We need to open our eyes. We need to see what's happening around us. When our leaders use hate and fear to bully voters. When our news programs inflame instead of inform. They do it for a reason. To feed our fears. And fear leads to one place . . . hatred.

"If we just look at the people around us, no matter how different they may seem, they are not. They are like you. They are human. All this fear, all the hate, it strips our humanity away. Although we don't see it happen, it makes us less than what we are meant to be.

"When I think about Michael, and I think about that day, I know he must have been scared in his last moments. But he didn't give in to his fears. Instead, he acted out of kindness and selflessness. As so many of us grasp for everything we can, fight endlessly to get *ours*, he gave. He acted out of love, not hate.

"Is there a lesson to all this? I don't know. Nor do I know if I'm the one to share it. All I can do is tell you what I learned. Tell you how I vowed to change. I vowed to never vote for a leader who preys on my fears. To stop watching programs that sell drama in the guise of news. Alone, my choices may be in vain. Alone, I am sure I won't make a difference. But if enough people see it. If enough people notice. And if they all take a stand. If we all stand together, maybe then, things might change."

———————

Julia sat behind a table. Atop it, stacks of her book rested on a crisp white tablecloth. She thought she was done, yet one last person approached the table. She glanced toward the exit, making eye contact with Evan as her boys spoke with the woman who had introduced her. She winked and he smiled.

Julia greeted the last person in line. Then she noticed that the woman, a twenty-some-year-old with glasses and inexpensive clothes, didn't carry a copy of her book. Instead, she had an iPhone in her hand and it looked to be ready to record their conversation.

"Are you a reporter?" Julia asked.

"A blogger," the woman said without a smile. "Did you know that Schmidt is scheduled for a psych evaluation this week? How do you feel about the fact that he's in a cushy mental health hospital instead of in jail? Is that fair?"

Julia stared at her. She said nothing.

"Will you provide some testimony? Anything? Don't you think you should be spending time making sure he pays instead of"—she swept an arm over the ten books still remaining on the table—"making money off your husband's story?"

Julia stood. She looked the woman right in the eye. She noticed the hunger there, the need to be noticed. She imagined the story she might write, the judgment and fear she might lead with, all in an effort to get her words read by strangers. She imagined those reading her article, their fear spiking, their anger flaring. Maybe it was righteous. But what did it get them, really?

"Excuse me," Julia said as she rose from the table.

She turned and walked to the hallway that led backstage. Once out of sight, she sagged against a wall, her head throbbing. She felt utterly spent as she stared up at the drop ceiling over her head.

"Michael," she whispered.

Slowly, she pulled out her phone. Holding her breath, Julia went online. It took her less than a second to find the video. For the second time that day, she touched play.

She watched her husband in tones of gray and green. The clip only lasted a few seconds. In it, he seemed to notice something amiss with his bag. Maybe the handle felt wrong. Maybe it was too heavy. She would never know. She could never ask him. Whatever it was, it gave him pause.

Michael's hand lowered and what looked like a phone slipped from his hand. Julia's throat tightened, for she knew without a doubt that she was the last person he spoke to. Through watering eyes, she watched her husband stoop and carefully open the bag. Exactly what he saw, she would never know. Yet it clearly unnerved him. Almost instantly, he slammed it shut. He looked around, frantic, and ran toward the exit of the Acela lounge, carrying a strange bag full of explosives.

Julia forced herself to keep watching. She had to. In the video, Michael took five long strides. And then, flash. The screen went a blinding white. And the clip ended. Like millions of others, Julia watched her husband die.

Alone in a dim hallway, she cried once more.

2

Marci Simmons closes the laptop once the screen flashed bright white. She just looks at me.

"Will she come to see me?" I ask.

The therapist shakes her head. "No, she won't. I told you that yesterday. I tell you every day."

"I wish she would," I say. "Every time I close my eyes, I see her. Her eyes were so filled with pain. I just wanted to take that from her. I'd put it on myself. I'd carry it for her, forever, if I could."

"Do you understand what you're saying?"

"Yes," I say. "I do."

"She's not your—"

"She wrote a book," I interrupt.

Her eyes widen. "How do you know that?"

"The newspaper."

"How did you get a newspaper?"

I look away. "I found it."

Honestly, I don't remember. In fact, it might not have been a newspaper. Maybe I just heard someone talking about it. I don't care, though, because I can tell I was right by the therapist's reaction.

"Can I have a copy?"

"You know you can't."

I have to. It's all I think about. There are just so many holes. So many questions. And I know she'll write about me. About her, too, of course.

"But don't you think it would help? We talk about it all the time. You want me to remember. Maybe if I read about—"

"It's not your story," she says.

"Well, I understand that. But it is. How can it not be?"

"You know how."

I nod. It's because I left her alone.

"It might help."

Marci Simmons doesn't say anything right away. She watches me, as if something might change. How can it, though?

"Have you been writing, still?" she asks.

I nod.

"Can I see it?"

I shake my head.

"You know," she says, "if I want to see it, I can."

"I understand."

We watch each other for a moment. I'm unsure why, really. Then the therapist tents her hands and she looks very earnest.

"What's your name?" she asks.

"Really?"

"Yes," she says.

I know what she wants. But I won't give it to her. Not today. Not ever.

"Michael Swann," I say.

Marci Simmons turns her head. She nods toward the door and two orderlies enter. They come into the room and release the shackle from the floor hook. The therapist does not look at me as they lead me from that room back to my cell. I sit on the bed as the lock snaps shut.

Once they're gone, I pull the notebook out. I want to go to the end, where I left off earlier. I want to write about the day she finally comes to visit. We'll sit across from each other and I'll apologize. I'd tell her I would do anything I could to get back to her.

I close my eyes and I picture how it could have been. I feel every minute that I lost. I whisper her name over and over again. *Julia. Julia. Julia.*

With a tear in my eye, I turn to the first page. On the top line, I let the pen touch the paper. It moves without me thinking about it. When I'm done, I stare at the title.

The Real Michael Swann
by
Michael Swann

And I wonder what it means.

ACKNOWLEDGMENTS

First and foremost, I would like to thank *rejection*. It has been my constant companion through this journey, and without it I would be entirely too well adjusted. More important, it has awarded me the two most important tools a writer can earn—improvement and persistence.

I would also like to thank the people at Barnes & Noble in Wilmington, particularly Kristen. I probably would have kicked me out for being some kind of creepy weirdo by now.

I thank the usual suspects—my Acer laptop, which still runs Windows 7; the kickass Epson laser printer I found for, like, $100; and tea, for helping me transition off coffee.

My wife and kids rock, although it would be nice if I got just a few cool points for all of this. Then again, you have to survive my peculiarities, so I guess we're even.

My parents, for showing amazing restraint in not asking me how my second book was coming along.

My agent, Stephanie Rostan: You are more clutch than Big Papi.

Jessica Renheim, Christine Ball, John Parsley, and Marya Pasciuto at Dutton: Thanks for inviting me to the table. I promise I won't steal any silverware. But seriously, I've enjoyed every minute working with you and your colleagues.

In fact, I want to thank everyone at Dutton who will work on this book at some time after I write these acknowledgments. I don't know who you are yet, but thanks in advance!

And to everyone I have not mentioned, including you. If you've gotten this far, then I thank you even more.

ABOUT THE AUTHOR

Bryan Reardon is the author of the *New York Times* bestselling novel *Finding Jake*. Prior to becoming a full-time writer, Bryan worked for the State of Delaware for more than a decade, starting in the office of the governor. He holds a degree in psychology from the University of Notre Dame and lives in West Chester, Pennsylvania, with his wife and kids.